THE
LOST
YEARS

THE
LOST
YEARS

COLIN WADE

Matador
9 Priory Business Park,
Wistow Road, Kibworth Beauchamp,
Leicestershire, LE8 0RX
Tel: 0116 279 2299
Email: books@troubador.co.uk
Web: www.troubador.co.uk/matador
Twitter: @matadorbooks

Web: www.colinwade.co.uk
Twitter: @CPWADE1

ISBN 978 1838591 588

British Library Cataloguing in Publication Data.
A catalogue record for this book is available from the British Library.

Printed and bound in Great Britain by 4edge Limited
Typeset in 11pt Sabon MT by Troubador Publishing Ltd, Leicester, UK

Matador is an imprint of Troubador Publishing Ltd

For Liz, Hannah and Thomas

1

Anya opened her eyes. Her heart was racing. She was in her bedroom. She was in her bed. Not in that place.

LEX.

Three letters. She had seen them somewhere...in that horrible place?

No, not again! The memories were fading.

She knew that whatever these dreams were, they had to be memories. Things she had blocked. The lost years rising up in her mind. Threatening to spill their secrets. Calling to her to remember.

A hand touched her shoulder. Rob, sleeping next to her. "It's OK," she said. "Go back to sleep."

He mumbled something and turned over. Oh, she loved him. She had from the moment they met, and yet she still couldn't talk to him about this. About the nightmares.

She lay awake, the darkness only pierced by the digital alarm clock that glowed out... 3.43 a.m.

The family home that she had known all her life suddenly felt cold and lonely. She played over how they met in her mind, trying to force happier memories into her psyche.

*

She was walking through the village, wrapped up against the bitter cold wind that reminded everyone that winter was here. Christmas was a few weeks away and the shops, houses and streets were pretty with festive lights. She hadn't walked down this end of the village for a while, certainly not since she had returned from her… she didn't know what to call it… bad times, nightmare, lost years?

Then, like a beacon of hope, she saw it. Simmons Art Gallery. Anya loved art. It is what university should have been about, until the tragedy that changed her life. She quickly walked towards it and went in.

"Hi, what can I do for you today?" said a rather handsome man, standing behind the counter.

It was like a thunderbolt to her heart. Did this really happen? Love at first sight?

Anya was a bit dumbstruck and stumbled over her words. "Oh, um, I love art and I didn't know this was here."

"Well, I have only been here a couple of months. I moved down from Hertfordshire to set this business up. It has always been my dream to sell art and own a gallery. I love to support local artists and get their work out to the wider world."

"Wow, me too," replied Anya, with the merest hint of gushing enthusiasm.

"Do you live round here?"

"Yes, in the middle of the village, just across the road from the river. How about you?"

"Yes, just around the corner, in a little end of terrace."

Anya felt herself reddening up. An inner glow. This was all so natural. She had only spoken to him for a few minutes but it just felt so right. He was tall with a tidy, short-cut hairstyle, clean shaven and a fit well-toned physique. God, he was gorgeous.

She must have gone into a bit of a dreamy trance because she suddenly realised he was looking at her, smiling, wondering whether she was going to say anything else.

"So, now we know where each other lives, can I help you with anything?" he said, breaking the awkward silence.

"Oh, er, no," she said stumbling over her words again. "I just wanted to see what you had." Oh God, what was she saying. "See what he had." Could she be any less subtle?

He just smiled again. "Well, please feel free to look around. We are still developing our full range but there should still be plenty for you to see."

Anya tried to look interested in the various pieces of art but she couldn't concentrate. Her heart felt like it was beating so hard it would burst out of her chest. She hadn't felt like this since her first stirrings of teenage lust.

She eventually made a decent fist of looking interested and after about ten minutes of browsing she went to leave.

"I'm Anya, by the way," she said, holding out her hand.

"Nice to meet you Anya," he replied, gripping her hand firmly. "I'm Rob. I hope to see you again soon."

Anya smiled to herself. The memories comforted her. She knew she would have to tell Rob about these dreams – nightmares – at some point but she was scared about what they meant. The darkness of those years was still there. The huge gaps in her memory. She fell back to sleep.

*

Rob and Anya were eating breakfast the next morning, the late summer sun streaming in through the window.

"What was the matter with you last night?" said Rob.

"Oh, nothing really," replied Anya, the classic deviation phrase to give her time to construct the lie.

"I have been thinking about Mum and Dad a lot recently. I think my subconscious is playing mind games with me and disturbing my sleep."

"Well, I guess that is understandable. Grief is a strange thing. You never really told me what happened to them. I am here for you, if you ever need to talk."

"I'm fine."

God, Rob hated that word. 'Fine'. Nobody who said 'fine' was ever fine. The dictionary definition should be changed to say 'word used to deflect from what you are actually feeling'.

He didn't push it but sensed that Anya was hiding something from him.

Anya was unnerved by this exchange. When she had met Rob, for her, it had all been about looking forward. Forgetting the past. She didn't want the past to draw a wedge between them. She didn't know how to deal with it. She didn't understand it herself.

They both busied themselves, trying to ignore the awkwardness that was left hanging in the air, and got ready to go to work.

As they left, Anya was still fretting. She had been working with Rob at the gallery for a little while now. The bad period of her life that was now invading her sleeping hours had also affected her employability. A university flunky and someone with her issues was not top of anyone's list. The gallery job had been a godsend but, after this morning, the constant proximity of Rob was going to make this a difficult day.

2

Clark tapped away at the keyboard. He had almost done it. Hacked the bank. He would do to them what he had done to many other corporate lepers. Replace their public facing web pages with a picture of a penguin holding a banner saying:

'Hello greedy corporate bastards, welcome to your new website. The penguin is now in charge.'

A few minutes later it was done.

Clark punched the air.

Let's see how long it takes you to fix that, you scumbags.

Clark was only twenty-two, but what really drove him on in life was getting revenge. Against the corporate bastards that had ruined his father's life and the dirty, sleazy politicians that never did anything to hold these people to account.

He would never forget the day at ten years old when he walked in after school, to find his mother cradling his father's dead body. Crying uncontrollably with a piece of paper in her hand. A suicide note.

'I am so sorry but I can't carry on. They have taken everything. I have no job, no savings and they have stolen the money from the pension. I can't support you, so I must stop being a burden, being a failure.'

Clark's father had worked for Jakeman's, the local factory in Mansfield, close to where they lived. It seemed like it employed half the town, making all types of quality handmade furniture. Things went wrong when due to deteriorating health, old man Jakeman had to sell up to a couple of millionaires. The Brady Brothers. They asset stripped, killed the business, took all of the money out and left the company pension scheme with nothing in it. They left the country leaving 5,000 workers out of a job with no pensions. The criminal case was hopeless. They had disappeared, somewhere where UK extradition did not work. The parliamentary enquiry was a whitewash, with many accusing the local MPs of being on the Brady's payroll, to make it all go away.

The injustice of it burned inside of Clark. His mother was never the same. It was one of the reasons he had to move away. To university in London, and later a job and home in Reading.

And then of course, there was the final thing. Something he had subsequently forgiven his parents, Mr and Mrs Kent, for. His name. Clark Kent. What were they thinking?

School was so predictable.

"Here comes Superman," they would chant.

"Fuck off," Clark would retort.

"Is it a bird, is it a plane, no it's Supernerd," they would continue.

"I hope you never need your printer fixed," was often the best next response he could muster.

This was always followed by the pants outside the trousers gag after numerous PE lessons. It all got a bit tired. Schoolkids' humour; just so basic.

All this had shaped who he had become. In adult life people liked him, but he preferred the company of his technology, the awesome technology-rich 'man cave' he was now sitting in.

The penguin hack was one of his favourites. Clark always believed that animals were so much better than people. It wasn't too malicious but it wiled away many an hour and proved how much he could control the type of people he hated.

He spent most of his time looking for conspiracies, tracking the type of people that had killed his father. Any companies that had politicians connected with them were ripe for his attention.

He became obsessed with any conspiracy. He believed all the famous ones. The fake moon landings, Princess Diana, JFK, aliens at Roswell. He wanted one of his own.

3

The phone rang. He picked it up and a voice he had not heard for a while said, "We have some more customers."

"I told you, I am not doing this anymore."

"You don't have a choice."

"I do and I won't bow to your bullying tactics anymore."

"You piece of shit. We kept your failing business afloat with our previous deal and now we need you to step up and sort this out."

"And what if I refuse?"

"Do you really need me to spell out the obvious? We have the evidence of your depravity. I don't think you or your business will survive a leak to the press."

He sighed. They would always have him, playing this card. "We'd better meet in the usual place."

A follow-up call was made to the boss. "He is going to do it."

"Did he take much persuading?"

"No, I just had to remind him what we have on him. He soon agreed and said we should meet in the usual place."

"Good. I assume he wants his usual £200k?"

"I presume so."

"Actually, tell each client that the cost is £700k, so we get a clear £500k to share between the rest of the team. If this ever goes pear-shaped, I want to make sure that our offshore accounts can't be traced. I also don't need to remind you that we will finish you if you betray our family."

"Don't worry Boss, I understand. You can trust me. After these ones, I don't plan to stay in this country. I want to live somewhere exotic and live off our profits."

"Good, make the arrangements to meet tomorrow. I assume our field agent is nurturing the right type of girls."

"Yes, he is still running his network. I'll get him to support the meeting."

"Agreed," said the boss. "Thank you. Let me know what happens."

4

Anya was dreaming. Nice dreams. Nice memories.

*

She had made an excuse to go back to the gallery. Rob was pleased to see her and after a few minutes he said exactly what Anya had hoped for.

"Anya, I hope you don't think this is a bit forward, but would you like to get coffee? I am closing in about half an hour."

She almost squealed with excitement. "I would love to."

They went to the local tea room. She had a chai latte, he had a cappuccino.

Anya leapt right in. "Tell me about yourself."

"Well, I was brought up in Hertfordshire by two loving, hardworking parents who you would probably describe as a bit 'conservative middle England'. My mother was the artist, which is where my love for art came from. My father was a good, hardworking businessman selling insurance, which I think is where I got my business brain from. I think these two influences and my Economics uni degree probably led me to the art business. So, all quite normal. God, I sound dead boring, don't I?"

Anya laughed. "No, not at all. Boring might be just what I need right now."

Rob laughed back. "OK then, let's hear about your *not* boring life."

Anya was excited but apprehensive. Rob was the first real thing that had happened to her since she got out of that place. How did she handle this?

"Oh, I don't know. I am an only child. I lost both my parents just under three years ago. It is still quite raw. They were wonderful people. I had such a happy childhood. I flunked uni and ended up back at the family home, which I inherited when they passed away."

"God, that is terrible. I am so sorry to hear that. What are you doing now?"

"I am still considering my options. Our family solicitor was great, sorting out the house for me and the little bit of inheritance that was left after…"

She stopped. She couldn't say it.

"After what?" Rob probed.

"Oh, um, after uni. After I flunked, I found it hard to get a job. The house was paid for but I had living costs. I guess the money just helped me live during that period. It's surprising how quickly you can go through money."

Lies. Lies. Lies. What was happening? The dream was changing. Rob's face was changing. His brown hair was changing colour. It was fair. His face was changing, morphing into someone else.

"Don't lie to me Anya." The new face was taunting her.

What, who, where? It was Bradley. Evil Bradley.

"Where is my stash? Have you snorted it all up your nose again, you bitch? You aren't paying me enough to keep doing this. We'll have to have one of our special parties. I am sure my mates will enjoy you again. The little slut paying her dues."

The dream was fading, changing again. Where was she now?

LEX. LEX. LEX. LEX.

She was being taunted. The face changed again. An old, wiry little man. That place.

She screamed. She sat bolt upright in bed. At home. With Rob.

"What the hell?" Rob was startled. "What is wrong?"

"Sorry, another nightmare. I am fine. Go back to sleep."

He stared at her with real concern. Real fear.

"We need to talk about this. Twice in a week. Something is wrong. What are you not telling me?"

"Not now. Please. Leave me alone."

Anya rolled over. Her back to Rob. Trying to stifle the sobs.

He looked at her back. Went to touch her. Stopped. He would have to be patient.

*

Breakfast the next morning was awkward. Again.

"Rob. I am sorry about last night. I don't know why I keep having these nightmares. I am sure it is only temporary. My crazy mind playing up. Would you mind if I didn't come into the gallery today? I am a bit washed out."

"Please don't shut me out Anya. I am always here for you. I love you."

"I know. I am sorry. I love you too."

Rob gave her that smile. The one that always melted her heart.

"Have a day off. No problem. See you later."

Rob left for work and Anya got straight onto the internet.

She had to confront this. That place was invading her dreams. The Loughborough Clinic. The letters 'LEX'.

She found the website of the Loughborough Clinic and searched for anything on their website with the letters LEX. Nothing.

She searched the wider world. She found references to car leasing, the *Financial Times*, the baddy in *Superman* and someone selling computer software, but nothing that would tell her what LEX was.

She logged out. She had to get some air. She went for a walk. She had to think. For the first time in a very long while, she was craving a hit.

She walked along the towpath by the river and found a seat. The air was a bit cooler but she didn't notice. Her mind was racing. Her body was lurching. Her mind wandered to where it all began. The tragedy. University. Bradley.

*

She couldn't focus on the words. Her parents – dead. No, this was a dream, a joke. The Dean of her college was talking to her in that voice. The hushed one you always hear people using on the TV when bad news is being delivered.

She didn't know how she had got from that room to the college bar but she was now sitting there. Crying. Dazed.

"Are you OK?"

A tall, rather handsome fair-haired man was standing in front of Anya. She had seen him around but didn't know his name.

"No. I... I... I have had some bad news."

He sat down beside her.

"Tell me."

"My parents are... dead. Killed in a car accident."

"Oh my God, I am so sorry."

He placed his arm round her. She buried her face in his shoulder and sobbed.

She had no idea how long he had held her. She was all cried out. For now. She looked into his eyes. God they were nice eyes.

"Do you want some company tonight?"

What the fuck. Was he hitting on her? At a time like this.

"What do you mean?"

He held his hands up.

"Oh God. I didn't mean *that*. Did you want someone to stay with you in your room? 'On the couch', so to speak."

"Oh, I see. That would be nice. My name is Anya by the way."

"Bradley. Bradley Williams."

From that first meeting she was hooked. Her heart was broken, her motivation for life lost. The deep profound grief and uncharacteristic loneliness led her in the wrong direction. Bradley consumed her. She relied on him more and more. The university tried to do the right things but the spiral of decay was irreversible. He exploited it.

She couldn't really remember when it started. The images were there. The rolled-up £5 note. The mirror. The white lines. The rest was a blur.

She didn't live her life any more. Uni was a distant memory. She lived for the next fix. Bradley pushed her further and further. He got nasty.

"Come on Anya, you know you want to snort all that lovely inheritance up your nose, don't you? Now give me the fucking money."

There was violence. Sexual assault.

Then, the clinic. Had he put her there? He wasn't there when she got out. She never saw him again.

*

"Anya. Anya. Are you OK?"

Anya jumped. She had been staring into space. Playing over that horrible period of her life. She forgot where she was.

"Oh, hi Mrs Strawman. Sorry, I was miles away. I'm fine thank you. Just enjoying the fresh air."

"OK, dear. As long as you are all right."

She wasn't all right. She was scared and she was pushing Rob away. She got up and walked back home.

5

The three of them met in the usual place. A pub in the middle of the Berkshire countryside, on a road which only led to the little hamlet where the pub dominated local life. It was not a place that many people found by chance. The landlord knew them and was always discreet.

They sat in a quiet corner all nursing pints of the local beer. One would be fine even though they were all driving. At least they hoped so. It would be a bit of a bother if they had to get the boss to get them off another drink-drive charge. Their police contacts could always be bribed for the right amount. They all sunk half of it in one drag and got on with the business in hand.

"So, Doctor, the boss has agreed to two more transactions."

"Why isn't he here to do his own dirty work?" the doctor replied with thinly veiled contempt.

"He is a bit busy at the moment."

"Yes," said the doctor, "he and his family have a lot more to lose now, don't they?"

"I hope you are not threatening us?"

"Oh no," said the doctor, "but I think this means my price should go up."

He grabbed the doctor by his collar and pulled him so close that their faces were almost touching. "Look you pervert, you do not have any negotiating room here." He let go quite quickly as the other punters in the pub starting looking over, wondering whether there was going to be a dust-up.

"You can keep playing that card but at the end of the day, you need me. No one else knows how to do these procedures. I won't betray you but just want a bit of recognition for the risks I am taking."

They were both surprised by his bravado, considering they could ruin him by exposing his secret, but they did need him.

"I'll talk to the boss. How much more do you want?"

"I think 25k per transaction should do it," the doctor replied.

He told the doctor to wait in the pub while he stepped outside to make the call to the boss. "He wants £25k extra per transaction," he said when the boss answered.

"Really. Did you remind him of our leverage?" the boss replied.

"Of course, but this time he seemed less frightened by the prospect of being exposed."

"Well well, maybe our doctor is getting some balls. Pay him what he wants, after all he will be dealt with as a loose end once these last two are done."

He returned to the pub and told the doctor what had been agreed.

The doctor's heart was pumping at an alarming rate but the bravado had worked and he tried to show a cool expression. He had decided he would disappear after these last two deals and the extra £50k would set him up nicely, somewhere exotic and far away from this place and all his demons.

"The girls will be ready to be admitted in a few days," the other one said. "I will bring them to you on Friday."

"OK," said the doctor. "I will get things ready."

6

Clark sat eating his favourite takeout pizza. The barbeque chicken one from Giovanni's. That name always made him laugh because 'Giovanni' had the broadest West Midlands accent he had ever heard.

The sustenance set him up for another night in his man cave. Alone, but happy with his own company.

As he pondered what to do next in his search for a juicy conspiracy, he watched the news streams that he had flashing up over his numerous terminals. One caught his eye.

'MP for Battersea, George Walker, tops league table of greedy politicians in the latest expenses scandal,' the scrolling headline read.

'£53,000 in dodgy expenses claims by Battersea MP puts party to shame,' another one exclaimed.

Another greedy bell-end MP. What a surprise, Clark mused to himself. *OK, Mr Walker, maybe you will be my little project tonight. Let's see what other dirty little secrets you have.*

Clark navigated to George Walker's local constituency website to get his parliamentary email address. Once he had this it would be a 'hop, skip and a jump' through the dark web to hack the government email server. Their security was so lame it was like taking candy from a baby.

Clark opened up TOR, the hacker's tool of choice for navigating the dark web and for keeping all your 'dark surfing' nice and anonymous.

He quickly found the perimeter firewall of the government website. A quick test of the usual vulnerable network ports soon found his favourite back door. TCP Port 21. Open and willing, like a baby bird waiting to be fed.

Clark scoffed at the screen. *God, these government IT people are such amateurs. They might as well just leave all their doors open, physically and virtually.*

He quickly hacked through to the exchange server and found George Walker's email history.

Right, let's see whether you have any more skeletons in your closet.

Clark started scrolling through his received emails. Nothing of any great interest. He looked through his sent items. He stopped. One caught his eye.

'Consultancy Services', the email title read.

He clicked on the email and read it out loud.

To Dr Felix Normandy,
Please find attached my invoice for non-executive consultancy services at Fairport Medical.
Regards, George Walker

Clark opened up the attachment. The invoice was for £10,000.

He set up a separate browsing session and logged onto the public website of Fairport Medical.

A company specialising in private psychological and addiction recovery services. Hmm, private healthcare. A cash cow if ever I saw one. Just the type of thing to attract this greedy bugger.

He navigated around the site. Dr Felix Normandy was the CEO but there was no mention of a board. No mention of George Walker being a non-executive director. It seemed like Dr Normandy ran this as an autocracy, so where did George Walker fit in?

Clark changed his focus and logged onto the public list of parliamentary interests that should provide the vehicle for all MPs to declare these types of private arrangements.

He was not surprised in what he didn't find. *Nothing to declare about Fairport Medical, Mr Walker?*

Clark had the bit between his teeth. *Right, Fairport Medical. Time for your examination.* He laughed at his own joke. *God, I am hilarious.*

TOR helped Clark get through similar network vulnerabilities on the Fairport Medical servers and he was soon on their email exchange server. He found an email alias for Dr Normandy and one for George Walker.

Interesting. So, you do have a role in this little venture.

But, as Clark went to navigate to their email history, something bizarre happened. There was nothing there. He tapped away, searching for answers.

Hold on. It is there but encrypted. Why only their history? Shit, this looks like asymmetrical encryption. Jesus, what are you trying to hide?

This had suddenly become a challenge. Sniff, sniff, sniff. Clark had a scent.

Clark looked at the picture that always sat prominently on his desk. Reminding him. Driving him.

Don't worry Dad, I won't stop looking for justice. I will avenge you. I think we have just hooked a live one here.

7

It had been a little tense when Rob got home. Their relationship had always been based on a deep love and respect for each other, despite the relatively short time they had been together. The very definition of soulmates.

The last two nights and mornings had shaken them both. They had not yet experienced the type of kink in their relationship that recent events had brought to the surface. Anya tried to defuse it straight away.

"I'm sorry Rob. I am just a bit cranky at the moment. I need to clear my head. Thank you for letting me have some alone time today."

"You're shaking. Are you sure you are not coming down with something?"

Shit. Anya couldn't believe it. Were the withdrawals coming back? Was she sick? Physically? In her head?

"I'm OK. Let's eat and have a quiet night in."

Rob's bullshit radar was now on full alert. Throughout his life, from quite an early age, people always complemented him on his calmness and kindness. Good parenting. But these qualities, that had so attracted Anya, did not mean he was a pushover. He knew when he was being played. When he was being lied to.

Rob was now convinced that there was something about the time before they met that was haunting Anya. He decided to let it go for now but he was going to keep an eye on this beautiful, fragile creature that had made him so happy.

They ate, cleared up and settled down for a night in front of the telly. They sat watching the evening news, which was dominated by the announcement that James Hardacre had been appointed the new prime minister, winning the snap leadership contest caused by party disunity about Brexit.

He was being filmed outside 10 Downing Street with his wife and their two-year-old daughter, looking all smug and doing the full 'I am a family man and I know what life is like for normal people' charade, when everyone knew they had an army of servants and nannies looking after their every whim.

"Ahh, the kid's really cute," said Anya.

"Yes, she is, which is surprising, because her parents are a bit visually challenging," mocked Rob.

Anya laughed and gave him a friendly slap for being so mean. This was nice. Laughing together. Easing the tension.

"Do you think our children will be beautiful?"

Rob looked at Anya pensively. "We've never talked about this."

"I know, but what do you think? I have always wanted children and we haven't exactly been careful these last eighteen months."

Rob paused for a bit, which made Anya nervous, but then that cheeky smile came over his face and he said, "I would love to have children with you Anya and yes, they will be beautiful!"

She playfully slapped him again, grabbed his neck and kissed him passionately. "Oh, we're starting right now," quipped Rob.

Anya smiled and pulled away. "Do you think we should get ourselves checked out, you know, if we are serious about this baby-making lark?"

"I am sure everything is fine. It can take a while for people to get pregnant but if you would feel better getting checked out we can both go to the GP and talk to her about it."

"I think we should. I'll phone up in the morning and see if we can get an appointment."

Rob sat there a bit stunned. Where had that come from? Was she deflecting again? They both shared strong family values and he always thought that marriage and kids was an inevitable part of his life plan, but this all seemed a bit sudden. Was she expecting him to propose as well?

Anya got up and went to the loo. What a strange few minutes. Admitting she wanted children. Rob's first reaction was fantastic but...afterwards, his expression had changed. He looked troubled. *God, why was life suddenly so complicated?*

8

Clark had been distracted all day at work. The sophisticated encryption on the two stooges' email accounts had pricked his conspiracy radar. He couldn't wait to get home to crack it and find out more.

Asymmetric encryption. I guess I should be vaguely impressed, Mr Fairport Medical IT person. The problem for you though is that, at the end of the day, it is all just based on clever maths, which means it is a job for SnapDevil's maths worm.

Clark may not have kept much physical human company but he did have a bunch of 'mates' in the virtual world. They called themselves Proton, an online hackers' community that joked and did things 'for the bantz' like any social group, but with no names, no identities, no locations and a code that said they respected each other's boundaries. No hacking each other. They exchanged hacking stories, tips, tools and anything that would get them where they wanted to be, in the virtual world. Without any irony he called himself Krypto.

SnapDevil had created a cool programme that constantly bombarded encryption with mathematical formulae to work out the algorithms and crack the access keys. It would sometimes take days for the programme to run and de-code the secrets but it always got there in the end.

OK, let's see what this little bad boy can do.

The length of time the programme would take to get results would really depend on how sophisticated the encryption configuration was.

So, Fairport Medical. My record is three hours twenty-four minutes with this lovely maths worm. Will you be my new besty?

The answer came after three hours and twenty-eight minutes.

Ooh, so close but no cigar.

He logged into Proton.

KRYPTO:	'Sup Snap.
SNAPDEVIL:	Smoking Krypto. Watcha doin?
KRYPTO:	Using your maths worm to crack another dodgy corp. 3 hours 28 minutes.
SNAPDEVIL:	Wah, not bad. You still ain't gonna beat my 2 hours 45 minutes any day soon.
KRYPTO:	Super LOL. Will do one day. Nuff respect though. This worm is a legend.
SNAPDEVIL:	You is welcome. Update me on the juicy stuff.
KRYPTO:	Will do. Laters.

He grabbed another coffee and rubbed his hands in glee.

Time to party.

The configuration had been pretty basic and he now had the algorithms to allow him to move freely in Dr Normandy and George Walker's emails. The first curious step, as he tapped away, was the redirecting of his access from the local UK server to another discreet server, in a different physical location. He pinged the IP address.

Holy shit. The Cayman Islands. Why have a server in a different country, especially one renowned for offshore secrets?

Clark didn't really need to answer his own question. Crime. Greed. Secrets. Conspiracy.

He could feel the adrenalin coursing through his body. His mouth was drying up.

A few minutes trawling through Dr Normandy's emails and he found what he was looking for. A three-year-old email from Dr Normandy to George Walker.

'The five patients are: Rachel Hermitage, Lisa Benbridge, Charlotte Kay, Marjit Ahmed, Anya Novak. It will be £200k for each medical procedure. The clear up is your domain. I don't want to know what you do after our deal is completed.'

Clark stared and stared at the screen. He had hit 'pay dirt'.

He took another gulp of his now cooling coffee, awestruck but trying to focus on his next step.

He found the medical records system. All the girls mentioned in the email had been treated as drug addicts between 2013 and 2015 at Fairport Medical's main centre. A place called the Loughborough Clinic in Warwickshire. They had all stayed in the clinic for well over a year and often up to two.

Clark started to look at their wider lives and to his horror, but no great surprise, he found another pattern. Four of these girls were now dead, all killed in 'accidents' within a few months of leaving the clinic. Anya Novak was the only one still alive and although she had been discharged from the clinic almost two years ago, Clark was convinced her life was in danger. He had to find her.

He rubbed his eyes, trying to take it all in. He looked at his dad's picture.

This could be it Dad. My own conspiracy. Our revenge.

He started closing down the various browsing sessions he had opened. As he was about to close down the one with the email, he suddenly spotted something he had missed.

He literally gasped. There was a name in the CC box of the email.

Oh, my holy mother of God. This can't be.

He stood up and jumped around like some five-year-old on too many E numbers. *This has suddenly moved to DEFCON 1.*

9

The doctor sat opposite the two new girls that had been delivered as promised. Bianca Mavroudis and Sam Clarke stared vacantly at him, searching for some relief from their agitated state. They were both drug addicts but had the genetics that would suit the main reason they were here.

The doctor started explaining what he was going to do, although he doubted they understood half of what he was saying to them.

"Bianca, Sam, I am going to be your doctor whilst you are here. You are both drug addicts and by the time you leave here you will be fully cured of your addiction. I will put you through an extended methadone programme that will gradually wean you off the drugs. You cannot leave or have contact with anyone from the outside during your treatment. We will control your diet, exercise and withdrawal. If you get violent, the staff will restrain you and we may need to put you into induced comas to treat the worst of your withdrawal phases. You will get better but you have to trust me and follow my instructions. Do you understand what I am saying?"

Bianca and Sam stared at him blankly. He took that as the best consent he was going to get and, anyway, he was way past the point where consent meant anything to him and the people that were bankrolling his 'other work'.

He got them settled and started the girls on their 'methadone programmes'. He had lied to them. The first of many lies. The programme he had devised would get them well within a few months, not the extended period he had suggested. It was all part of the deception.

"Well ladies," he said, as they both lay on their beds in a state of mild sedation, "time for the magic to start."

They drifted in to full unconsciousness. He could leave them now. They would be out for a long while.

He went back to his suite, turned on his private computer. More images had been uploaded.

He opened them one by one.

He breathed deeply. He was getting hard.

Two ten-year-olds together. Naked. Just what I like.

10

The nightmares came again. The third night. The demons would not let go.

*

Anya tried to duck the fist, but it landed on the left side of her head. She was dazed. She stumbled and fell hard against the coffee table. More cuts and bruises to add to the many that were all over her body.

"Get up you bitch."

"L… L… Leave me alone."

"Leave you alone. I thought you wanted this."

Anya grabbed for the little white bag of powder.

"Ah, ha, ha. I don't think so. You owe me money and I won't stop hurting you until you give it to me."

Anya pulled herself up, fumbled in her bag. She had got £200 out of the bank earlier in the day. For food or something, but nothing could stop her urges. She had to get a fix. She thrust it at him like a grumpy child.

"Now that is better." He slapped her and threw the packet on her crumpled body.

*

Anya woke. Darkness. Another disturbed night. She couldn't look at Rob. Had she disturbed him again?

No. "Thank God," she whispered to herself.

Anya got out of bed as quietly as she could and looked out of the window. The street was dark and quiet. She was shaking.

"You don't need it. You don't need it. You don't need it."

She kept chanting it to herself. Where would she get some? At this time of night. In Goring. That wasn't the kind of thing you did in Goring.

She willed herself through it and gradually the shakes subsided.

She got back into bed and tried to get some undisturbed sleep.

When Anya came downstairs for breakfast, Rob seemed back to his old cheery self.

"Hello sexy, a better night last night?"

The lies were now coming easily.

"Oh, yes, great thanks. I'll ring the GP surgery after breakfast and then we can go into the gallery."

"Cool, my little precious."

OK, now he was acting weird. Weird but happy. Anya would take that for now.

Anya made the call. "So 12.30 p.m. on Friday. We can shut the gallery for a couple of hours, can't we?"

"Yes, of course. I look forward to discussing how my pecker is working."

They both smiled. Rob's sense of humour had always been cheesy but she loved him for it. At the moment, Anya would take any happiness she could get.

11

Clark was still reeling from what he had found. He was convinced he had finally found his own juicy conspiracy.

The list of girls' names. Four dead. The money and *that* name. On the email. As the kids would say, "OM fucking G".

He had to contact Anya Novak.

Clark prided himself on 'walking the walk' when it came to cyber security. He was a supreme hacker and with his cyber mates' help he knew that no one was safe in the digital world. Your secrets could always be found by someone.

His first golden rule... be paranoid.

Right Miss Novak. We are going to have to go with snail mail. I can't risk any sort of digital footprint on this one. Now, how the hell do I write this without freaking you out?

He walked around his man cave. Watched the news. Played FIFA 18 on the Xbox. His brain constantly racing, trying to find the right words.

He finally sat down and wrote out the following, freehand:

Dear Miss Novak,

I know you don't know me but I am going to be blunt and get to the point. I believe your life is in danger. I have uncovered what I believe to be a conspiracy which you are unwittingly involved in. We

need to meet and I will tell you more. Please write to
me at the address below stating when and where you
want to meet. Do not try to contact me by any other
means.
Regards
Clark Kent
Flat 13, Windrush Plaza, Reading, RG1 4EP

He looked up her address on the Fairport Medical records; she was registered to a flat in the centre of Oxford. He guessed this was her address when she was at university. A quick trawl of various public records soon found her current address as 23 Willow Close, Goring, Oxford. He popped the letter in an envelope and slapped a first-class stamp on it.

I think this deserves a first-class stamp.

He would post it on the way to work tomorrow.

Clark's mind settled. That was done, but what next?

He thought about all the conspiracies he had read and researched. His father's sorry story. The greed. His second golden rule... follow the money.

He hacked back into the Fairport Medical network and hopped onto the remote Cayman Island server. He went beyond the emails, trying to find files, documents, evidence... *follow the money.*

He found a folder under George Walker's private profile, simply marked 'Bank'.

"Well, lame arse, I guess this might just be what I am looking for," quipped Clark to himself.

He opened up the most recent file. A bank report, from a Cayman Island bank.

What have we got here? Five transactions paying money out of this account in 2013 and 2014, each of £200,000. Jesus, that matches the email.

He scrolled down the report.

Four payments before these, paying in £550,000 each time and one of £375,000. Holy crap. This is some heavy shit. What the hell is this money for?

There were more transactions going out.

Five sets of transaction for £50k, five for £125k and four for £175k. Hold on.

The symmetry hit him. He checked the maths.

£2.575m in. £2.575m out. This was big. Multi-million pound big.

Follow the money.

12

They would not let go. The fourth night. Worse and worse.

*

LEX. Those letters again. She could see them over a person's shoulder, the rest of the word obscured. Someone was hovering over her. That wiry little man. She was lying down. Tubes, machines beeping, cannulas in her arm.

What was this? Like some nightmare smear test but not pleasant. Not right. She was being violated, down there.

Please stop. Please stop. Please stop.

*

She came to. The darkness enveloped her. She was cold. Sweating, but cold. Rob was snoring. Thank God for small mercies.

He was her soulmate but she just couldn't tell him the truth. She didn't understand the nightmares, the dreams, the years she had lost with no proper memories. She had to process them before she could reach out to him.

She lay in the darkness staring at the blackness, trying to orientate her eyes to make out the shapes in the room. The wiry old man in her dreams kept disturbing her thoughts. It was the doctor from *that* place.

"What was his name?" she whispered to herself. "Dr... Dr... French. That was it. Dr French."

Her memories of him were limited. She began to think about the few memories she had. At the end of her time in that awful place.

*

"Miss Novak. I am pleased to say you are cured of your addiction. You have been with us a long time but I hope you see that it has been worth it."

Anya had seen herself in the mirror that morning. Worth it! She looked a shocker. Her beautiful hair was lank and lifeless. The sharp, attractive facial features crafted from her Czech father and English Rose mother were somehow collapsed, battered and bruised. Sunken.

"What have you done to me?" she shouted at him with a firm, accusatory tone.

"What have I done to you? Miss Novak, you are a drug addict and for nearly two years I have been curing you of your addiction. You were one of the most addicted people I have seen in recent times."

She didn't trust him. She had no memories of her time in the clinic.

"Look at me. Battered, cuts and bruises all over my body. I have no memory of what has gone on in here."

"You had violent withdrawal rages. I am afraid we had no choice but to restrain you. This did mean some cuts and bruises. As for the memories, the addiction affects your short-term memory and we did have to put you into induced comas at times to manage your withdrawal and recovery. You may never fully recover your memories from this period of your life. I suggest you go home and focus on the next stage of your life. The gift I have given you."

The gift! Anya hated him. He was a horrible, creepy little man. She didn't believe anything he said. There was something wrong about this place, about him. Nothing felt right. She had to get out. Go home.

*

She snapped back to where she was. In the cold and dark. Safe but petrified. The same thoughts went over and over in her mind. Meeting Rob had all been about the future. Looking forward and forgetting the past. But, the past would not let go, pulling her back like some naughty child wanting just one more go on the swings. She would have to confront this. Go back to the clinic? Get answers from Dr French?

She fell back into a troubled sleep.

13

James Hardacre sat in his office at 10 Downing Street, a few minutes away from his first full Cabinet meeting.

He had finally done it. Got the top job. Six years an MP, the last three as Environment Secretary. He mused to himself.

"Thank you, Dad. I think."

He was worried. His dad was one of the most powerful men in the country. Part of the so-called Deep State. The Establishment. The king-makers with the billionaire lifestyles and influence to match. He had undoubtedly helped James get the top job, but there was always a price to pay.

God, what have I done? How can I lead the country when he is still pulling my strings?

"Daddy."

His inner turmoil was broken by his daughter Sophie, bounding into the room like the Duracell bunny.

"Hello Princess. How are you?"

"Err, good. Can I have ice cream?"

"Not for breakfast! Go and find Mummy. Daddy has got to go to an important meeting."

"O… kkkkkkk."

Sophie bounced out and went down the corridor back to their personal apartment.

He thanked God for Sophie. Their little miracle from so much despair.

14

Anya and Rob went to their GP appointment. As they sat in reception they did one of their favourite things. People watching.

It seemed all the clichés were there. The frazzled mum with the kid that wouldn't sit down, must be ADHD, the heavily pregnant woman who looked ready to pop at any second, the two old ladies talking loudly to each other about how they were getting new hearing aids… go figure… the young woman clutching a blood test bag looking like she wanted to be anywhere else but about to have a needle put in her arm and a long line of people queueing at reception behind an old geezer who was taking all the receptionist's time trying to book a doctor's appointment for some time next week and constantly changing his mind about when he should have it. The terribly British thing of people in the queue muttering to themselves and mildly seething, but without saying anything, was playing out for all to see. Anya wondered what people made of her and Rob.

Fifteen minutes after their scheduled appointment time their GP, Dr Isabel Fleming, called them in. Anya explained their desire to have a baby and the lack of birth control over the time they had been having sex.

The doctor was sympathetic, discussed their family backgrounds and health history. Anya was tense. Her drug addiction was not on her records. She was not going to tell them. Not now.

Dr Fleming was satisfied that there was no obvious reason why either of them could not produce a child. She said all the usual things about it taking time with some couples and if they just relaxed and forgot about it they would probably fall eventually. She agreed to do some blood tests for Anya to make sure the right hormones were being produced, as her cycle seemed regular enough for that not to be a factor.

She handed Rob a little pot for his 'tadpole deposits' so that some poor lab technician could watch whether they were all swimming fast enough and in the right direction. Rob smiled at the prospect of working with Anya to fill it up.

The doctor sent them on their way and said the test results would be back the next day. She would call them.

They went out for a late lunch in the local pub and then reopened the gallery for the afternoon. Later they cooked up a quick evening meal of stir-fried chicken and vegetables with soy sauce and then gorged on an apple crumble for afters.

It was now late September and the weather was unseasonably cold for early autumn. They decided to light up their lovely open fire for the first time in a while and soon the reassuring crackle of burning wood and smell of fire and smoke was soon filling the cottage.

Rob seemed happy. Anya was relieved that she had not woken him for the last two nights. She needed his love, not the drama. They cuddled up on the sofa.

As they sat watching *Holby City*, Anya suddenly realised the day's post was still on the side.

As she picked up the pile she was immediately struck by a hand-written envelope, addressed to her. She opened it up to reveal a handwritten letter.

At first, she just stared at it, trying to take in what it said. She then let out a mildly hysterical laugh.

"What is it?" said Rob.

"Superman has written to me and says my life is in danger."

"What, let's see that." Rob examined the letter. "Clark Kent? This has got to be some nutter."

"Why would he be writing to me?"

"I don't know. How odd."

Anya studied it a bit longer then crushed it up and threw it on the fire. That satisfying sizzle and blast of fire energy erupted in the hearth as it landed dead centre.

"You should be a basketball player," quipped Rob.

Anya didn't answer, just stared at the fire, not responding, rattled by this weird note.

Rob watched her. She was worried. Was this more weirdness about her past? He was not going to let this go on much longer.

15

The name on that email was haunting Clark's thoughts. How could he possibly be involved? George Walker was clearly a greedy bastard and it was no surprise to see him apparently involved in dodgy dealings, but the other guy?

Clark had to remind himself that the evidence he found was three years old, when this man was not such a prominent figure, but now, he was one of the most powerful men in the country backed up by a family name and fortune that had undoubtedly got him where he was today.

Clark didn't know what to do with this information. He was beginning to feel overwhelmed. Should he share it with Snap? A problem shared and all that. No, not at the moment.

He decided to follow his third golden rule. *Follow the evidence trail.*

The email and bank report had given him something. Girls' names, huge amounts of cash changing hands and apparent culpability of a dodgy doctor, dodgy politician and *that man.*

Clark decided to delve into the life of the first girl listed on the email, Rachel Hermitage. He searched her social media presence and up until a few months before she was admitted to the clinic there were lots of pictures of her partying hard with a wide group of different people.

Well Rachel, you are clearly a party girl enjoying life to the full, but where are these pictures being taken?

He suddenly found one with her standing outside a bar with a group of friends.

Bentley's Bar.

He quickly searched for their website.

Oxford. Now that is interesting.

He searched the public alumnae records of Oxford University. She was there. Listed as an undergraduate.

Undergraduate? So you didn't finish uni. I guess it is obvious why.

He had a sudden thought.

Anya Novak was living in Oxford. Were they at university at the same time?

He went back to the alumnae records. Anya was listed the same – undergraduate. They were in the same year and neither finished uni.

He did a search on Anya's social media profile. The first picture of her made him stop in his tracks. Rachel was gorgeous but Anya was something else.

My God, she is stunning. A beautiful face, an amazing body. Wow.

He looked back at the pictures of Rachel. His instincts were right. Anya was there, with Rachel, in many of the pictures.

They were friends.

Clark's conspiracy radar was now on full alert. Had these girls been targeted as a group?

He hacked back into the Fairport Medical records. He wanted to see if they had been admitted together.

Right, Anya was admitted in September 2013. Rachel in November 2013. Shit, they WERE targeted together.

Clark pored over the rest of the social media pictures of Rachel and Anya. He realised that the closer it was to when they were both admitted to the clinic, the more drawn and spaced out they looked. Anya in particular had lost some of her gloss. In her early pictures she was a knockout but it was now obvious that drugs had shattered their lives.

He put his head in his hands. How tragic.

There was one thing that still unnerved Clark about these two girls. Why was Rachel dead and Anya still alive? Was this just another tragic moment in Rachel's life, or something more sinister?

Clark now had the bit between his teeth. He had a strong evidence chain already and had to see if the other girls were somehow linked.

He looked at the next girl on the list. Lisa Benbridge. He found her social media profile and the photos of her, like Anya and Rachel, showed a very attractive woman. She had long, blonde hair, a pretty face and a great body.

He had printed out a number of Anya and Rachel's social media pictures and laid them out on a table at the end of his man cave.

As soon as he saw Lisa's picture, he knew. She was in the ones he had printed out.

"There. There. There." He jabbed his finger at the pictures on the table, pointing to Lisa in each one.

He checked the same sources. There she was. Oxford University alumnae records – undergraduate. Same year as Rachel and Anya. Admitted to the clinic in November 2013, the same month as Rachel.

Jesus. Three out of five. Beautiful women. All friends. Targeted as a group.

Clark's realisation that he was actually onto something real made his stomach lurch. This is what he'd always wanted. To find a conspiracy. Uncover it. Get some revenge. Make his dad proud, but the reality was something different. He was shit scared.

Every creak in the flat made him jumpy. He had watched all the films. Wasn't this the moment when the government spooks crashed through the window, apprehended him with a black hood over his head and took him off to a secret location to torture out of him what he knew?

He shivered and turned off his computer. This was all getting a bit heavy.

16

They came again. Night five. No let-up.

*

LEX... LEXI... she could almost see the word. Where was she? The machines. Lying down. She was restrained. Was she in a hospital? It was all so clinical.

There were screens round her obscuring her view. She wrestled against the restraints. Woozy but still able to fight a little bit.

"Le... m... go!" Her speech was slurred. The full sentence wouldn't form.

She thrashed and thrashed and thrashed.

*

The scream could have woken the dead. Her eyes bulging, thrashing about in bed. Her bed. Not the bed in the nightmare.

She looked straight over at Rob.

"What the hell?" said Rob, as he was woken by the commotion.

Anya bolted out of bed and made for the bedroom door.

Rob leapt after her. Caught her at the door.

"No, you don't. You are not running away from this again. You damn well tell me what is going on."

Anya looked at him with a mixture of fear, hatred and sheer panic.

"Leave me alone."

He grabbed her tighter.

"You are hurting me."

"Tell me what is wrong."

"I can't. I have lied to you."

"I know."

Anya looked at him with disbelief. Why was he so fucking perfect? How did he know?

"Let's go downstairs, make a coffee and *talk*." Rob's accentuation of that last word frightened Anya. She had never seen Rob so angry.

She relented. She had nowhere to go. This was the moment. The moment when she had to tell Rob. Tell the truth.

*

The mood was strained. It was 5 a.m. and the day hadn't started in the sky. It was still bleak and dark, much like the mood in the kitchen as Rob made coffee and Anya sat at the table deflated and broken.

Rob placed the coffee in front of Anya, grabbed her face tenderly and said, "I love you Anya, with all of my heart. You have made my life complete. I will not let you suffer on your own. Tell me. It's about your past, isn't it?"

She looked at him. Mr Bloody Perfect. She didn't know whether to smash his face in or kiss him.

There was a short, uncomfortable silence. Anya eventually broke it.

"I am a drug addict."

Rob's face crumpled. "Oh my God Anya."

"My parents died. I was in despair. I couldn't concentrate on uni. Got in with the wrong crowd and got addicted. This is why I flunked uni."

"But you haven't been using since we met. Have you?"

"No, I was 'cured' and meeting you kept me straight. Stopped any cravings. But, these dreams, these nightmares, they are drawing me back to what happened. I am so scared."

"What did happen?"

Anya started crying. "This is the problem. I don't know. I have huge gaps in my memory. There is about eighteen months of my life I just can't remember. The dreams seem to be real, like my brain is trying to recover the lost memories, but they are horrible and unsettling."

"So, is there anything you remember?"

Anya didn't answer. She just stared at the ground, not wanting to catch Rob's eye.

"Anya. You have to tell me."

She stayed silent. She couldn't do it. Go back to those dark places.

"Anya. Come on."

After a few more uncomfortable minutes, Anya finally spoke.

"OK. OK. I know I was admitted to a place called the Loughborough Clinic, treated and apparently cured by a creepy little man called Dr French. I was in there for almost two years but only have memories of the last few weeks before I was discharged. He claims he was treating me for my addiction the whole time but I don't believe him. There is something wrong with that place. Something wrong with him. I don't know what he did to me but the nightmares are horrible. I keep seeing these letters LEX. I am woozy, restrained on a bed, wires and machines attached to me and even one where he was violating me. God, it is all so horrible and not the sort of memories that seem to link to any sort of drug addiction treatment I have ever heard of."

"Why have you taken so long to tell me all this?"

"I couldn't make sense of it. It was scaring me. When I met you Rob it was all about looking forward, forgetting my past.

Building a new life with you. I didn't want to lie to you but I just wanted to forget."

Rob was trying to process all she was telling him. His instincts had been right and he was hurt that she had not confided in him. It was fight or flight time.

He chose fight.

"OK. We need to deal with this thing head on. We have to be a hundred per cent honest with each other from now on."

Anya smiled. She felt like a weight had been lifted from her shoulders. She wasn't dealing with this alone anymore.

"Thank you, Rob. I love you."

They refilled their coffee cups and relaxed in each other's company for the first time in a while.

"Tell me. What do you want to do next? What would help?"

"I want to go back to the clinic and confront Dr French. We need some answers."

"Good, that is what we will do."

They made breakfast and then searched for the location of the Loughborough Clinic. It was in Warwickshire, about two miles outside of Leamington Spa in a countryside location. The route finder said it was sixty-nine miles away and would take about an hour and a half to get to.

"We'll close the gallery down for the day on Friday and go up there," said Rob. "I don't think we should warn them we are turning up. If what you think is true, there is something dodgy going on in that place."

The game was on.

17

Another day's work done and Clark was finding it harder and harder to concentrate. The evidence he had found about this conspiracy was invading his every waking thought.

The name copied on the email was still constantly on his mind but he wanted to complete his research on the five girls first. Rachel, Anya and Lisa were friends and seemed to have been targeted as a group. He wanted to see if Charlotte Kay and Marjit Ahmed were in the same group.

So, Charlotte, let's see what your story is.

He found another very prominent social media profile and her pictures showed another young, attractive woman, with bobbed, brunette hair, a sharp, angular face with a slightly fuller figure than the rest of the girls he had seen.

Hmm, another very attractive girl but I don't think I have seen you before.

He looked at the pictures he had printed out of Rachel, Anya and Lisa. Charlotte was not in any of them.

Now that is curious.

He checked the alumnae records of Oxford University. Would she be there? Would this be a connection?

And, there you are. Four out of five at Oxford. This is not a coincidence.

But, there was an interesting difference. Charlotte had started her second year of uni before the same pattern of degradation set in. She was in a different year and a different social group.

OK Charlotte, when were you in the clinic?... Admitted in January 2014. Interesting, a bit later. A second batch?

He took the same steps with Marjit and started with her social media profile. The pictures again showed a very attractive, slim girl of what he thought was probably Indian origin.

He knew as soon as he saw her picture that he had seen her before and, there she was, in many of the same pictures as Charlotte, but not with Anya, Rachel or Lisa.

Like Charlotte she was in her second year at Oxford University and again her photo history charted the same sorry degradation into drug addiction and a complete cessation of all social media activity once in the clinic, where she had been admitted one month after Charlotte.

Well, well, well, five out of five and we do have two distinct social groups. All at Oxford and all in the clinic at about the same time.

His stomach was lurching again because one question kept bothering him. He shouted at his screen.

"What the hell happened in that clinic to get four of these women killed and why is Anya still alive?"

Clark had to take a break, to eat and replenish his caffeine levels. He was feeling scared and isolated. He had always been happy in his own company, using his virtual mates in Proton if he wanted some banter and some human contact, even if it wasn't physical. But the reality of this, finally finding a conspiracy, what he'd always wanted, was unnerving him, taking him to emotional places he had never been. Snap would help and understand but something was holding Clark back from sharing what he had found. Was he becoming too paranoid?

He decided to try and finish the girls' stories before he moved onto the alleged conspirators. He started to look at the 'accidents'.

Clark looked for any public records of how Rachel died. He found newspaper reports in the local Berkshire paper referring to the car accident. The report said she had been driving down a local B-road in the late evening when her car was in a collision with an unidentified black car, thought to be a 4x4. This seemed to be based on a witness statement at the time from a driver who was about half a mile away from the accident, saw the collision but by the time he reached the scene the black car had gone. Rachel's car had plunged into a ditch and burst into flames. She had no chance and all the witness could do was alert the emergency services to clear up the scene.

Jesus. Was this a tragic accident... or something else?

Clark trawled the papers over the weeks following the first report and despite a few half-hearted attempts by the police appealing for information about the mystery black car, the case seemed to drift off the public conscience and out of the newspapers pretty quickly.

Come on Rachel. Help me out here. Were you murdered and where are your parents in all this? Is no one looking out for you?

He did the same for Lisa, Charlotte and Marjit's accidents. Looked at the public records and as he did his heart sank. His inner monologue playing out the frightening similarities. Accidents or murder?

Every accident the same. A car accident. The car leaving the road in similar circumstances with similar horrific results. A black car mentioned in some of them. No credible witnesses. A lame police investigation. Just another statistic. And, no parental appeals in the papers or on TV. What the hell happened?

He looked again at Rachel's life. She was an only child and it appeared had much older parents. It seemed they had Rachel very late in life. Clark found death records for her father who appeared to have died from natural causes at the age of seventy. No car accident, just life. Her mother was still alive but was registered in a nursing home for dementia patients.

OK Rachel, so that is why no one is looking out for you.

Lisa Benbridge was next. She was a product of the care system. She had no parents and no siblings. They had given her up as a baby and she was moved from foster family to care home and back again. Somehow, despite this terrible start in life, she was academically gifted and had managed to excel at school and get a place at Oxford. She was a fighter but the fire that had driven her to get out of social poverty had been extinguished.

"Fucking hell," he screamed at the empty room.

The injustice burned in Clark. If this wasn't an accident but murder, this had suddenly got extra personal. His dad was in his thoughts again. Evil people destroying innocent people's lives.

He looked at the last two girls, Charlotte and Marjit. They were also only children, no siblings.

It came as no surprise to Clark that Charlotte's parents were not alive. Both seemed to have died in their fifties from a respective heart attack (father) and brain haemorrhage (mother). Tragic, but no apparent 'accidents'.

Marjit's parents appeared to be alive but living in India. Clark couldn't find anything that suggested they had been to the UK to deal with their daughter's death. It seemed from the paperwork around her death that her body had been shipped back to India for burial. He guessed they had been fobbed off and told their daughter's death was just a tragic accident. The distance had probably put them off, especially as they got her body back home so easily and efficiently. Clark was convinced someone had made this happen quickly to avoid too many questions, leaving her parents to grieve well away from where it had all happened.

The table at the end of his room was a mess, full of photos of the five girls. He had a large whiteboard that was serving no purpose. He mused to himself. He had seen all the crime series on TV. When there was a killing, they made a murder board.

OK, time to get serious. This is murder times four. I am sure of it.

He started to write on the board and put up pictures of the girls, linked to the Loughborough Clinic, which he had written in bold in the middle. He added the names of the two conspirators, Dr Normandy and George Walker and linked them to the clinic. He detailed the financial transactions under their names.

He wrote the key points under the pictures of the girls:

'All only children and no one looking out for these girls – targeted deliberately?'

'Why were they murdered? Car Accidents – black 4x4'

'What is the money for?'

He gazed at it. It was good. Quite professional. There was something missing though. That name. He couldn't avoid it any longer. The third conspirator? He wrote his name on the board... *James Hardacre.*

18

Anya's phone rang. It was their GP. Anya listened intently and then a smile spread across her face, a rare sight in a traumatic week. Anya thanked the doctor.

"We are both fine. There is no reason why we can't produce as many babies as we want."

"Cool," said Rob, "shall we get on with it then?"

The kitchen table was suddenly an impromptu love prop as they went at it fast and furiously, easing the pain of the last week.

"Phew," said Rob, "maybe we should get the GP to phone us with good news every morning."

Anya laughed, adjusted what clothes she had left on.

"Come on handsome, let's go see this dodgy doctor."

They had a leisurely breakfast and set off just after 10 a.m., hoping to avoid the worst of the traffic. They got on the M40, which was moving at a reasonable pace, and after about an hour took the turn off the motorway to Leamington Spa. They navigated their way through the pretty town and eventually found the road out towards where the route map said the clinic was located. After fifteen minutes on the A-road, going west out of Leamington Spa, they found the turning into the minor no through road which apparently led to the clinic.

The road was almost two miles long, with no other buildings or habitation on the route. This was properly remote and added to their air of suspicion. In the last half a mile, they realised they were being watched by CCTV cameras which lined the route up to an imposing walled institution that looked more like a prison than a health clinic. There was a huge, unmanned security gate that remained securely shut as they drove up to it. There were a number of parking spaces around the entrance and it was evident that they had to park up and communicate by an intercom system before they could go any further. They were being watched by some unseen bodies who were not going to let them in without a fight. Rob and Anya suddenly realised this might not have been their best idea.

They decided to carry on. They had obviously been seen on the CCTV and might as well front it out. They parked up and walked to the intercom on the gate.

Anya pressed the buzzer and a lady's voice came back over the intercom: "Hello, can I help you?"

"Hi," said Anya, "my name is Miss Anya Novak and I was treated at this clinic several years ago for drug addiction. I was treated by Dr French and I really need to speak to him. I have been having recurring dreams about my time at the clinic and need to understand what they mean."

There was a brief pause and the lady on the intercom said, "Umm, Miss Novak, I am afraid we don't have anyone here called Dr French and we never have. I have been here for over seven years and no one of that name has been a doctor here in that time."

Anya looked at Rob with disbelief. "There must be some mistake," she said to the faceless voice. "I was here for almost two years between 2013 and 2015, treated by Dr French for drug addiction, which he cured me of."

There was another brief pause and the voice said, "I am sorry Miss Novak, but I can assure you that there is no one called Dr French here and, I am sorry to make this more stressful for you, but I have just checked our patient records and you were not treated at this clinic. Are you sure you have the right place?"

"Of course I have the right place. I might have been out of my head for most of it, but I was coherent for the latter part of my treatment and I know I was at this clinic. The Loughborough Clinic."

"I don't know what else to say to you," the voice replied. "I have no records of you ever being a patient here or the doctor you allege you were treated by."

"Let me in," said Anya, "and I will find the man that treated me and prove you wrong."

"I am sorry, I can't do that. You were not a patient here and you do not have an appointment. We do not allow people just to turn up like this, whether they have been a patient or not. We need to tightly control the environment for our patients and can't have strangers just barging in. Please leave or I will call security."

Anya let out a frustrated scream, which must have burst the eardrums of the person at the other end of the intercom. Rob ferried her away from the button, fearing what she might do next. Rob coaxed her back in the car and drove away as quickly as possible.

Anya was sobbing uncontrollably between bouts of screaming things like, "What the hell is happening?", "How can they say I wasn't there?", "Dr French is real." Rob drove to the end of the approach road and found somewhere to stop in a vain attempt to listen and calm her down.

"I think this probably confirms what you already expected," said Rob. "They are obviously lying or covering up the fact you were there. Something definitely dodgy went on in there, but we are not going to find the answers by trying to barge in. We'd better go and rethink what to do next."

Anya wanted to hurt something at that precise moment but she knew Rob was right and she wasn't going to take it out on him. "OK," she said, "take me home."

*

Janet Wall, the receptionist at the clinic who had spoken to Anya, phoned Dr Normandy.

"Dr Normandy, I have just had a woman come to the gate called Miss Anya Novak, claiming she was treated by a Dr French for drug addiction several years ago. She says she is recovering memories from the time she was here and wants to talk to the doctor about it. I told her that we have never had a Dr French work here and when I checked our patient records we have never treated her. I sent them away threatening to call security and that seemed to work. I thought I should let you know."

"Thank you, Janet," said Dr Normandy. "Do you have her on CCTV?"

"Yes, we do."

"I'll come and have a look at the pictures."

He arrived in reception within a few minutes and Janet showed him the CCTV.

"I have never seen that woman in my life," said Dr Normandy. "Well done for getting rid of her. She is clearly deluded about being here."

The receptionist was pleased with herself. Staff knew not to get on the wrong side of Dr Normandy as her colleague Janice had found out when she opened one of his confidential parcels. She was sacked and escorted off the premises before anyone knew what had happened. He was a creepy bully but he paid well and people learnt to keep their mouths shut and do what he said.

But, there was something about that woman's face that Janet recognised. The office staff generally did not interact with the patients once they were in treatment but she was sure she had seen Anya Novak at the clinic. She pondered on it for a bit but soon dismissed it, as after all her records would be on the system if she had been there. Wouldn't they?

19

A week had passed and Clark had not heard from Anya Novak.

"Damn," he muttered to himself, "she can't have believed my letter."

He looked at his new 'murder board' and pondered how to handle this. He decided he would have to try again, add some more evidence of what he had found to try and hook her in.

He knew what he was doing was weird but he was convinced this was a serious conspiracy, led by people that didn't hesitate to kill to protect their secrets.

He started to freehand a new letter. After a few screwed-up versions, which landed in various places around the bin – his basketball career would have to wait – he landed a version he was happy with.

Dear Miss Novak,

I am sorry if my previous letter freaked you out. I am sure my name didn't help. I bet you thought I was some nutter but my name genuinely is Clark Kent. My parents really didn't get what they were doing naming me Clark!

I really do believe your life is in danger and I think you can help me in sorting out what I think is a big criminal conspiracy, which you are unwittingly involved in.

I have been searching through the people and events that I have found connected to this conspiracy and I hope by giving you further information you will be convinced that I am not some conspiracy nutter. So, here goes.

Anya, you are one of five girls that were admitted to the Loughborough Clinic in 2013 and 2014, treated by a Dr Normandy. All of you were admitted as drug addicts and you were all at Oxford University in your first or second years, at that time. Two of your friends, Rachel Hermitage and Lisa Benbridge were admitted within a few months of you. Two other girls, Charlotte Kay and Marjit Ahmed were also admitted during this time. I don't think you knew them but they were together in a separate social group in Oxford. All four of these girls are now dead, all killed in suspicious car accidents. I don't want to frighten you but I don't understand why you have not been targeted for an 'accident', which is why I am scared for your safety.

I have found a money trail back to Dr Normandy that suggests he was being paid a significant amount of money to treat you and the other girls. I have not yet been able to find out what the money was for. There are two prominent public figures with their grubby hands all over this, linked to the clinic.

Please help me Anya. Write to me at this address and we can agree a time and place to meet that suits you.
Regards
Clark Kent
Flat 13, Windrush Plaza, Reading, RG1 4EP

He popped it in an envelope, indulged in another first-class stamp and nipped down the road to the post box.

"Come on Anya. Help me out," he muttered under his breath as he dropped the envelope in the post-box hole.

He got back to his flat and logged onto Proton.

KRYPTO:	Snap. You out there?
SNAPDEVIL:	Yo dude, what can I do for ya?
KRYPTO:	That dodgy corp. I hit pay dirt. Totally dodgy. Money, murder and names.
SNAPDEVIL:	OK, I am intrigued. Who?
KRYPTO:	James Hardacre.
SNAPDEVIL:	Holy shit.
KRYPTO:	I know. Can you dig for me? Find out about him and the family.
SNAPDEVIL:	Consider it done.

Clark was relieved at finally sharing it with someone. Snap was the best at mining people's personal secrets. If there was something about the Hardacres to be found, Clark was sure Snap would find it.

He drank some coffee and ate four Jaffa Cakes. He stared into space. Thinking. Worrying. Waiting.

20

His phone beeped. A text message.

'Anya Novak needs to be dealt with.'

He smiled to himself. He wondered when the fifth one would be 'tidied up'. He couldn't understand why they had waited so long. He put his normal plan into motion.

At 2 a.m. he drove slowly up to the bottom of the close where Anya lived. He was in full black attire to make sure he wasn't noticed and, thankfully, street lighting at this end of the village was quite sparse. He would be in and out within a minute. He moved quickly and stealthily up the pavement to get a fix on Anya's car. He had to be sure he was going to 'hit' the right one. There were two on the drive. He guessed it was the smaller of the two. Men always had the bigger cars. Something about size and all that.

As he walked away, he jumped as their neighbour's dog started barking. He hadn't made a sound. How had he spooked the dog?

"Shit," he muttered under his breath.

He hurried away, no point in hanging around to be seen. He was back in the car and off down the road within thirty seconds.

21

Anya woke with a start. For once it wasn't the bad dreams. The next door's dog was barking. She got out of bed and peered out of the window.

There was a dark shape moving away from her house. She strained to see more but it was too dark and very quickly the shape was gone. She didn't know whether to worry about it or not. The visit to the clinic had unnerved her and she was seeing suspicious things around every corner.

"Stop being silly," she said to herself and got into bed next to her human hot water bottle. She hoped the bad dreams wouldn't come again, now that Rob knew.

*

It was Saturday morning and Anya had not had any bad dreams the previous night. She had been woken by the dog barking but the demons hadn't invaded her sleeping hours for the first time in a week.

She was still rattled by recent events, including the horrible visit to the clinic but, as Rob was busy doing some gallery stuff, catching up from yesterday, she had the opportunity to be on her own with most of the day to play with. She hoped it would give her some head space to work out what to do next. She decided to go food shopping, got in her car and set off.

Anya decided to take the B4526 out of the village and take the long way around to get to Waitrose in Pangbourne. It was much prettier and she wasn't in any rush. As she drove through the lovely countryside, she began to feel better and smiled to herself about how faux-upper class she had become. Shopping at Waitrose, living in a posh Oxfordshire village and running an art gallery. The class thing had always been her parents' minor obsession.

Her dad did his two-year conscription in the Czech army before becoming a trainee chef in a Michelin-star restaurant in Prague. He was very good and soon moved up the ranks to sous chef, delivering world-class food. He moved to England at twenty-three and worked across a number of Michelin star restaurants in London and Berkshire. He loved the accolades, the famous diners, rubbing shoulders with the right level of people. He felt he had achieved a level of class mobility that allowed him to act like someone in the upper classes. Anya's mother was just the same. She worked as a window dresser at John Lewis in High Wycombe. She had worked for the firm pretty much all her life, stopping only to have, and bring up, Anya. She always talked about how the shop attracted the right level of people. She was actively involved in village life, the WI, the church fundraising, Neighbourhood Watch. She acted like she belonged at the class level she had created for herself and others seem to accept her and Dad for what they were. Anya loved that they acted posh.

"God, I miss you," she said, articulating her inner sadness as the memories of her parents shone bright.

Her mood had turned a bit melancholy but a sudden stomach cramp jumped her back to the present and a smile returned to her face.

So, body. What are you doing to me? I'm late, so am I pregnant? Wouldn't that be wonderful? I bet it was the great shag we had on the table.

She giggled to herself. This was nice. Maybe after all the nightmares, her life was going to get back on track. She still wanted answers about her past but being pregnant would refocus on the future. She drove on, much happier than she had been for some while.

He had been waiting and saw her drive out of the village. He had clocked the right car. He caught up with Anya's car quickly. She was up ahead toddling along one of the numerous back roads in these parts. Perfect killing territory. He glanced in his mirrors and up ahead. No cars around. He would have to be quick though. This was broad daylight on a Saturday morning and there was bound to be other cars around any minute.

He put his foot down and sped up right behind Anya. Anya looked in her mirror.

Who is this arsehole tailgating me?

It was a black 4x4. Suddenly the driver made a move to overtake and Anya slowed a bit to let the prat pass, but to her horror, just as he got alongside her he wrenched the wheel to the left and smashed into the side of her car. She lost control immediately. Her car veered off the road and started hurtling down a bank towards a group of trees. She wrestled for control as the car bumped and tipped on the rough surface. There was an impact and then total blackness.

He sped away, pretty sure no other cars had seen the accident. He would get the damage sorted quickly at the normal place. The one that was on Dad's payroll, who didn't ask any questions.

22

The doctor was pleased. He already had Bianca and Sam well entrenched in his special drug programme. At the start, they were so spaced out he could pretty much do what he wanted but as he controlled the withdrawal phase with his special concoction of drugs, he put them into induced comas to save all the hassle of the violent rages. He had told all the girls that the scars and bruises they suffered were as a result of restraint after withdrawal rages. This was another one of his blatant lies.

Once they were in the programme they hardly left their beds. His special programme allowed him to keep them pretty much comatose the whole time. The scars and bruises came from the next phase of the programme.

He did bring them round for short periods to give their brains some semblance that they were being treated but really, one of the positive side effects of the coma drugs was the suppression of memories. He wanted them to remember being there but not much else, as after all the clients were relying on them not remembering what had happened to them.

He did occasionally feel guilty about what he was doing but it never lasted for long.

"Guilt is for poor people," he said out loud as if he felt the need to answer the challenge that his brain was creating from the so-called good part of his soul. He laughed at this thought.

I don't think there are any good parts left. Straight to hell for me!

The thought reminded him. His online pals would almost certainly have uploaded some more images. They had promised him some much younger ones this time.

23

Rob was busy in the gallery, dealing with the latest batch of art from local artists. This had been one of the foundations of his success, connecting with local artists that needed an outlet for their talent and selling their stuff locally and through the European art dealer collective he was part of. He took a slice of each sale to cover his costs, and make a profit, but the artists did well out of the deal. He had always had a head for business and the gallery was booming.

As he was allowing himself a minute to wallow in his ego, his phone suddenly rang.

"Hello, Rob Simmons speaking."

"Mr Simmons, are you the next of kin for Anya Novak?"

He was stunned. What sort of question was that!

"I'm sorry, who is this and why are you asking me about Anya?"

"My name is Judy Belbin and I am a nurse at the A&E Department at the Berkshire General Hospital. Anya has been admitted and I am trying to contact her next of kin. Your name was in her phone."

He could hardly bear to say the next sentence.

"Is she... dead?"

"No, but she is in a coma. She has been in a car accident."

Rob didn't know whether to laugh or cry. He had always thought that asking about next of kin meant people were dead. He took a moment to compose himself.

"Mr Simmons. Are you still there?"

"Yes, yes, sorry. Just a bit of a shock. I am on my way."

He quickly ushered out his customers, closed the gallery and got straight in his car.

It took forty excruciating minutes to get through the busy Saturday traffic and find a parking space at the hospital. Rob rushed into A&E like some madman and asked for Anya. She had been moved into an ICU bed on another ward. He rushed up to the next level and found his beautiful Anya, lying unconscious in a bed connected up to all sorts of machines and drips that were keeping her alive. The doctor came and spoke to Rob.

"Mr Simmons, my name is Dr Barkley. I treated your partner when she was admitted. She is alive but has not regained consciousness. She has a head injury, broken ribs and multiple bruises over her body, due to the car accident. She is in a coma and I have to admit it is difficult to say what her prognosis is at the moment. We will have to monitor her over the next few days."

"Do we know what happened?"

"It appears a member of the public came upon the accident and called an ambulance. They were able to get her out of the car without incident but she was unconscious the whole time."

"Why won't she wake up?"

"I am concerned about the head injury. It is almost certainly the cause of her comatose state. We need to monitor her closely and hope that her being in a coma is just the body's way of healing."

"You think she is going to die, don't you? Why are you not being honest with me?"

"Look Mr Simmons, I know you are upset but I can assure you I am not holding anything back. I am concerned about her but we must remain positive. Despite her comatose state, the rest of her vitals are good at the moment."

"Can she hear us, if we speak to her?"

"Well, as with most coma patients, medical evidence suggests that her brain is still cognisant and can receive sounds, even if the body will not allow a conscious state. I would encourage you to talk to her."

Rob sat by the side of the bed and held Anya's hand. He started nattering away, trying not to show the pain in his voice, when all he wanted to do was shout, scream and cry.

As Rob continued to talk to Anya, the machines kept beeping, the drips kept dripping, but Anya didn't stir, didn't change position, just lay there small and vulnerable. Rob had been there almost five hours. He hadn't eaten, gone to the loo, moved from the position by her bed.

"Come on love, I think you should go home, get something to eat and have some rest. We will ring you the minute something changes."

Rob looked at the friendly face of the ward sister with a mixture of exhaustion and anger.

"I can't leave her."

"You won't be any good to her if you wear yourself out. Please go home and come back tomorrow."

He reluctantly agreed, kissed Anya on the forehead and walked away, tears welling up.

As he drove home in a daze, his thoughts turned to the gallery.

What the hell am I going to do? I can't look after Anya and run the business.

As he tried to process what to do, the image of Anya lying in that bed kept invading his thoughts. Suddenly, the fog cleared and an idea hit him.

Elisha?

Elisha was one of the local artists who had previously shown an interest in working at the gallery. They had politely declined her offer as the business could only sustain Rob and Anya, but now things had changed. He called her after eating a quick dinner and explained what had happened. She was delighted to help.

24

Clark was sitting eating Chinese out of those groovy square takeout boxes. Chicken in black bean sauce, egg fried rice and some prawn crackers. He was slouched back in his office chair, feet on the desk, watching the feeds from the early evening news.

As he shovelled more and more food in, a headline from BBC South East stopped him in mid shovel.

'Young lady badly injured in car accident just outside Goring. Police believe another car involved did not stop at the scene. Woman in coma.'

He put down the takeout carton and quickly logged onto the local BBC news website.

'Car accident on a B-road heading out of Goring. Woman's car driven off the road and crashed into a tree. Police appealing for witnesses, especially anyone that saw a black car in the area.'

Clark almost saw the Chinese food again far too soon.

This can't be. Just like the others. Is this Anya Novak?

He sat staring at the screen, not knowing what to do next. He found the number of the Berkshire General Hospital and asked to be put through to admissions.

"Hello, can I help you?"

"Yes, I was wondering whether an Anya Novak was admitted today?"

"Are you a member of the family?"

He had to lie. He knew they wouldn't confirm if he said he wasn't family.

"Yes, I am her brother." He winced at the lie, hoping the tone of his voice would not give him away.

"Yes, I can confirm that Miss Novak was admitted today. She is in ICU. Please phone the ward before visiting."

Clark hung up and went straight for the drinks cabinet. He didn't drink as a rule but dusted off an old bottle of whisky and downed two measures, one after another. The taste was horrible and didn't settle well with the Chinese. He sat down.

What the fuck is going on? This is just like the other four. Someone has tried to wipe out the last one. God, I didn't really think this was going to happen. Why now?

He sat with his head in his hands. Shaking. The alcohol had not calmed his nerves. He had to shut down for the day, both digitally and emotionally, and work out what the hell to do next.

This has suddenly got frighteningly real.

*

His phone beeped. A text message.

'You did not get the job done. Anya Novak is still alive. Get it sorted!!!!'

Shit.

25

Rob bolted up the next day, after a troubled sleep. Although it was Sunday and the gallery was closed, Rob met up with Elisha and gave her a whistlestop tour of how to run the gallery, ready for Monday. He then rushed to the hospital to be with Anya.

When Rob arrived at the hospital the police were there, checking with the doctors whether Anya had woken up.

"Mr Simmons, my name is DC Stephanie Bellows. I am investigating the accident your partner was involved in. Is there anything you can tell me?"

"No, I wasn't there. I only know what the doctors told me."

"We believe another vehicle was involved but did not stop at the scene. There is a black paint transference mark on the side of your partner's car."

"OK. What are you doing about that?"

"Do you own a black car Sir?"

"What? Yes, I do. Are you seriously suggesting that I was somehow involved in this accident?"

"Just routine Sir. Many attempted murders or murders are committed by people known to the victim."

Rob could not believe what he was hearing but had to stop himself from adding 'assaulting a police officer' to the current list of absolute fucked-up things that had happened over the last few days.

"I am really offended but I guess you are doing your job. My car is in the hospital car park and you are very welcome to examine it now."

Rob had to escort the officers down to his car before he could see Anya. His heart was breaking but he had to get these arseholes off his back.

They examined his car and quickly ruled it out of being part of the accident.

"Thank you, Sir. Your co-operation is appreciated. Our forensic teams are working on trying to identify the car brand that the paint came from. We will let you know when we have more. If you think of anything, you will let us know."

"Of course."

Rob left them and rushed back up to the ward. Anya was still there. No change but thankfully no deterioration. He sat by the bed and started nattering away again.

*

Anya was confused. She was hearing voices but couldn't see anything, except blackness. Was this one of her recurring nightmares? LEX, the restraints, the violence. No, this was different. She could hear Rob's voice. He was nattering away about the gallery but she couldn't respond, couldn't move. What was going on? She was trapped in her body. She willed herself to see but nothing would work. His voice faded and she went back to the dark sleep.

*

Rob returned home to a Chinese takeaway he had bought on the way back and a bottle of white wine. He slumped in the chair, turned the TV on and watched nothing in particular. God the place was empty without Anya.

As his mind wandered around he suddenly realised there was a large pile of post on the side, a victim of the stress and strains of the last few days. Other priorities.

Rob picked the pile up and started to leaf through them. Junk, junk, junk, electric bill, junk, Waitrose vouchers, junk, the latest Matalan catalogue and… Rob stopped and stared at a hand-written envelope addressed to Anya.

What the hell is this? It looks like the same handwriting from that previous letter.

He stared at it for a few minutes, not knowing what to do. Eventually, he decided the only thing he could do was open it. After all, Anya was in no state to read it.

He ripped open the envelope and stared at the words in disbelief. It was this Clark Kent character again, but this time he was writing with details of what had happened to Anya and the other girls who had been treated at the clinic, and they seemed to tie in with what she had been telling him.

Rob was stunned. Was this man for real?

He read it over and over again.

God, so much of this fits with what Anya told me, but he is implying that these other girls were murdered in car acc…

He couldn't finish the sentence. Car accidents.

The police said they thought someone else was involved.

Rob's heart started to race and his stomach was in knots. He stood up and started pacing the room.

What is going on?

He wanted to cry, scream and shout but he had to get his head together.

The Loughborough Clinic. The car accidents. The drug abuse. Oxford Uni. This can't be a coincidence.

He read the letter again and again, hoping that somehow this would all make sense. He needed Anya. He needed her to explain.

After what seemed like the fiftieth time of reading it, he suddenly focused on what the penultimate paragraph was saying.

Who is Dr Normandy and what is he being paid for?

He picked up his tablet and found the website of the Loughborough Clinic, within the website of the company running it. Fairport Medical. He navigated to the main information page.

'Dr Felix Normandy, CEO.'

Rob was confused.

Anya was treated by someone called Dr French but they claimed yesterday they had never employed a Dr French. How is that possible?

He just couldn't process it all. Who was Dr French? Who was this strange man Clark Kent and why was he looking out for Anya? Was this some vicious arsehole just playing sick mind games?

Rob sank the rest of the bottle and before he knew it fell into an alcohol-fuelled sleep. The letter fell out of his hand, landing unceremoniously on the carpet, next to the empty wine bottle.

Now Rob was the one who was going to have the nightmares.

26

The doctor examined Sam and Bianca's latest blood tests.

"Good, good. You should both be ready in about five weeks."

The girls didn't answer. They were comatose. Again. Courtesy of the doctor's magical drug cocktail. He goaded them.

"Oh, you poor sweet, innocent girls. How perfect you are."

He texted his contact.

'The girls are progressing well. They should be ready in about five weeks. Please can you arrange for the usual packages to be sent to me, marked strictly confidential.'

*

His phone beeped. He read the text message.

'Excellent.'

He texted the boss.

'All systems go. Doctor says 5 weeks. I will meet the clients.'

The boss texted back straight away.

'Good. Let's meet at my club. I would like to be there. Sort it for tomorrow night about 8 p.m. We also need to chat about the other situation.'

He got straight onto the clients. He knew they were both personal friends of the boss. There was no margin for error. He was under no illusion that the boss would have any hesitation in taking him out if he sniffed any disloyalty or cock-ups. He spoke out loud to the empty room, feeling the need to justify his loyalty. Almost as though his every move was being filmed and he was having to play to the camera.

"Don't worry Boss. You can trust me. After all, you are paying me enough not to make mistakes."

*

His phone rang and, as soon as he answered, the caller launched straight in. Pissed off and aggressive.

"What is the situation with Anya Novak?"

"I have been into the hospital a couple of times to see if there is any way I could access her room but the ward is pretty much locked down. I think it is too risky to try to get to her in the hospital. If she wakes up, my best bet is to hit her again when she is out in public."

"I am not happy leaving these loose ends. You had better pray she doesn't wake up, but if she does you need to make sure you do the job properly next time. Don't try to access her in the hospital. I agree it is too risky and I can't afford for you to make more mistakes."

The phone was promptly hung up and he cursed to himself. He had never made a mistake but his dad was not prepared to cut him any slack with the Anya situation. Just because he was one of the most powerful men in the country, it didn't stop him being an asshole.

Once he had dealt with Anya he was gone. His so-called family could sod off. He would make sure he was the other side of the world before the shit hit the fan.

27

Rob woke up the next morning. Still on the sofa with a thumping headache. He tried to reorientate himself. Where was he? Where was Anya?

His brain soon caught up and the deep pain in the pit of his stomach reminded him.

He looked at his watch.

Shit. Eight-thirty.

He was supposed to be meeting Elisha at the gallery at nine.

He willed his stiff, hungover body to get off the sofa. He saw the letter lying on the floor. He picked it up and placed it on the table.

Sorry Mr Kent, I can't deal with you at the moment.

He jumped in the shower, dressed quickly, sunk a glass of orange juice and ate two pieces of toast faster than was probably healthy.

The gallery was only ten minutes away and he was only about five minutes late. Elisha was waiting outside.

"Sorry Elisha."

"God Rob, you look terrible."

"Bad night."

"Is there anything I can do? How is Anya?"

"Look Elisha, you are doing it. Just being here is more than I can ask for. Anya is really bad and you helping me out is just what

I need. I can do the mornings but if you can do each afternoon, I can go and see Anya."

"Of course."

Elisha smiled at him, seeking some sign that the Rob she knew might still be in there.

Rob noticed the smile. Almost flirtatious. In another life, he might have cracked onto Elisha. She was just his type. Arty, quirky and incredibly cute. But he had his Anya, his soulmate.

They got down to work and got the gallery business sorted out. At lunchtime, Rob left to go and see Anya, starting what would become a demoralising routine of work, Anya, lonely house.

When Rob got to the hospital nothing had changed. The machines were still beeping, the drips kept dripping and the nurses kept checking her vitals. Anya just lay there. Small and fragile.

Once the room was clear, Rob started nattering away.

"Anya. That man has written to you again. Superman. Clark Kent. He says you were one of five girls treated at the clinic as drug addicts. Two were your friends, but Anya, they are all dead, killed in car accidents."

Rob had to stop, stifling the tears.

"What do I do Anya? I think someone tried to kill you. Do I trust this man?"

28

Clark was agitated. The attempted murder, because he was sure that's what it was, on Anya Novak had been the biggest endorsement yet that he was onto something. He studied the murder board.

The girls are all linked and deliberately targeted. We have Dr Normandy being paid big money for something. Other big money transactions. George Walker involved. James Hardacre, involvement unknown. Snap onto that. What can I do next?

He stood and stared, seeking inspiration from the pictures and words he had written. A thought came to him. He started to look back at the pile of social media pictures he had printed off. The ones he had not put up on the board.

Someone was targeting you all. Whoever it was must be in these pictures.

He looked at the pictures of the first group. Anya, Rachel and Lisa. He spread them out on the table.

He soon found what he was looking for.

Hello blondy. You seem like someone who was active in this group and you look like a proper stuck-up posh boy.

A man, tall, fair haired with what seemed like good breeding was all over the group's pictures. It was a leap of faith but something about his face twitched Clark's conspiracy radar.

You look like just the type.

He pinned up the clearest picture he had of the man and put him next to the pictures of the five girls, with a big question mark next to him.

He looked at Charlotte and Marjit's pictures. He wasn't there. He looked over them again.

Hold on.

He picked up one picture and had to get a magnifying glass out. The image was blurry, but magnified it was a definite maybe.

Hmm, is this you blondy? You look like you are trying not to be seen. Are you the finder? Are you one of the people being paid out of this Cayman Island bank account?

Clark sat down in his 'kick arse' office chair, poured himself another coffee and stared at the board, taking it all in. The little grey cells, à la Poirot, doing their thing.

Clark suddenly realised his main terminal was flashing with a Proton message. SnapDevil?

He logged on.

SNAPDEVIL:	Dude. Here is the FTP site link. That is one serious heavy family.
KRYPTO:	Thx. May need you again. How about a Cayman Island bank?
SNAPDEVIL:	WTF? How heavy is this shit getting?
KRYPTO:	Heavy. Will read and let you know when we need to do the bank.
SNAPDEVIL:	Wait your instructions dude.

Clark followed the secure link that Snap had sent him, which contained his initial findings on the Hardacre family. He started to devour the words.

JAMES HARDACRE

PM, obvs. No obvious skeletons on the dark web other than plenty of speculation that his dad got him the

PM job. Seems quite a weak-willed man, propped up by his dad's power and influence. Had his first kid in March 2015. Typical public school upper class knob.

ANNABELLE HARDACRE

James' wife. Well connected. Rich family. Obvious marriage material for someone like James. Completely shuns the limelight. Very rarely seen in public. Only comes out to be by his side when she absolutely has to.

WILLIAM HARDACRE

Multi billionaire playboy. Owns huge swathes of property in Mayfair. Seriously well connected, nationally and internationally. Presidents. Sheiks. Rumoured to be part of the 'Deep State' and, as above, lots of speculation that he got James the job by using his influence with the other king-makers in this country. Married, with one kid (James, obvs), but rumours that he can't keep his dick in his pants. Definitely the real power in this family and a nasty piece of work. Rumours he has some dodgy connections with major crime groups, including your old pals the Brady Brothers.

Clark was stunned and before he realised it, tears were rolling down his cheeks.

Bastards, Bastards, Bastards.

He couldn't contain his emotions. Somehow, after all his searching he had found a conspiracy with loose connections to the men who had killed his father.

He sat and stared at the screen, reading the words over and over, his resolve strengthening by the minute. Now this really was personal.

29

They met up in the swanky London gentleman's club. The type of place where nobody asked any questions. Perfect for the meeting with the new clients.

The boss and the fixer sat sinking large glasses of brandy as they waited for the first client. The door opened.

The boss stood up to greet the visitor.

"Charles, a pleasure to meet you again. How is life?"

"Not too bad. Keeping the wolf from the door."

They all laughed. The sort of laugh that the filthy rich could make when telling lame jokes about money. There were no wolves near any of their doors.

"Charles. We have had notification from the doctor that he is about five weeks away from being able to start our little... arrangement."

"Good, what do you need?"

"Well old boy. A payment of £725k into this off-shore bank account would be a start. After that you need to get your son to provide the necessary and send to the doctor in this packaging."

"OK, seems fine. I'll transfer the money tomorrow and get this package to Edward."

He got up, holding the details of the bank account and the supplied packaging. "Nice to do business with you."

"Our pleasure."

The boss smiled at his fixer and raised his glass.

"Here's to more lovely money. When is Castro coming?"

"He should be here in about ten minutes."

Sure enough, after about ten minutes, the door opened and the second client walked in.

"Castro. How are you and how is your father?"

"Very well, thank you. He sends his regards and can I thank you so much for doing this. We just can't take any more. You are going to make our lives complete."

"No problem. The doctor is ready to start in about five weeks, so you need to supply the necessary in this packaging."

Castro took it and looked away, a bit embarrassed.

"We also need the payment Castro."

"Oh, yes, of course. How do you want it?"

"Transfer £725k into this account." He handed him the details on a piece of paper.

"OK, fine. We'll get this sorted out."

"I guess your father is paying?"

"Well, sort of. We are sharing the cost. I don't have enough yet to cover it all. My job pays well but I can't pay it all."

"Hmm, fathers should be good to their sons. We have to show you the way. Make sure you take the right forks in the road, so to speak. I usually find money has a lot to do with that."

Castro didn't know what to say and nervously shuffled out of the room.

"God, what a spineless idiot. Why don't they make them with backbone anymore?"

The fixer just smiled and nodded. The boss carried on rambling.

"Talking of spineless. Are you keeping an eye on what my son is doing? I hope he can count on your support when the important votes come along."

"Well, you know it will mean me voting against my party, but with the amount you are paying me, I am sure I can be persuaded."

"Don't get sarcastic with me boy. You'll do as you are damn well told."

The fixer pushed back in his winged chair and decided not to say anything else. After a few minutes of uncomfortable silence, the boss spoke again.

"Oh, and as for the other 'issue', I presume you know he didn't get the job done?"

"Well, yes, I gathered from your text messages. Why did you decide to hit her now? I thought she wasn't a threat?"

"She visited the clinic, asking for the doctor. Thankfully the security protocols he had put in place worked and she was sent away, but it means she is recovering memories like the others."

"So, the doctor's approach to our little scheme isn't as foolproof as he first suggested. That is all five now."

"I know. Once he has done these two, we will deal with him. I don't accept failure. We need to eliminate Anya Novak, get these deals done and finish this thing."

"Message received."

He looked at his fixer with the stare that intimidated most people he met.

And I will deal with you too, when the time is right, he thought to himself.

30

Rob returned home after another demoralising visit to the hospital. He grabbed a coffee and walked into the living room.

It was still there. The letter. Kind of sneering at him.

He picked it up and read it again for about the sixtieth time. He rubbed his hand over his face.

What the hell should I do? I don't know this man with his weird name. This has to be a sick joke.

He sat down, his head spinning.

How does he know about Anya? This just doesn't make sense.

He tried to take his mind off the letter, off the hell his life had suddenly become. Just as Anya had told him about her previous life and the awful trauma she had been going through with the dreams, she was gone. Not able to talk to him. Not able to explain. He couldn't shake the fear that her life was in danger, that the car accident was like the others. Murder, or thankfully in Anya's case, attempted murder.

He phoned Elisha and discussed gallery business and Anya. He got off the phone and channel surfed. Nothing was working. The letter still sat there. Goading him.

After much soul searching, Rob made a decision. He had to find out about this man. 'Clark Kent' or whatever his real name was. He had to visit him and see if he was for real and find out how he knew so much about Anya.

This Clark person lived in Reading and his flat was not that far from the hospital where Anya was still lying helpless. He decided to write to him, suggesting they meet up one evening.

Dear Mr Kent, or whatever your real name is,

I am disturbed by your letters. How do you know so much about my partner Anya and, if you are for real, why haven't you reported your findings to the police?

I am prepared to meet you, only because much of what you say seems true to Anya's situation. I truly believe that her life is in danger and that someone tried to kill her in a car accident. The bottom line is that I need an explanation from you. You had better not be some sick prankster.

I am in Reading every day at the hospital seeing Anya. I will come to your flat on Saturday evening around 7.30 p.m. If this is not acceptable, please leave a message at the hospital for me.

Rob Simmons

31

Snap's preliminary findings on the Hardacre family were still spinning in Clark's head. When his dad took his own life, Clark had been too young to do anything about the Brady Brothers. He hadn't acquired the skills he now had or the access to the virtual friends that he could always count on to find what needed to be found. Now though it was different and, whilst he hadn't set out to find a connection with the Brady Brothers, fate had somehow given him the chance to bring down somebody that had clear associations with them. Revenge by association, unless of course they could find some firmer connections.

He was also concerned that he hadn't heard back from Anya Novak and was unsure whether she had even received the letter before her 'accident'.

He decided all he could do was to keep on building the case.

Follow the money.

Follow the evidence.

He decided to search further on the secure Cayman Island server of Fairport Medical for more evidence.

Right, Hardacre. Let's see what else we have on you.

He did a rudimentary search through the file structure for any mention of the Hardacre name. Nothing. He logged back onto Dr Normandy and George Walker's email accounts. Apart from the one email he had already found… nothing.

How odd. Why is James Hardacre's name only on one email and no mention of William Hardacre?

He changed tack and started aimlessly trawling through the file structure, looking for anything interesting. He found a sub folder under George Walker's main folder called 'Dr Normandy – pictures'.

The folder had hundreds of picture files. He clicked on the first one. The shock of what he saw made Clark's body convulse, which forced the chair he was sitting on to roll away from the desk on the slick wooden floor.

From the few feet away he now found himself from his computer screen, he fixed his gaze on the most depraved thing he had ever seen. A child being sexually abused. He guessed all the others were the same. He couldn't bring himself to look at another one, but he had to see if these were all what he thought they were. Evidence of paedophilia.

He forced himself to look at a few more and sure enough the same horrific pictures came up one by one. When he got to the fifth picture something else took the wind out of him.

Oh my God, that is Dr Normandy. Abusing these children.

He looked at a few more and sure enough there was Dr Normandy in many of the pictures.

What is this? How does this fit in with what I have found so far?

He had to close the pictures down. He couldn't bear to look at any more. It was making his stomach lurch. He sat in his chair, trying to make sense of this new revelation.

Dr Normandy. A dirty fucking paedo.

Clark was now spending most evenings staring at his murder board, seeking inspiration. He knew the Cayman Island bank account was key. If he could somehow hack in and find more on the money trail, he was sure this conspiracy would be blown wide open.

But, that was easier said than done. He would need Snap's help. Banks did good cyber security and Cayman Island banks probably had the best around. People like the Hardacres and the

Brady Brothers used institutions like this to protect their dirty little secrets and would not tolerate some two-bit hacker getting at their information easily. Clark smiled. He and his friends were no two-bit hackers.

He logged onto Proton.

KRYPTO: Snap. You out there?

SNAPDEVIL: Always Krypto. What can I do for you?

KRYPTO: This thing. The conspiracy. Getting really fucking real. We need to hack that Cayman Island bank account.

SNAPDEVIL: Loves me a challenge. Send me the details.

KRYPTO: Here is the IP to the outer firewall. I'll send you a Bitcoin.

SNAPDEVIL: Appreciate dude, but the thrill of the hack is still enough.

KRYPTO: I know but if this goes all the way it will be like nothing we have ever done. You deserve some payment.

SNAPDEVIL: OK, leave it with me. This won't be fast.

Clark logged off. He knew Snap would love the challenge. Knowing he was onto that would give him some head space. Once again, he sat in his office chair staring at the board.

The reassuring thud of the post on his hall floor brought his wandering mind back to the present. Clark's heart skipped a beat as he came upon a hand-written envelope.

She must have written before the accident.

He ripped open the envelope and read the contents. It wasn't from Anya. It was from her partner Rob. Clark was glad that Anya had someone looking out for her.

The letter was a bit terse. Rob was clearly sceptical about Clark and what he had said in his letter but wanted to meet. The next evening.

OK, Rob, I get why you are sceptical but I look forward to meeting you.

Clark was glad he could finally share this nightmare with someone else.

32

Saturday came and Anya's condition was unchanged. Rob had not heard from Clark so assumed it was OK to go and see him. He grabbed a quick meal in the hospital canteen and set off for Clark's flat. He lived quite near the centre of town in a swanky riverside complex. He parked up in the multi-storey opposite and made his way up to his flat.

Rob found Flat 13 and buzzed on the door. The door was opened by a lanky, slightly dishevelled character with mad curly hair and glasses. Rob thought he really could be the Clark Kent in the movies.

"Hi, I'm Rob," as he stretched out his hand in greeting.

"Hi, I am Clark," he replied as he shook his hand with a confident, firm grip. "Please come in."

They both sat down in his living room and for a moment there was an uncomfortable silence as neither knew how to start the conversation.

Clark broke the silence. "How is Anya?"

"No change. The doctors don't seem to know when she will wake up."

Clark launched in. "Look Rob, I am so glad that you came to see me. My head is exploding with the amount of stuff I have found. When I read about Anya's accident it all suddenly became too real. I knew I was onto something the minute I found the first email mentioning the girls and finding out that four of them are dead."

"Whoa, Whoa, slow down. You can't just launch this at me. I mean, who are you? How do you know about Anya? Why haven't you been to the police? I don't know you from Adam. Are you just playing some sick joke on me? On us? Look mate, I need a bloody explanation before I start listening to your fantasies about my Anya."

Clark had to check himself. He was bursting to tell Rob everything but he realised how weird this must all seem, but then why had he come?

"Look, I am sorry. I know this must seem strange but I needed to see you, Anya, to explain what I have found."

"I'm sorry, that is not good enough. Why haven't you gone straight to the police?"

"The way I have found this information is… let's just say… not by conventional methods."

"What does that mean? I know about the internet. You can find out anything these days. What did you do, find it on Reddit?"

"Err, no. You don't find what I found on the conventional web."

"Oh shit, so you are a hacker. A criminal. Jesus, this was a mistake."

Rob moved to the front door to leave. He had never broken the law in his life and was not about to start now, however much he wanted to help Anya.

Clark was mortified. He was about to lose the only physical person that could help him with this nightmare. He grabbed Rob by the arm.

"Please Rob, don't go."

"Get off me. I do not break the law."

"Rob. Please. Give me five minutes. I need to show you why I do this."

Rob stopped and glared at Clark. Trying to read him. He didn't seem like a scammer. He seemed genuinely concerned, frightened even.

"Five minutes and then I am gone."

Clark breathed a sigh of relief.

"Please come through to my office. I need to show you something."

Clark invited Rob through to what could definitely be referred to as a man cave. Rob was overwhelmed by the gadgets on show. Clearly this guy didn't get out much. It might have been impressive, but Rob also thought it seemed kind of sad. There was no hint of a life here – just screens and terminals and exposed wires, along with takeout boxes. He clearly didn't entertain much.

"This is why I do it."

Clark thrust the picture of his father at Rob.

"Who is this?"

"This is my father. When I was ten, he took his own life, because greedy corporate bastards asset stripped his company and ran off with the pension scheme money. He was left with nothing. Then, the politicians who were put in charge of holding these men to account brushed it all under the carpet and let them get away with murder. Literally."

"Oh."

"Yes, Oh. At the time I was too young to do anything about it but I made it my life's ambition to nail these bastards or people like them, including dirty, sleazy politicians."

Rob was overwhelmed by the sudden passion and mild aggression coming from Clark. He could see tears in his eyes. He was either completely genuine or a great actor.

"It all started with the news story about George Walker fiddling expenses. I started to look at his life and yes, I broke the law by hacking his private email but it didn't take me long to find exactly the type of conspiracy that I have been searching for all my life. It led me to Anya and now to you. Now I would like to tell you more, but you have given me the five minutes I asked for and if you want to go, then go."

Rob was stunned. He didn't know what to do. Another fight or flight moment. For the second time in a week, he chose to fight.

"Look, Clark, I am sorry. You have to understand how bizarre and overwhelming this all is. Someone has tried to kill my darling Anya and we get these weird letters from you seemingly referencing things that no one else should know."

"I know. I know, but I think we are on the same page here. I also believe that someone is trying to kill Anya because of links to that clinic and that is why I wrote to you. All this evidence. The four other girls, all dead in car accidents. All five girls at Oxford Uni, drug addicts admitted to the same clinic, big money changing hands. I am convinced we are in some heavy shit."

Rob sat down. Deflated by the stressful exchange of words and the realisation that Clark was genuine. Anya really was in danger.

33

The doctor was pleased. Sam and Bianca were nearly clean and ready for the next stage. He brought them round.

"Sam, Bianca, your recovery is going well. I am going to move you into my private clinic for the second stage of your drug addiction rehabilitation."

Another lie. They were nearly ready for the stage that paid the big money.

Sam and Bianca stared at him blankly. Woozy, confused, with little energy. He was rambling on about the next phase of their treatment.

They guessed he must know what he was doing, as they didn't feel desperate for the drugs anymore but were still not functioning. They followed him zombie-like to another part of the clinic. They both had very nice private rooms with a bed, nice comfortable chairs and a flat screen TV. He encouraged them to rest.

He got an email from reception stating that a medical package had arrived by courier.

"Fantastic," he muttered to himself. "Now we can really get started."

He collected the package and took it into his private clinic. All was in order and nicely frozen. He transferred the contents to his medical store.

He was the only person who accessed this part of the clinic. He had a complete living area for himself, which meant he didn't need to leave, if he didn't have to, and did not need any more staff to help. One less risk, given the nature of what went on in here. The staff were told to contact him on the internal telephone number if they needed him in the main clinic. The staff knew he had a private clinic which no one was allowed into but they had learnt not to ask too many questions.

He went back in to see Sam and Bianca. They were chatting away, watching TV. Within seconds, he had injected them both with more of his special cocktail. Back to a comatose state within minutes.

He went back to his private quarters and logged onto his special site. His friends had promised to set up his next physical encounter with a seven-year-old boy.

Yes, it's arranged. Brilliant.

34

Clark made Rob some coffee, as they both sought to recover from the rather lively opening exchanges of their first meeting.

As he had decided to stay, to listen to what Clark had to say, Rob started looking around his man cave. At the end of the room was a large whiteboard covered in photos, arrows and writing, just like one of those murder rooms you see on all these detective shows.

Clark came in with the coffee and saw Rob staring at the board.

"I have tried to summarise the key players and key points I have found so far."

"This is quite impressive," said Rob, as he stared at the picture of Anya, smiling and beautiful. "Talk me through it."

Clark took a deep breath and started offloading all that he had found.

"Right, let's start with the girls. As you already know from my letters, there were five girls, including Anya, admitted to the Loughborough Clinic as drug addicts, all within a six-month period of each other. Anya was the first but was closely followed by her two friends Rachel and Lisa. I am sure they were targeted as a group at university. Charlotte and Marjit followed, seemingly as a second targeted group."

Rob interjected. "Why are you saying they were targeted?"

"Well. The money. I have found evidence of big money changing hands between Cayman Island bank accounts and secret details which yes, I had to hack, on a secure server in the Fairport Medical network, again located in the Cayman Islands. That does not suggest normal transactions for medical services. This Dr Normandy character may charge top dollar for his services but nothing on his website suggests he charges the sort of money that is changing hands."

"How much is it?"

"Around half a mill per girl."

"Bloody hell."

"You see. Something dodgy is going on here and the fact that we have four murdered girls and an attempted murder on Anya, tells me we have stumbled on something massive."

Rob sat down. The use of the word murder took the wind out of him.

"I'm sorry. This is all so fucked up. You should take this to the police now. Anya is in danger."

"Look Rob. I agree. Anya is in danger but regardless of how I obtained this information, I don't think it is enough and with the people involved in this conspiracy I would not be surprised if there are some corrupt police officers on the payroll."

"Oh, come on. You have to believe that the police, of all people, can be trusted."

"I am sorry Rob, you are being naïve. Look at the car accidents. None of them solved. A flaky investigation. The only lead is the mention of a black 4x4. Someone is covering these up."

"Look Clark, I get your life mission is to find a conspiracy and avenge your father but we don't have time. Anya needs to be protected."

"She should be safe in hospital. The police are investigating and this should keep some presence around her for a bit."

"You just said we can't trust the police!"

They both stared at each other, their heckles rising again like two stags ready to rut.

"OK. I know you are frantic with worry. Why don't you speak to the ward sister rather than the police and make sure the ward is secure?"

Rob's head was spinning. He still wasn't sure about this nerd but there was something about him that made Rob want to believe him. To make him feel less alone.

"Fine. I will speak to her tomorrow."

Rob got up and looked at the board again. He suddenly spotted something he hadn't noticed before.

"Holy crap. Why is there a picture of the prime minister on the board?"

"Well, therein lies a mystery. His name was copied into the email I found that started this all off. The one between Dr Normandy and George Walker that listed the girls' names and referred to the money. I have trawled the rest of the files and emails on the secret server and can't find anything else with his name on it."

"He can't be involved. Surely. How on earth would he get away with it, being PM and trying to run the country?"

"Well, the email was three years old, before he was PM, but I agree it seems strange. I did get one of my online mates to look at his family though and the real dodgy one looks like his father, William Hardacre."

"Never heard of him."

"No reason why you would have unless you run in his circles. By all accounts he is a nasty piece of work with shit loads of money. Definitely seems like he used his connections to get James the PM job and…"

Clark had to stop. Trying to compose himself. Rob noticed.

"What's the matter?"

"Sorry, this is where it gets really personal for me. It is rumoured he has connections with the men that shafted my father and forced him to commit suicide."

"Oh my God Clark. Really?"

"Yes."

"Jesus. If the Hardacre family are involved, this is really heavy. It just makes me more worried about Anya."

The personal torment for both of them was now evident and it hung heavy in the room. After a few minutes where neither of them said anything, seemingly lost in their own thoughts, Rob went back to the board.

"OK, we know about George Walker. Seems to tick your box for the sleazy politician and clearly implicated by the email. The Hardacres are a worrying link but there is limited evidence they are involved. So, what about this doctor. Anya said she was treated by someone called Dr French and when we went to the clinic, they claimed he never worked there. You keep referring to a Dr Normandy."

Clark snapped out of his daydream and tried to focus on what Rob was saying.

"Umm, Dr Normandy is the CEO of the clinic the girls were treated at. I don't know who Dr French is. There is nothing in any of the files mentioning that name."

"Do you think he was the one doing the dodgy deals behind Dr Normandy's back?"

"Well, no, the email to George Walker was from Dr Normandy. He is definitely implicated."

"This doesn't make sense Clark. Your evidence trail does not match with Anya's memories. We went to the clinic and they denied she had been treated there, or that Dr French ever existed. The day after we visited, someone tried to kill her."

"Sorry, I don't know what else to say but there is something else about Dr Normandy."

"What?"

"He is a paedophile."

"No. How more fucked up can this get. How do you know?"

"George Walker has a folder on the secure server with depraved pictures of Dr Normandy abusing children. It made me sick having to look at them."

"What does this mean? Are they all paedos?"

"No, I don't think so. My best guess is that George Walker and whoever is running this conspiracy are using this to make the doctor do what they want."

Rob suddenly realised how tense he was. His stomach was in knots. He just couldn't handle any more. He picked up his jacket.

"I have to go. It's late."

"But Rob, there is more we have to talk about."

"Look mate, give it a rest. You are lucky I am still here. I need some time to process all this. Everything you said sounds plausible but it just makes me more worried. I need to go home, get some sleep and go and see Anya tomorrow. To make sure she is safe."

"OK, but please come and see me again soon. We do need to talk some more. Here is my phone number."

Rob left, got back to his car and drove to Goring in a daze.

How had he got in the middle of something so bad, so scary? Clark did seem genuine but he needed to see Anya again. Talk to her about all of this, even if she was only hearing him. As he drove along, he realised he was crying. He sniffed away the tears.

God, what the hell is going on?

35

The dreams came again.

*

LEX... LEXI... LEXIC... she could almost see the word. The screens were still obscuring it. She strained to see but she was tied down again. Restrained. A horrible face, the wiry old man. Dr French. He was injecting her. She was getting woozy... nothing but blackness.

The dream changed.

Hands were all over her. Several men. Forcing themselves on her.

"Come on you whore, you know you want it."

Bradley and some other men.

She was high but could still feel everything. The pain. The sexual abuse.

Anya's brain was racing, mixed up with these awful dreams. She would wake up in a minute. Like all the other times and Rob would be there. Hold her. Make them go away, but... she couldn't wake up. She was trapped in the blackness, her body paralysed. What was going on? She could hear Rob's voice.

*

Rob had got through the morning in a daze and could have hugged Elisha to death when she turned up to relieve him, so he could come and see Anya.

After the previous night, he was so relieved she was safe. He had spoken to the ward sister about his fears and she had promised to keep everything secure. People could not get in the ward without pressing a buzzer and being let in by a member of staff. He was mildly reassured but took up his now regular place by her bedside, closed the door to her room so he couldn't be heard and started to natter.

"Oh God Anya. It is all so terrible. I met him last night. Superman. Clark Kent. I am still not sure about him. He is driven by revenge, for his father's suicide. Nothing seems to stop him. He is a criminal, a hacker. He found out about you by hacking websites, getting information he shouldn't be able to have access to. But, everything he found seems to add up. It seems to ring true with your experiences and the awful dreams you had. There are four other girls and they are all dead. My God Anya, someone was trying to kill you. You are the last one of the five."

He had to pause for breath. She just lay there. No response.

"This is really bad Anya. Big money has been changing hands. We don't know what for. There is a doctor involved but not the one you remember, a sleazy politician and, Jesus, I can't believe I am saying this, but we think James Hardacre could be involved or his dodgy father."

There was a knock at the door. Rob jumped out of his skin and stopped rambling. It was the ward sister.

"The police are here again. They would like to speak to you."

"OK, send them in."

Two police officers walked in. One was the female DC who had pretty much accused him of attempted murder, until Rob had shown her his car. The other one he had not met before. A man, looking like he owned the place.

"Mr Simmons, my name is DI Peter Welmsley. I have overall responsibility for investigating your partner's accident."

"OK, what have you found?"

"Not much. Our forensic teams have matched the black paint transfer to a 4x4 type vehicle but can't distinguish the make. We have had no witnesses come forward despite our appeals. Is there anything else you can tell us?"

Rob felt like someone had punched him in the stomach. A black 4x4. Just like the others. This confirmed it. Anya had been hit. Someone was trying to clear up the last remnants of this conspiracy.

"Mr Simmons."

Rob jumped out of his daze.

"Oh, sorry, no. As I told your colleague, I wasn't there. I don't know what happened."

The DI stared at him, trying to read his manner. Trained to spot liars.

Rob tried to stay cool. If Clark was right, he couldn't trust these officers.

"OK, Mr Simmons, but please let us know if you think of anything that might help."

"No problem."

They left and Rob breathed a huge sigh of relief. He wasn't sure whether they were dodgy or just still felt he was the 'murderer'.

He resumed his previous position and started nattering away. Anya just lay there. He really hoped she could hear him.

36

Rob felt like his life was on a hamster wheel. The same every day. Gallery in the morning, the hospital in the afternoon and home to a lonely, quiet house in the evening. He had to break the routine and decided to go and see Clark again.

Clark was relieved. He still had so much to discuss and waiting was making him nervous and impatient.

"Rob, it is so good to see you again. How is Anya?"

"No change. The doctors say she can hear me but I get nothing back. She just lies there. The machines are keeping her alive."

"What about the security on the ward?"

"I did speak to the ward sister and she does have the place pretty secure. Every visitor has to buzz the door to get in."

"That is good. What about the police?"

"Huh, those bastards. They seem more interested in fitting me up than trying to find the real killer."

"I told you, they can't be trusted."

"Don't fret. I told them nothing, especially as they confirmed the paint transfer on Anya's car was from a black 4x4. I almost shit myself when they said it, but I think I managed to hide my horror. This just confirms that the same person that killed the others tried to kill Anya."

"Well yes, I am sorry to say it confirms all that we have found so far."

Rob looked drained and Clark wasn't sure how far he could push him. Their first encounter had been volatile but some of the fight seemed to have gone out of him. He decided to press on.

"Rob, you started telling me about your visit to the clinic, before you went last time. What made you go there?"

"Anya had been having bad dreams for several nights before we decided to go to the clinic. She was trying to keep them from me and it did cause some tension. For the first time since we got together, I didn't trust her. She kept lying to me."

"What changed?"

"Well, I bloody well forced her to tell me what was going on."

"Which was?"

"Well she finally admitted that she was a drug addict and had been admitted to that clinic for treatment. Apparently, her parents were both killed in a car accident in her first year at uni. She was devastated, sought support from the wrong crowd and started taking drugs."

"OK, I can kind of understand that but what about the dreams?"

"The dreams she was having seemed to be recalling real events which her brain had forgotten. She told me that she has limited recall of her time at the clinic but she is convinced the dreams are actually recovering memories. This Dr French character told her that the drug addiction had supressed her memories and that she may not ever recover them. Anya said she always felt uneasy in there and the doctor was sleazy."

"What did she say she dreams about?"

"She keeps seeing the letters LEX as part of a longer word. She is often restrained and seems to be connected up to lots of machines and drips. She definitely feels like she was in a hospital setting. She also had one dream where he seemed to be violating her."

"Oh my God, really!"

Clark paused, trying to process all this new information. Rob just sat there. Crestfallen. The experiences of the last week clearly lying heavy.

"Well, I guess it sounds feasible that she is recovering real memories but it is strange that they claimed she wasn't treated there when I found her records on their system. This just adds to the conspiracy. They are trying to cover up the fact that any of these girls were ever there."

There was another uncomfortable silence. Everything Rob had said was hurtling around Clark's brain. The information sat there. Festering. Something about what he had said was niggling away but Clark couldn't connect the dots. He needed time to think it through.

Rob broke the silence.

"Show me what else you have found."

They walked into the man cave and looked at the board. Rob pointed at the picture of the mystery man.

"Who is this?"

"I don't know but I think he may be part of the conspiracy. He seems to have been around three of the girls regularly, including Anya, and popped up in one picture of the other group. If I am right, he may have been the one targeting the girls."

"Was he being paid from this bank account you found?"

"I don't know yet. The information we have is only at a summary level, on a bank statement. It shows several transactions going in and out of the Cayman Island bank. It is feasible that one set of transactions was being paid to this bloke."

"Show me the statement."

Clark opened up the hacked access route into Fairport Medical. He was a bit nervous as Rob had clearly been pissed off about his 'criminal activities'. He didn't seem to bite this time.

"Here is the statement. There is complete symmetry between the payments going in and going out. The only anomaly is that the first of the bigger payments in is £175k less than the four others. I can't explain it without hacking into the bank and finding the details behind them."

Clark looked at Rob a bit sheepishly as he realised what he had said.

"Shit, Clark. I can't be associated with how you are doing this. I am not going to jail for anyone."

"Not even to save Anya?"

"Oh, fuck off. That is low."

"I am sorry Rob, but life doesn't work like that. We are dealing with criminals and we have to work in their world. I will not find the evidence we need without breaking some laws. I am working with a mate. We are good and won't be caught. You just have to trust me."

Rob was torn. He was beginning to trust Clark but everything they were doing made him nervous. He sat down, trying to process his inner turmoil.

Clark shut down the form, hoping that Rob would come around. He was just about to shut the file folder when he spotted something.

"What the hell is this?"

Rob perked up. "What?"

"There is another bank statement. Dated yesterday. Holy crap. More payments have been made into this account."

"Eh? What for?"

Clark looked at Rob in horror.

"Oh my God. I think they may be starting again."

37

His phone rang.

Oh, shit. Here we go again.

He answered it and the caller launched into his tirade, just like he always did. No 'Hi, how are you?', just volume and abuse.

"My contacts at the hospital are telling me that Anya has someone visiting her every day. She isn't married, so is he a boyfriend or a relative?"

"I don't know."

"My God, your job is to deal with this stuff. How do we not know who he is? How do we know he is not a threat to us? Your sloppiness is pissing me off. He may know about her time in the clinic. You need to find out who he is and what he knows."

The phone was once again disconnected abruptly, with the sense that the handset was being virtually slammed down.

He sat there, shaking his head.

Why the fuck do I put up with this?

He was due to be paid for the latest two 'recruits' and was really tempted to make a run for it as soon as the money was in his account, but Anya was unfinished business. She had always been the special one and he really wanted to give her 'special treatment'.

He decided to find a willing bimbo who wouldn't mind him snorting a line off her cute ass. Tomorrow, he would go to the hospital and try and find out who this man was. Maybe it would be a bit of fun. Killing two for the price of one.

*

As he lay in bed, after the first round of rampant sex, the girl he had picked up would not shut up. Prattling on about more drugs, more booze and more sex. Her voice was grating on his last nerve. He snapped. He leapt up and straddled her. At first, she looked excited, ready for another session, but her expression changed as he put his hands round her throat. Her eyes bulged as she struggled against the force he was exerting. He eased off and she punched him in the mouth. It didn't faze him. She had made his mouth bleed. He liked the taste of blood. He smiled at her and put his hands back round her throat. He loved it when they fought back.

*

It was getting late. Rob and Clark didn't know what to do with the new information.

"How much has gone in?"

"Two payments of £725,000."

"Has any gone out?"

"Yes, two payments of £225,000, which I guess are the payments to the doctor, and it means he has got an increase."

"What do you mean?"

"Well, the original email with Anya's name on it and the other four girls had the cost of services as £200k each. If this is the same trail, he is getting £25k extra for each one."

"So, the other payments haven't been made yet?"

"Which means, this is live. Something is happening now."

"Bloody hell, Clark. Can they really be doing this? If these are the same people that are trying to kill Anya, are they doing it to clear up their old scam before they start on a new batch?"

"I am sorry to say it mate, but yes, I think this is exactly what is happening and your visit to the clinic probably accelerated their plans."

Rob sat with his head in his hands. He didn't know how much more he could take. Clark gave him some time. He knew their relationship was on a knife-edge. Rob finally spoke again.

"How do we find out more? Prove that this is the same conspiracy?"

Clark knew this was the moment that would make or break their relationship.

"Well, you have to be happy with me hacking to get wherever I need to go, to find out whatever we need to know. I have to continue to break the law and you need to be happy with that, if you want to protect Anya and have any chance of exposing this thing. You have kind of condoned my behaviour by being here... twice... so I need you to make a decision. Are you with me or not? Do you trust me that we won't get caught or are your morals just too damn compromised?"

It was a great speech but Clark still couldn't tell whether it had done the job.

Rob sat there, gazing out of the window. He knew Clark was right but he was so ill-equipped to deal with this. His life had been so simple. Meeting Anya was the latest step in a nice ordered life that had not experienced any real kinks. The solid law-abiding foundations that his parents had brought him up on were now being tested beyond his limits. He just didn't have it in him to break the law but he had never experienced such horror, such apparent evil. If he was going to stick with Clark, he was going to have to operate way out of his comfort zone. Eventually, he decided.

"Oh, fuck it. Let's do it. I will not have anyone hurting my beautiful Anya. Let's nail these bastards."

They agreed to finish for the night and reconvene soon. This opened up a whole new set of leads and if this thing was happening now, the clock was ticking. They both knew that this presented as much of an opportunity as it did a threat. Could they somehow catch these bastards red handed?

38

He wrestled his hungover body out of bed and set off for the hospital. He knew his dad would not tolerate any more mistakes.

As he went up to the level where Anya was incarcerated, he tried not to raise suspicion as he edged as close to the outer door of the ward as he could. The door was operated by a security buzzer that had to be released by one of the staff but there was a small window in the door that he could look through, which gave him a decent view into Anya's room. As he had when he had scouted the ward before, he could see Anya lying down, apparently still in a coma.

There was a man sitting by her bed. That must be the man his dad was talking about.

"Can I help you?"

He almost jumped out of his skin at the voice behind him. He turned around to face a rather stern-looking nurse. He had to think quick.

"Oh sorry, I think I am lost. I am looking for Ward 5c."

"It is down one flight of stairs and turn right as you come out of the stairwell," she helpfully instructed him with a look that said she wasn't sure she believed that is what he really wanted.

He made a rapid exit in the direction she had instructed and cursed himself for being sloppy again. His dad would not be impressed. After such a successful run, he was dropping the ball all over the place.

He stopped in the stairwell and composed himself. He would try to watch the ward door from as inconspicuous a place as he could. He wanted to follow this man and find out where he went.

The nurse went into the ward and immediately spoke to Rob.

"There was a man outside peering into this room. When I asked him what he wanted he said he was looking for another ward. He left as soon as I gave him directions."

Rob's heart sank.

"What did he look like?"

"Quite handsome, looked posh, fair hair, about six feet tall."

Rob dashed out of the ward and looked around. No one seemed to be out of place. The description the nurse had given sounded alarmingly like the mystery man in the picture gallery that was on Clark's board.

It was nearly time to go. He went back into the ward, said goodbye to Anya and thanked the nurse for her vigilance but said he couldn't see the man anywhere.

Rob wasn't seeing Clark tonight so decided to go straight home.

*

He had been peering out of the stairwell door at the ward door when, all of a sudden, the man appeared, wide-eyed and desperate, scanning the space outside. He quickly closed the door he was standing behind. He hoped he had not been seen. He waited a couple of minutes and risked peering out again. The man had gone. He was just considering his options when the ward door opened again and the man came out, bag in hand, as if he was leaving. He watched the man go to the lifts and press LG. He was going to the car park on the lower ground floor. He quickly ran down the stairs hoping he could get to the car park, where he too had his car, before the man appeared.

He was really out of breath as he emerged into the car park, just as the lift dinged to announce its arrival. He ducked behind the nearest vehicle and peered over it to see the man step out of the lift and approach his car a few feet away. He would have to stay where he was and run to his car, which was somewhat further away, hoping he could get out and catch the man's trail before he got too far ahead.

The man quickly got in his black Audi A3 and drove away. He jumped out from his hiding place and ran to his own car on the far edge of the car park, got in and sped off in pursuit. He couldn't see the Audi anywhere and the Reading traffic along the A4 was chock-a-block. He joined the crawling traffic and pondered his options. He knew where Anya lived and thought it was a pretty good bet that this man lived with her. This would mean he would be heading to the A4074 towards Oxford.

He crawled through the rush-hour traffic and followed the roads out of Reading, over the Caversham Bridge, to pick up the road that would eventually become the A4074. As the road emerged out of the built-up area and the procession picked up speed, he peered ahead to see if there was any sign. At first, he thought he had made another cock-up, but as the road weaved its way along, he thought he caught sight of it. He was five cars behind and the twists and turns were not helping but as they emerged out of a wooded area onto a long, straight bit of road, two cars slipped into a right-turn lane and he was left with a clear view of the Audi. He did a fist pump and followed at a distance.

Rob was tootling along the road contemplating what to have for dinner when he looked in his rear-view mirror and did a double take. About four cars back, he was sure he could see a black 4x4. He kept driving, trying to keep an eye on this car, which seemed to be going in the same direction as him.

Jesus, am I being tailed?

He kept looking every few seconds. It was still there. He tried to talk himself down from the growing terror he was feeling.

Come on Rob, stop being paranoid. There are hundreds of black 4x4s.

It didn't work. His stomach was in knots. He felt sick. He had never felt terror like it. A level of vulnerability that he often saw in others but had never felt before. He continued driving, almost immobilised by fear when he realised the turn for Goring was coming up.

OK, Mr black 4x4, let's see if I am being paranoid or if I really am in the shit.

He took the turn and kept an eye on his rear-view mirror. The black car did not follow. He almost cried with the relief and tried to stop himself shaking as he drove home.

Rob got home, made his dinner and phoned Clark. He was still having small panic attacks as he thought about the events of the afternoon.

"What do you think? Am I being paranoid?"

"No. I don't like the sound of this. The fact he didn't follow you home doesn't mean he wasn't the man. I know there are lots of black 4x4s but I don't believe in coincidences, especially after the incident at the ward door. We need to be more vigilant. If these people are as ruthless as they seem, they probably have someone keeping an eye on things at the hospital. I reckon someone has told them about you visiting every day."

"Shit Clark, I really needed you to reassure me about this. I was absolutely terrified."

"Well, I am sorry mate but we knew this thing would get heavy. This suggests to me that they are still trying to clear up anything related to Anya."

"What do I do?"

"You'll just have to remain vigilant. If you see the car again, see if you can get a registration number or a picture of the driver."

"Bloody hell Clark. I didn't sign up for this. To have a murderer following me. Do you know what this is like?"

"Look, we don't know for sure it is anything to worry about. Just keep vigilant and ring m—"

Clark stopped in mid-sentence.

"What's the matter?"

"Shit, how could I be so stupid?"

"What!"

"We have been using our phones."

"So?"

"If the Hardacres are involved in this, you can bet they have access to people like me. People that can mine our digital footprint. If they know your name, they will surely be monitoring your phone calls, which will lead them to me."

"Oh magic, you just told me not to worry!"

"For God's sake Rob, grow up. I know you are frantic with worry but you need to man up. We are in this thing whether you like it or not."

There was another uncomfortable silence. Rob broke it.

"What can we do?"

"I can sort out the digital footprint. I just need to hack into the records and delete our call history. You can keep using your phone for normal stuff but, tomorrow, buy a burner."

"A what?"

"A burner. A pay-as-you-go mobile phone with no contract, which you don't register to your name. I'll buy one too and we can swap new numbers when you next come to see me."

Rob left the call with an uneasy feeling and double checked that all the doors and windows were locked. He had never felt so alone. So scared. So out of control of his life.

*

He had watched the Audi take the turn for Goring. At that moment, that had been good enough. He could be pretty sure that this man lived with Anya and decided not to take any more risks by following him any further. He had carried on past the turn and went home.

At 2 a.m. he drove up to the bottom of the close that Anya's house was in. He got out and moved quickly into the cul-de-sac towards the house. There it was. The Audi the man had got into earlier was parked on the drive.

Well, well, well. So, you do have a boyfriend Anya. What a shame you will never get to see him again.

He got back in his car and texted his father the update.

'Anya Novak has a man friend. Lives with her and is the man who visits her every day. Shall I kill him?'

His father texted right back.

'NO! I want to know where he goes, what he does and who he meets. We need to know if there is anyone else linked to Anya that we should have known about. Follow him for a few days and let me know. You can kill him when the time is right. WHEN I SAY SO.'

He looked at the text and shook his head.

God, Daddy, you spoil all my fun.

39

The next morning, he followed the man from his house and watched him go into a building in the village called Simmons Art Gallery. He looked up the website and found the proprietor was called Rob Simmons. Anya was listed as a partner in the business.

So, this is how you make your money. I shall soon put a stop to that.

He sat in his car and watched the gallery from an inconspicuous distance and texted his dad.

'His name is Rob Simmons. He owns an art gallery with Anya Novak.'

His dad responded.

'Good work. I will get my people to put a digital trace on him. Keep following him and tell me what he does.'

He sat and waited. Time dragged on and he was getting impatient. Just after lunch, Rob emerged from the gallery and headed back home. He followed at a discreet distance. Rob had retrieved his car and was on the move, taking the road towards Reading. He followed and was not surprised to end up at the hospital. He gave up the tail for the day and went home. He really wasn't sure following this man was part of the deal. He was impatient for another kill, to clear this mess up and bugger off to South America. He would do as his dad asked, for now, but he wasn't sure how long it would last.

After another day doing his IT job 'standing on his head', Clark got back to his obsession. The conspiracy. He touched his dad's picture. He was in the zone.

He contacted Snap.

KRYPTO: Snap. You out there? How ya getting on?

SNAPDEVIL: Yo Krypto. This bank is some serious shit. Cypher encryption. 1028 bit. The maths worm won't beat it. I had it running and given me part of the answer. Need to supplement with own knowledge. Will get there but is gonna take some time.

KRYPTO: Understand. Keep going. Bank is key. Conspiracy growing. Lives in danger.

SNAPDEVIL: Hear you dude. Laters.

Clark was as satisfied as he could be. Snap had never let him down and he knew he would get through the security eventually. He would just have to work on the other leads and try to keep Rob alive and as calm as he could in the meantime.

He had erased their phone histories and bought a burner. He was pretty sure if Rob was being followed that he was now under surveillance and his life was almost certainly at risk. Despite that, Clark had to protect himself. Stay off the radar if they were ever to break this conspiracy. The familiar butterflies played in his stomach. He looked at his dad's picture again. It calmed the butterflies and kept him focused.

Clark resumed his Poirot mode. Staring at the murder board. Letting the little grey cells work their magic. The foundations were all there but the bank was vital. His mind snapped back to the most recent revelation... *it's starting again.*

Clark hacked back into the Fairport Medical network. He was sure that the secure medical records he had found, which confirmed the five original girls had been at the Loughborough Clinic, would tell him whether some new 'victims' had been admitted.

He found the admissions records for the last ten days. Five admissions. Two that had been 'red flagged', almost certainly the security feature that had stopped the normal staff seeing Anya's and the other four girls' records.

He rubbed his hands together. *Come to Papa.*

He clicked through to their individual records.

Bianca Mavroudis and Sam Clarke. OK, so maybe two new victims. Let's see what they are in for. Huh, surprise, surprise... drug addicts. This can't be a coincidence. They ARE doing it again.

He opened up a browser session and started to look at their wider lives. It didn't take long for them to tick all the boxes.

Drug addicts. At Oxford University. Only children. Dead or distant parents. Young and beautiful. Holy crap. I think this has nailed it. We have a live situation. This might just be the way to crack this conspiracy. Catch the bastards in the act.

He sat in his chair. Poured himself a coffee and stared at the information he had found. He was itching to tell Rob but, as he hadn't visited with his new phone details, he had no way of contacting him... safely.

He got up and wrote the girls' details on the board. He finished his day with a mixture of fear, apprehension and a little bit of excitement. Was this really payback time?

40

William Hardacre sat in the private office of the prime minister at 10 Downing Street, waiting for his son to emerge from whatever lame meeting he was involved in. His boredom was broken by the sound of tiny feet bounding into the room.

"Grandpa!"

"Hello Sophie. How is my favourite granddaughter?"

"Good. Do I have a present?"

"Oh, you are a cheeky one, but I just may have something in here."

He rummaged in his bag and pulled out a soft toy.

"Peppa Pig. Thank you, Grandpa. I will love it always."

She bounded out of the room, Peppa in tow. He smiled to himself. She really was a gift, amongst all the shit he had to deal with on a daily basis. His happiness was brief as James walked in.

"Hello Dad and what can I do for you?"

"Have you got that Chinese trade deal nailed yet?"

"We are getting close. The final commons vote is tonight. We should be all right."

"Well, I bloody well hope so. I have paid enough people off to make sure you get a free ride."

James Hardacre sighed inwardly. His relationship with his dad seemed only to be about what he could now do for him. He wasn't sure of the last time he had acted like a father, rather than a ruthless businessman.

"What are you sighing for? I have given you everything you wanted. It's no time to have cold feet."

"That's just the thing isn't it, Dad. I am constantly in your debt and you are never going to let me forget it are you?"

William Hardacre stood up to leave.

"Get some backbone son and deliver me that trade deal."

James sat and stewed. What the hell was he thinking allowing himself to get into this position?

41

He followed Rob for the next three days. His life was a routine of gallery, hospital and home all evening.

God this man is boring. I can't see how he is a threat to us. He just wants to see his little Anya get better. Ah well, I will enjoy snuffing you both out when the time is right.

He sat in his car and texted his dad.

'Been following Rob Simmons for several days. Same old routine every day. He is no threat to us so it won't matter if I just deal with him. Will it?'

His dad responded.

'Where the fuck were you when patience was handed out? The digital trace shows some strange activity on his phone records. His history has recently been deleted. My people can't retrieve the data. I am sure somcone with some technical knowhow is helping him out. You need to keep tailing him. Do not kill him… yet.'

He read the text and cursed. This was getting really old and his rage was building. His old man might be a ruthless bastard but he was being a right pussy about this Anya and Rob situation. He would keep an eye on Rob when he could be bothered. After all he had several other things to do, including those Swedish twins he bumped into the other night. They were definitely up for it.

42

The next day, Rob continued on his hamster wheel. Gallery, five-minute handover with Elisha, hospital to see Anya... not getting any better.

He was a constant nervous wreck. He thought he had spotted the black 4x4 at odd times over the last few days. Fleeting glimpses, or was he just being paranoid... again? Clark had told him to be vigilant but he had never seen it for long enough to really be sure.

He had decided to see Clark again that evening. He had bought the new phone and had to go there so they could exchange new numbers. They had to stay dark after Clark had said he was sure Rob was being watched, digitally and physically.

He nattered away to Anya about the gallery, the latest news, anything to take his mind off the fact that she lay there, non-responsive.

*

"I can hear you. I can hear you." Anya wanted to scream it out. Tell Rob she was here, but her body was locked down. The darkness would not lift. Those horrible dreams were still coming, mixed with the pain of hearing Rob's voice. Was this hell? Was she dead?

Rob kissed Anya on the forehead and set off for Clark's. He was a bit concerned about the black 4x4. He kept looking around as he drove out of the car park. Kept an eye on his rear-view mirror. As he got nearer and nearer to Clark's flat his apprehension grew. He couldn't lead them to Clark. He got to the car park near Clark's flat. He couldn't see anyone following him. He hoped he was in the clear.

He bounded up the stairs to Clark's flat and rang the bell.

"Oh, hello Rob. I wasn't expecting you."

"I know. Sorry. Just had to break the routine. Do something different. I have the new phone."

"Good, come in. Were you followed?"

"No, I don't think so. I do think I have seen the black 4x4 around Goring but never for long enough to be sure. I kept a close eye behind me when I was driving over here and couldn't see anyone suspicious. I have been a complete wreck. I am sure the terror is making my mind play tricks on me."

They convened in the living area and agreed to get some pizza in. Mr 'West Midlands' Giovanni was getting more business from the Clark household.

As they waited for the pizza to arrive, they talked about the new revelation. *It's starting again.*

"I did some digging Rob and found the names of two girls who I am certain have been admitted under the same conspiracy."

"Really?"

"Yes, Sam Clarke and Bianca Mavroudis. They fit the same profile as Anya and the other four girls. Drug addicts, at Oxford, only children, distant or dead parents and critically they seem to have the same security markers on their medical records, meaning the general staff can't access them. Dr Normandy is hiding their records and with the money trail starting up again, this can't be a coincidence."

"So, let's ring the police. Catch them at it."

"And tell them what?"

"That two girls are being..." Rob paused, not able to complete the sentence.

"Exactly, we don't know what is happening to them. If the police go in there now, Dr Normandy will just say he is treating two girls for drug addiction. Unless there is something completely obvious happening to them that is criminal when the police go in, I can't see they would have anything to go on."

"But that's crazy. Can't we tell them what we have found? The emails, the money trail."

"Look, we could. I had always envisaged sending an anonymous crime file to someone when the time was right but I just don't think we have enough yet to give the police a watertight case. We are the only ones that know about this. I really think we have to do our own investigations."

"Fine, but all the while Anya and, now probably me, are being pursued by killers."

"I know. I don't really have an answer to that. My mate is trying to hack the Cayman Island bank but it is going to take time. While we are waiting, we need to be careful and think about how we can find more evidence, whilst keeping you and Anya safe."

"And keep *you* off the radar."

Clark sensed the accusatory tone but tried to ignore it.

"Um, well yes. I think it is vital that the trail doesn't lead back to me. Like you, I don't really want to spend any time in jail."

Clark was getting used to Rob's brooding look. It was just Rob's way of processing the utter shit that he was being constantly bombarded with. Clark had learned to keep quiet at these moments. Rob would come around when he was ready.

"OK Clark, I am not sure I completely agree with you, but if the police can't go in there, we have to find a way to get in there ourselves."

"Hmm, that is not a bad idea. How would we do it?"

"Could we go in as fake relatives?"

"They don't seem to encourage visitors, so not sure that is going to work. I can definitely hack their security system to get us past the exterior doors but without knowing the layout of the place, we are running a high risk of being caught if we don't know where we are going when we get in there. I haven't checked but I bet the whole place is covered by CCTV. Again, I can turn that off but this will only mobilise their security staff to find out what is going wrong. That might buy us a few minutes at a time but is not a sound plan."

"What about going in as delivery drivers?"

"That might present us with a small window of opportunity but our movements would still be restricted. That could be part of a wider plan. We need something more permanent. Something that will give us more regular access to case out the place."

"You are a technical whizz. Can you go in as IT support?"

"That is a better option but really depends where they get their IT support from. You may though have stumbled on the best plan Rob. We need to get in there as a member of staff."

Clark navigated to the Fairport Medical website and found the job vacancies page. 'There are no current vacancies at the Loughborough Clinic.'

"Damn, nothing available. I will put an email alert to let us know when vacancies arise. I really think this might be the best option but we might have to be patient."

"There is one thing though," said Rob. "Who is going to apply?"

"Hmm, it can't be Anya, as in theory they will know her face."

"And the little matter of her being in a coma!"

"Yes, sorry. I guess I was working on the assumption she will wake up."

Rob was clearly hurt by the exchange but Clark pushed on.

"I have a full-time job, which I can take leave from but it really depends on how long we would need to case the place out and execute any plan."

"I could do it. If Elisha could cover the gallery, I could in theory take as much time out as we need."

"Yes, but don't forget they have you on CCTV."

"Oh Christ, surely they won't have kept that."

"Hmm, I don't know. If you triggered something by visiting there is every chance someone at the clinic has you and Anya's identities as a red flag."

They pondered on this for a bit longer as the pizza arrived. After they finished off most of the food, Clark spoke.

"I can make you a fake ID but we need to change your appearance somehow. Maybe grow a beard, wear some glasses."

"OK. Sounds feasible."

"We just need to hope the email alert works quickly."

They both seemed to be happy with the plan and Clark could sense an intensity about Rob that he hadn't noticed before. Clark pushed on in the hope that he was reading the situation right.

"What else can we do? I have got the bank work underway. We have got this new idea of getting a job at the clinic. Both might take some time and patience. We need some other ideas."

"What about targeting the staff at the clinic? See if anyone would tell us more about the sleazy doctor and what he is up to. I am sure that receptionist we spoke to at the gate was covering for him. Her responses seemed too rehearsed."

"Yes, that might be an angle."

Clark moved into 'mission control', his fingers quickly dancing over the keyboard at his usual blinding pace.

"Right, I have hacked back into the Fairport Medical systems and have the staff database up. The staff list is quite small but there is a receptionist called Janet Wall. I bet that is who you spoke to." Clark flicked onto another screen and found her home address. "She lives in Leamington Spa. We could give her a visit to see if she would talk."

"That might be an idea, but do we run the risk of raising the very suspicions we said we need to be careful to protect? What if she is loyal to Dr Normandy?"

"Yes, you may be right but there may come a time when we have no choice."

"What about disgruntled ex-employees?"

Clark tapped away again and found a list of staff that had left over the last three years. It was a very small list but one name jumped out, Janice Silverman, another receptionist whose reason for leaving was marked as 'Dismissal for Gross Misconduct'.

"Now this looks promising. Why was she dismissed? Did she cross the dear doctor and lose?"

They both looked at each other excitedly. Could this be their smoking gun?

Clark found her address. She lived near Warwick. A visit to see Janice went to the top of their 'to-do list'.

"What else?" said Clark. "You are on fire with the great ideas!"

Rob ignored the blatant attempt at flattery and instead sat staring at the picture of Anya on the board. His beautiful Anya. God, she needed to wake up soon.

Clark saw Rob gazing at her picture.

"She will be all right you know."

Rob looked at Clark, moody and aggressive. "You know that for sure, do you?"

Clark retreated again. He seemed to have developed a habit of triggering Rob at just the wrong time. After a few minutes he decided to take a chance by opening up the conversation.

"Look Rob, I am sorry. I do have one other idea."

"What?"

"The accidents. I am sure this is all part of the cover-up. I wondered whether there was a way we could make some enquiries to the police. We would need to think of a scenario that would not raise suspicion."

Rob nodded. A bit calmer. A bit friendlier.

"Yes, let me think about it. We need to come up with a plausible reason for doing that."

They decided to end it there. Both with plenty to think about and an ongoing test of their patience as they waited for Snap, and for the Loughborough Clinic to have a job vacancy.

As Rob left, Clark sat in his chair, thinking. Talking about the car accidents had pricked that little niggle in his head again, which had started when Rob was telling him about Anya's spiral into drug addiction and her horrible dreams.

It was something about Anya's parents. Niggling away. What was it that didn't seem right about their deaths?

43

The blackness was still all around her but the dreams kept coming.

*

She rolled the £10 note up. Carefully laid out the white powder on the mirror in two nice, neat lines. She snorted them one by one. Ahh, relief from the pain, from the beatings, from the constant sexual assaults. In that moment, she was floating, out of her body. The drugs giving her the hit she so craved. She lay on Bradley's sofa, in the swanky riverside flat, hoping that he wouldn't be home any time soon.

The images flickered away. This was when she woke up. Wasn't it? Anya struggled against the blackness. Why was she dreaming but not waking up?

*

Rob sat by Anya's bed holding her hand hoping for something. He jumped. Her finger had moved. Hadn't it? Was he imagining it? He called the doctor.

"Doctor, I am sure her finger just moved."

"OK, let me examine her."

The doctor looked at the machines, at the constant stream of information coming out of them, keeping Anya alive. He opened her eyelids and shone a torch in each one. Checked her pulse and vitals.

"I'm sorry Mr Simmons but nothing seems to have changed."

"But I am sure her finger moved."

"Look, it is possible and, if it did happen, it is a good sign. Her neurological capacity may be repairing itself. You just have to be patient."

"It *did* happen."

The doctor walked out, leaving Rob in absolute turmoil. Was this good? Should he be jumping for joy? He sat down again and held her hand. Willing for her finger to move again.

*

Clark was getting impatient. It seemed like suddenly he was waiting for everyone. Snap for the bank, the clinic for job opportunities and Rob to come up with a plan about contacting the police and visiting Janice Silverman. He pondered what he could do next.

Follow the money.

The new money. He wondered. Had any more payments been made?

He hacked back into the folder on the Fairport Medical Cayman Island server, where he found the original bank statements.

"Bingo. Another statement."

The symmetry was back as the remaining £500k per transaction was split into three payments of £225k, £175k and £100k.

Interesting. It seems like everyone is getting a pay increase.

44

A few more days had passed and Rob continued his hamster-wheel existence. He focused on the ray of hope that Anya's finger movement was a sign she was on the way back to him.

He'd had a text from Clark on the new phone. The rest of the money had been paid out. The game was definitely on.

As it was Sunday morning he had a rare change of routine. He would still visit Anya in the afternoon but for now he could 'enjoy', if indeed he could ever enjoy anything at a time like this, the laziness of the only day he had off. The text from Clark had reminded him about the two things he said he would consider. Visiting this Janice Silverman person and maybe contacting the police.

How can I contact the police without raising suspicion?

He picked up the Sunday paper and tried to get some inspiration. He read about the latest Brexit arguments, the Premier League results from yesterday and the cow that had got itself stuck in a ditch. Suddenly, a story gave him some inspiration. A disgruntled relative was bringing a civil lawsuit against a company that had got away with what the relative had thought was criminal health and safety breaches against their father who had been critically injured at work. The police and the Health and Safety Executive had not ruled in the family's favour. The relative was determined to get justice.

I hear you mate. But, your situation does give me an idea. I could approach the police pretending to be a solicitor following up a civil claim.

He phoned Clark. He answered straight away.

"Hello Rob."

"Hi Clark. I have an idea about the police. Why don't I contact them pretending to be a solicitor with the pretence that I am starting a civil claim against the hit-and-run driver?"

"Hmm, that might be a good plan but still a bit risky. This conspiracy definitely has some dodgy police officers on the payroll. The difficult thing is working out which ones are in on it and which are clean."

Clark went back over his notes about the accidents. "They cover four different police forces as the accidents were in Berkshire, Wiltshire, Hertfordshire and West London. I guess you could target one and see how you get on."

"Which one though?"

"I reckon the police in West London. Marjit Ahmed's so-called accident. It is the biggest force and probably maxed out with work. They probably didn't bat an eyelid at a cold investigation. They must have hundreds every week."

"OK, give me all the details that you have and I will make a call into their contact centre to see if I can get the name of the investigating officer."

"OK, let me know how you get on."

Rob decided to strike whilst the iron was hot and contacted the police about Marjit Ahmed's accident in West London.

He phoned 101 and got through to the contact centre. He started the cover story spiel and gave the date and details of the accident that Clark had supplied him with. The contact handler found the unique reference number for the incident and sought to verify further why Rob was seeking information about this case. His explanation seemed to satisfy the very helpful lady and she agreed that she would get the police officer who had been assigned the investigation to phone him, as she could not give his direct contact details out to Rob. She confirmed his name as PC Jason Fellows and gave him the reference number for the incident. Rob supplied a false name.

Rob was just getting ready to visit Anya after a quick lunch when his mobile rang and the voice at the end of phone asked to speak to Simon Bentley.

"Oh, hello," said Rob, jumping quickly into character, "I am Simon Bentley. How can I help you?"

"Hi, my name is PC Jason Fellows. I understand you were enquiring about a road traffic accident that I investigated."

"Yes, thank you for coming back to me so quickly. I am a lawyer representing the parents of Marjit Ahmed who was killed in that accident. They are distressed that criminal proceedings don't appear to have progressed in this case and they have asked me to review the civil route. In essence, they would like to know the status of the case and the name of the other driver, so we can try to serve legal proceedings against him."

"Um, this might be an obvious point, but if we had identified the driver he would have had a criminal charge against him. I have reviewed the case notes and the real issue is that we never identified the other driver."

Rob hesitated for a minute. That was a good point and maybe their cover story was a bit rubbish. Just as he was about to panic about what to say next, the PC continued.

"However, what I can tell you is that this case was closed as our local police enquiry. About six weeks into the investigation my inspector told me we had been contacted by a superintendent in the National Major Crime Agency, who said he headed up a Major Crime unit that was investigating a series of these types of crimes and asked us to pass all case notes to them."

Rob was intrigued by this and pushed a little further. "What was the superintendent's name?"

"Err, let me have a look." After a brief pause, as the PC tapped away at the system he was using, he came back with "Superintendent Hassan Chandra."

Rob thanked him and disconnected the call. He had to phone Clark about this new development. Was there really somebody looking at these as a series of connected cases or was this all part of the conspiracy?

Rob phoned Clark and relayed the information he had found. Clark asked Rob to hang on and he heard the familiar sound of Clark banging away at his keyboard.

"Well, Hassan Chandra does exist and he is a superintendent in the National Major Crime Agency. Now, whether he is one of the dirty cops on the payroll is difficult to judge but his rank and the status of the NMCA would probably be enough for him to sound plausible to local police forces about taking over their cases. I reckon you need to approach another police force about their case and see if there are any similarities or patterns of behaviour."

"OK, good idea. Which one do you think I should do next?"

"I would suggest going to the police in Hertfordshire and ask about Lisa Benbridge's accident."

They agreed that is what Rob would do and he wrote down all the information that Clark gave him over the phone. No email. They still needed to *be paranoid*.

He got in his car, desperate to see Anya again, but with a little bit of excitement that maybe he and Clark were beginning to get somewhere.

"Hmm, maybe this nerd isn't so bad after all," he said to himself as he started the now familiar journey down the road from Goring to Reading.

45

The doctor checked Sam and Bianca's latest blood tests. They were ready, earlier than he had predicted. The packages from the clients had already arrived, he had been paid and he was ready to go.

Right, let's get this moving. The sooner this is done, the sooner I can get away from all this. At least with all this extra money, I can relocate to the Far East where my friends have me all set up for...

He didn't need to finish the sentence. He just smiled to himself. The latest pictures of young boys and girls from this secret Far East 'arrangement' had really got him excited. This was where he wanted to go. Where he wanted to be. To play out all his fantasies.

He had brought Sam and Bianca round from their semi-permanent drug induced comatose state to try to fool them into thinking they were still progressing through the tough drug recovery programme. It seemed to be working. He explained their long periods of sedation as necessary for their recovery.

The girls seemed to believe his every word. Just like all the others. Except for...Anya Novak. She was always the troublesome one. He wondered what the boss and his cronies were doing about that little problem.

Bianca and Sam were together chatting and watching TV. They seemed oblivious to what was going to happen to them. The doctor asked Sam to return to her room for some medical checks. They obeyed like the little lab rats they had become.

He started examining Bianca on the pretence of giving her a general medical check, but without warning injected her with the drugs that would sedate her... again. She was out within seconds. He went into Sam's room and did the same.

He wheeled them both into the treatment room, prepared the first samples from the package he had received from the clients and started their first cycle of treatment.

They were both more or less where he needed them to be to make the treatment cycle work but there was no guarantee it would take first time. If it did, this ordeal would be over much quicker and he could get on with his life.

He wheeled them both back to their rooms. More than ever, he would keep them in an induced coma for long periods. The less they were cognisant for this phase the better. He would make sure they came out the other side with some time to adjust. Just with no memories of what had happened to them... hopefully.

46

Rob got home after another day of the same old routine. There had been no more body movements from Anya, leaving him a bit deflated.

"It just needs time."

That mantra from her doctor was beginning to wear thin. He was excited by the progress he was making with Clark, but it would all be for nothing if she didn't wake up.

Rob decided to put a call into the police in Hertfordshire, as Clark had suggested.

The call into the Hertfordshire contact centre went without a hitch. The cover story was holding up. Within a couple of hours, his phone rang.

The caller asked to speak to Simon Bentley and Rob once again lied that he was indeed that person. She introduced herself as PC Sarah Whalley and confirmed that she had been in charge of the investigation.

The conversation followed a similar pattern, where Rob laid out the cover story about representing Lisa's parents in a civil suit. The PC seemed to understand and confirmed that the other driver had never been identified.

Rob knew he had to probe. "So, what is the current status of this investigation?"

The PC tapped away at the police crime system. "The case is closed as a Hertfordshire investigation."

Rob was stunned. Was this going to be the same situation as Marjit's investigation? He probed further.

"That's strange, how can a case be closed if the perpetrator has not been caught?"

"Sorry, the case is closed from a Hertfordshire perspective because my inspector told me we had been asked to hand it over to the National Major Crime Agency."

Rob almost couldn't contain himself. "Oh, so do you have a name of the person dealing with it?"

"Yes," she replied. "A Superintendent Hassan Chandra was the contact we were given."

Rob thanked the PC and disconnected the call. He was absolutely dumbfounded. He was now sure they had stumbled on another key part of the conspiracy. This superintendent was almost certainly part of the gang and had been the one to conveniently sweep these investigations under the carpet on the pretence that it was a National Major Crime Agency issue. Rob knew he would have to approach the other two police forces but he would put good money on the same story being played out.

He phoned Clark and relayed the information. Clark was not surprised and gave himself a pat on the back for being right again. They really were getting somewhere.

Rob made calls into the contact centres for the police in Berkshire and Wiltshire, using the same cover story for Rachel and Charlotte's accidents.

Both forces seemed content to support his request. Now all he had to do was wait.

Would this be four out of four for this Mr Chandra?

Rob was certain it would be.

*

His phone beeped.

'What is happening? What is Rob Simmons doing? Who is he meeting?'

He texted back.

'Absolutely fucking nothing. He just goes to that damn hospital every day and comes home. Just let me kill him. His life is so dull. He won't be missed.'

The response was swift and predictable.

'No. Keep following him. Something will come up. No one can be that boring.'

47

Clark was hyper. The information from Rob about this Hassan Chandra character had really cheered him up and he was bouncing around the room like a five-year-old. Maybe it was the five Jaffa Cakes he had eaten in quick succession.

He was certain this person was a key character in the conspiracy and the lead corrupt police officer. He had found a picture of him on the internet and posted it up on the murder board, next to the other alleged conspirators.

So, Mr Chandra. Are you one of the people receiving these big wads of cash?

Mention of the money reminded him that he was still waiting for Snap.

Come on dude. You are normally better than this. That bank must have some serious security.

He calmed himself, sat down and tried to get back to his more Zen-like Poirot mode. Relaxed and letting the little grey cells do their thing.

As he sat, staring at the board, the niggle came back. Anya's parents. What was it that was bugging him about their deaths?

He stared and stared and stared. Nothing was coming.

Niggle, niggle, niggle. Suddenly, the thunderbolt.

The phrase he had written on the board.

'All only children and no one looking out for these girls – targeted deliberately?'

No one looking out for these girls. Oh my God!

The realisation hit him like a massive punch to the stomach.

Anya did have functioning, loving people looking out for her... until they died.

Clark was shocked and suddenly scared out of his wits.

This can't be. Did someone do this deliberately? To isolate her. To stop anyone looking out for her.

He opened up a browser session and searched for any information about their deaths. Hadn't Rob said they died in a car accident?

As he found various newspaper reports about the accident, he started banging his head with his hands.

No, no, no... fuck no, this can't be happening!

The reports had an all-too-familiar M.O.

'... car driven off the road late at night... another driver thought to be involved... didn't stop at the scene... witnesses think it was a large black car...'

Clark didn't know what to do with this information. His relationship with Rob was volatile at the best of times but the last few interactions had been more positive. He didn't want to ruin the progress they had made by giving him some more shit to deal with.

As much as it would play on his mind, he decided not to tell Rob yet. There would be a time and a place for this bombshell. That time was not now.

He puffed out his cheeks and forced himself to move out of the man cave, to watch some mindless TV. This thing was taking over his life. He had to think and do something else.

He looked at his dad's picture as he walked out.

Sorry Dad. I need a break from all this.

48

Sunday arrived and Rob had decided to go and visit Janice Silverman. He was still waiting for the other two police forces to come back to him, so he had decided that today was about finding more dirt on Dr Normandy and the Loughborough Clinic.

He knew he was taking a gamble visiting her unannounced. She may not be even be in. He decided to drive up in the afternoon. She lived in Warwick which, with the quieter roads, would probably take about an hour. Clark had given him the address and he had it logged in his phone in case he got lost.

The trip did take just over an hour and he found the road that Janice lived in quite easily. He parked a bit down the road from Janice's house and got out. The street seemed like any other residential setting in this part of the country; quiet, respectable and very middle class. They had decided to go with complete truth when approaching Janice; no false names, no cover stories, in the hope that Janice was feeling aggrieved and would spill the beans with little prompting.

He walked up to the white front door past a very well-kept garden with the early signs of spring flowers peeping out from various places in the borders. He pressed the door bell and at first thought no one was home. Suddenly the side gate opened and a friendly faced, slim lady who looked like she was in her fifties came out to see who was calling at her door.

"Hello, can I help you?"

"Are you Janice Silverman?"

"I am," she said, seeming a little bit more guarded than her opening welcome greeting.

Rob steeled himself and, in the most unthreatening way he could, launched into his pitch.

"My name is Rob and my partner Anya was treated as a drug addict at the Loughborough Clinic. I wanted to talk to you about Dr Normandy and what is going on in there."

He could see Janice stiffen at the mention of the place and her expression changed from friendly to hostile.

"You have come to the wrong place. I can't help you. Please get off my property."

With that, she turned around and walked back around the side of her house, leaving Rob standing there. Stunned and not knowing what to do next.

Rob returned to his car. He sat staring at Janice's house.

Shit, this was a mistake. What do I do know?

He sat for another ten minutes, staring at her house, trying to work out what he could do. How could he convince her that he desperately needed her help?

He had to give it another try. He walked back up her garden path and rang the doorbell.

She emerged from the same place as before.

"I thought I told you to go away. Get off my property or I will call the police!"

"Look, I am sorry, but I am desperate. I need your help. Someone tried to kill my partner Anya and it is linked to her time at that clinic."

Janice stared at him. Trying to read him. Trying to work out whether she should trust him.

"I told you. I can't help you."

She started to walk away.

"Please Janice. Please help me. Dr Normandy did something to Anya. When we went to the clinic to find out what had happened, someone tried to kill her the next day. Four other girls who were treated by him were murdered and we think there are two more girls in there now."

Rob had been speaking a hundred to the dozen, trying to get the words out before she disappeared out of sight. He was relieved when she stopped walking away and turned around. Her expression had changed. She looked scared and horrified, all at the same time.

"OK, you had better come in."

She led him round the back of the house into a nice conservatory. No one else seemed to live there.

"How did you get my name?"

Rob looked a bit sheepish but they had agreed to tell her the truth.

"My friend is a computer geek and hacked into the Fairport Medical servers. We were looking for disgruntled ex-employees in the hope that someone might be able to help us dish the dirt on Dr Normandy and the clinic."

"What, and you thought just turning up on my doorstep unannounced, referencing a part of my life I would rather forget, would be the best approach?"

"Well, yes. I guess where my mind is at the moment, I am not thinking that clearly. My friend found out that you were sacked and we thought you might be just the type of person we were looking for."

Janice seemed uncomfortable and changed the focus of the conversation.

"You said someone *tried* to murder your partner. If she is alive, why isn't she here?"

"She was hurt in a hit-and-run car accident. She is in a coma."

"Oh, I am sorry to hear that. Do the doctors think she will recover?"

Rob decided to milk this for all it was worth. Not that he really had to try too hard to stir the emotions. He looked down to the ground, shaking his head.

"They just don't know."

There was an uncomfortable silence. Rob wasn't sure what to do next. He had at least got her to talk to him and had tried his best sorrowful look.

He looked up and she was staring at him. Sizing him up. Thankfully she broke the silence.

"Look, I am really scared to talk about that place. There is no doubt that Dr Normandy is a nasty piece of work. A real bully who runs that place with fear. As I said, I would just rather forget about it all. If he ever found out I had spoken to you, I am not sure what he would do."

"So you do think he is capable of... of criminal acts?"

Janice looked increasingly uncomfortable and didn't answer.

"Janice. Please help me."

"Yes, I do."

"What happened to you in there?"

Janice started to cry. Big, convulsive sobs.

Rob leapt up and put an arm around her, hoping that his over familiarity after only knowing her for five minutes would not seem inappropriate.

"Oh God Janice, I am so sorry. I didn't mean to upset you but I am just so worried about Anya."

Thankfully, Janice seemed comforted by his attentions. She wiped her eyes.

"Sorry but I have just never had someone to talk to about this. About the awful way I was treated. I wanted to sue him but didn't have the money, the knowhow or the courage. You turning up like this has just brought it all back. I have moved on and got a new job. I have tried to keep myself busy with work and my lovely garden. I am just trying to put it all behind me."

"Your garden is beautiful Janice. You should be very proud of it. As for the clinic, if you can just give me some information, I can get out of your hair and let you get on with your life."

She had calmed down and Rob sensed an inner resolve. Maybe finally getting it all out to someone was what she needed to do.

"OK. What do you want to know?"

"Why were you sacked?"

Rob was pleased that Janice suddenly seemed to be totally engaged in what he needed. The information started pouring out.

"Dr Normandy had a number of packages arriving by courier over several months. They were in large boxes, a bit like big cool boxes, sealed with a metal tie. They were also marked 'Medical Supplies – Handle with Care'. He had apparently told Janet, the other receptionist, that these boxes were not to be opened under any circumstances and he was to be notified the minute they arrived. I had noticed a few of these deliveries come through but Janet had always dealt with them and I hadn't been told about the 'not opening' rule. I can't say I really took too much notice of what she did with them. One day, Janet was on a day off and one of these deliveries arrived. I had assumed wrongly that we needed to cut the metal tie and take out the contents of the box. I was just opening up the outer box when Dr Normandy came into our office and went absolutely ape-shit at me. He sacked me on the spot and got security to walk me off the premises. I hardly had time to collect my stuff."

"Did you see what was inside?"

"Not really, but what I can tell you is that whatever it was had been frozen or needed to be kept very cold, because the moment I took the lid off, there was like a cloud of coldness erupting from it. He grabbed the lid from me and slammed it shut before I could do or see anything else."

Rob continued to probe as he sensed she was up for telling him all she knew.

"Is there anything else you can think of that seemed strange?"

She thought for a moment and soon more precious information was heading Rob's way.

"Do you know, yes, there are two more things that I always thought were odd. Around the same time that these medical boxes turned up, he got a number of packages from Poland that seemed like boxes of drugs, based on what was on the outside of the packaging. The strange thing is that I did all the ordering of the drugs for the clinic but I never ordered anything from Poland. Based on what you have told me, I would guess that is probably dodgy."

"What else?"

"Well, there is a part of the clinic that no one but Dr Normandy is allowed to go into. It is right at the back of the site, well away from the other clinics and is marked 'Strictly No Admittance'. All staff are told that they are not allowed to enter that part of the clinic, not even cleaners or other doctors. No one knows what he does in there and everybody is too scared to ask."

Rob was excited. Janice had confirmed their suspicions. This was gold dust.

He was just thinking about leaving, realising that he was probably pushing his luck asking for too much more, when Janice turned the tables.

"OK, Rob. I have told you all I know. Now tell me what you suspect happened to these girls?"

Quid pro quo. He had to answer.

"In truth, my friend and I don't know. We have found evidence that big money was changing hands and the doctor was being paid a good chunk of it to do something to the girls. Something that was dodgy enough to get them killed after they left the clinic. Their medical records are also hidden and all Dr Normandy's files are on a separate server in the Cayman Islands, along with the bank they are using to launder the money."

"My God. That is terrible. Do you have a picture of Anya?"

Rob got out his phone and scrolled to a recent picture of Anya.

"Do you remember seeing her in the clinic?"

Janice studied the picture hard. "She is very beautiful but I guess she didn't look like that when she arrived, if she was admitted as a drug addict. She does seem familiar but we don't have a lot to do with the patients other than when they first get checked in and when they leave. I do think I remember her though."

"That's interesting. When we asked at the gate the lady on the intercom said that she had no records of Anya being treated there, which I guess is explained by the hidden medical records. Anya was also told the name of the doctor she was treated by was Dr French but no one at the clinic has that name. However, Dr Normandy is definitely implicated by the evidence we have found."

"That all sounds very dodgy and from what you have told me you are right to be concerned, especially if someone is trying to kill your partner. I thought we had access to all the patient records so it sounds as though he had those records taken off our security profiles. There definitely wasn't anyone called Dr French working there when I was there."

"Do you think the lady we spoke to on the intercom is this Janet person you were talking about?"

"Yes, it could be. I didn't socialise with her out of work so I haven't had any contact with her since I was sacked. She did seem like his 'go to' person for admin stuff so it is likely she has remained loyal to him and is still there."

"Do you think she would talk to me about this?"

"Hmm, I am really not sure. If you did try to speak to her it would have to be outside the clinic and I am still not sure whether she would talk as openly as I have been. If she is part of his dodgy dealings you might be exposing yourself."

Rob made excuses to leave, thanking Janice again for all her help and left pondering everything she had told him. She gave him her phone number and offered to help in any way she could.

Rob sat in his car and phoned Clark, telling him about his chat with Janice. He relayed what she had said about the packages being delivered, the drugs from Poland and the out-of-bounds section of the clinic. Clark was excited. He was convinced this was more evidence of Dr Normandy's involvement in the conspiracy and would give them some more angles to follow.

Rob set off home, happy with the day's work.

49

He sat in his car and watched Rob come out of a house about fifty yards up the road from where he had parked. Rob returned to his car and sat there for about ten minutes, not seeming to do anything. Eventually he got out and went back to the house.

This time Rob was gone for longer, emerging about twenty-five minutes later. Whoever lived in the house had invited him in for a chat.

Rob got back in his car and it looked like he was on the phone to someone. About five minutes later he drove off.

He didn't follow him. He had been lucky on the way here. He had decided to do one of his periodic checks on Rob's movements when he almost ran straight into him driving out of the village. He decided to follow him, expecting another routine visit to see Anya in Reading, but when Rob took a different turn towards the M40, he decided to follow him and see what he was up to.

He was not in his usual black 4x4, which was in the garage for maintenance. He had borrowed his dad's Lexus. They were pretty sure that Rob didn't know he was being followed but he figured a change of car can't have done any harm. He still followed at a discreet distance.

This visit was the first unusual thing that Rob had done since they had been tailing him. He didn't know who lived in the house and he couldn't see who Rob was talking to, before they seemed to disappear round the back.

He texted his dad.

'Rob Simmons has just visited an address in Warwick. Can one of your computer nerds find out who lives there?'

As usual the response was fast.

'Good, finally we are getting somewhere. Give me the address.'

He texted the address and waited. As he was driving back down the M40 his phone pinged. He pulled into the next services and read the text.

'So, Mr fucking impatient. I told you I was right. He is trying to find out more about the clinic. The woman he visited was Janice Silverman, an ex-employee of Dr Normandy's. How the hell did he get her name? I know he is getting help from someone. You need to find out who and deal with this Janice person. If she is spilling the beans about the clinic, she needs to be dealt with.'

Once again, he was pissed off by the tone of his dad's text messages but at least he had given him the green light to kill someone. It was just a shame it wasn't Rob or that bitch Anya, yet.

He travelled home, planning his killing mission and hoped that Rob would soon lead him to whoever was helping them.

50

It was late on Tuesday afternoon as Rob was doing his usual daily visit to Anya for the day, when the call from the last of the police forces had come in.

The police in Wiltshire had given the same story. Hassan Chandra had taken over the investigation. Three out of four. This call was from the police in Berkshire.

"Hello, can I speak to a Simon Bentley please?"

"Yes, speaking," replied Rob, lying once again to the police. Oh, how his principles had changed in just a few short weeks.

"Mr Bentley, I understand you are enquiring about an RTC."

"Yes, I am a lawyer representing the parents of Rachel Hermitage who was killed in the accident. We are trying to pursue a civil claim against the hit-and-run driver, as they do not believe that justice has been served."

"Hold on."

He heard the now familiar tap, tap, tap of the keyboard as the officer searched their police systems for information.

"The investigation is closed."

"How can that be? The case was never resolved which is why the parents are pursuing a civil claim."

"We had no leads but about six weeks in, my inspector told me the case had to be closed and handed over."

"Who to?"

"I can't tell you that."

"Was it to Superintendent Hassan Chandra at the National Major Crime Agency?"

"How could you possibly know that?"

"Thank you, Officer. I think you have given me all I need."

Rob hung up quickly before he got too deep into the conversation. Whilst it wasn't a direct confirmation, the officer's reaction said enough. Four out of four.

*

DC James Carroll was concerned. Whoever this Simon Bentley was he knew information about the RTC that he shouldn't know. He was worried that in the heat of the moment he had given away information he shouldn't have divulged. He had to ring his inspector.

"Guv, its James. I have just had a strange call with a lawyer representing the parents of a girl that was killed in an RTC about three years ago. He came through 101 and they asked me to ring him. He was asking about the case and I told him it was closed. I don't know if you remember it but it was the one we handed over to the National Major Crime Agency. The problem is, I refused to give him the name of the agency or super we handed it to, but he seemed to know it anyway. I am afraid I may have slipped up by my reaction when he mentioned the name."

"Yes, I remember it. Part of a crime series wasn't it? We handed it over to that Asian superintendent."

"Yes, that is right, but how did he know that and the guy's name?"

"Don't worry about it. Old news as far as we are concerned. These lawyers are crafty bastards. Probably got some inside information. Can you email me the guy's name and phone number and I'll pass it on, in case it causes them any grief?"

"No probs. Cheers Guv."

Inspector Harry Li was unnerved by the phone call from his DC. He thought the little 'arrangement' he had been so handsomely paid for was long gone. How the hell had it suddenly reared its head again? He would have to phone Hassan.

"Hassan, it's Inspector Harry Li. I am sorry to ring you. I know we were supposed to keep off the grid with our arrangement but something has come up about our little deal from three years ago."

"What?" replied Hassan, clearly aggravated by this piece of business coming back to haunt him.

"One of my DCs who did the original investigation just had a call from a lawyer called Simon Bentley, representing the parents of the girl killed in the accident. Something about pursuing a civil claim because we were unable to bring a criminal charge. The problem is my officer didn't give your name or agency, but this bloke apparently already knew it. I thought you said this was all locked down?"

"Shit. This is not good. Thanks for telling me but do not contact me again. Text me his phone number. I will deal with it."

51

After another day on the hamster wheel, Rob decided to go and visit Clark to tell him about the good news from the last two phone calls from the police. Superintendent Hassan Chandra and his Major Crime Agency were now major players in this conspiracy. Clark would be stoked.

Rob texted him to say he was on his way and Clark agreed. He collected his car from the underground hospital car park and set off to battle across the Reading rush-hour traffic to get to Clark's flat.

He had only been going a few minutes when, after sitting waiting at the numerous sets of traffic lights that plagued Reading centre, his heart suddenly froze as three cars back he could see a black 4x4. The driver was wearing dark glasses and the whole set-up looked alarmingly similar to the car and person that had been following him the other week. The lights changed and he carried on towards Clark's to see if the car would follow him. It did. As he was about half a mile from Clark's flat, he got on the phone to him.

"Clark, it's Rob. I have a black 4x4 following me. I am sure it is the same one as the other week. The driver looks male but he has dark glasses on, so I can't make out his face."

The sound of terror in Rob's voice was obvious but Clark knew he had to protect himself, first and foremost.

"Do not come to me. If this is our guy we cannot afford to blow my cover. Find the next available turn and head back home."

Rob changed his plans and took the next left, taking him back towards the west of Reading and the roads towards Goring.

"I have done it. I have changed direction and I am now heading home. Fuck me Clark. Is this it? Is he going to kill me?"

"Just keep driving and try to calm down. Can you see the number plate?"

"Oh my God. Oh my God. Oh my God. He has turned with me."

"Come on Rob. Calm down. This could be the break we need to identify this dude."

Rob was terrified but he knew Clark was right.

"OK. OK. I will see if I can manoeuvre myself so I can see the plate."

Rob kept changing lanes as he headed west towards the roads that would take him back home, in an attempt to get the plate.

"Right Clark, I think I can see it. AW56... hold on he has gone behind another car, B... damn it, I think it is JM."

"Hold the line caller," said Clark trying to introduce some lightness to the obvious terror that Rob was experiencing. Rob could hear the familiar tap of the keyboard as he now continued over the Caversham Bridge with the car still a few vehicles back from him.

"The car with that number plate is black, yes a 4x4 model I think and is registered to a Mr Charles Jefferies, age sixty-seven, living in Fleetwood, Lancashire."

"Eh, how is that possible? This guy does not look sixty-seven and he must live locally."

"I think what we have here my friend is a case of false number plates. He has found a car with the same make and colour and copied the plate number. This explains why he is so brazen about driving it around and killing people in it. If anyone had reported the plate number the police would be sent on a wild goose chase to Lancashire. It is just more evidence that this guy and vehicle are a key part of our conspiracy."

"Oh my God. He is going to kill me, isn't he?"

"Just keep driving. Head for home. Try to shake him off. We need to think of a way to meet up without you getting tailed. I think this now confirms that they are onto you and... oh shit!"

"What?"

"Did you get followed to Janice's house?"

"Err, no. I don't think so."

"You don't think so! Fuck me Rob, you need to be more sure than that."

"No. I didn't get followed. I was keeping an eye out for a black 4x4. I am certain that no one followed me up there."

"Well, I hope you are right. Now we know they are definitely tracking you we need to be ultra-careful."

"Careful! That is easy for you to say. You are not the one with a killer following you!"

The tension was palpable but they stayed on the call. Rob kept feeding updates every few seconds to Clark, who knew he had to distract Rob somehow.

"Anyway Rob. Why were you coming to see me?"

"Oh, God yeah. I'd forgotten the good news in all this drama."

"Good news?"

"Yes, the other two police forces came back to me and they both confirmed they had passed their cases on to the National Major Crime Agency and our mysterious Mr Chandra."

"Ah man, that is savage. We now have another key player in this conspiracy and almost certainly the 'go to' person in the police environment that is pulling all the strings where the police are involved. Great work Rob."

They discussed what to do next. They needed to consider all that Rob had found from Janice and the police, whilst they waited for a job vacancy to come up at the clinic. Clark was also hoping that Snap would soon crack the bank.

"You need to break your routine," said Clark. "I suggest that we meet this Sunday. Go and see Anya in the morning and then get a taxi from the hospital to my flat. I reckon he is tailing you by knowing your car. I bet he sits in the hospital car park waiting for you to move."

Nothing that Clark was saying was helping Rob manage the overwhelming fear he was now feeling. He looked in his rear-view mirror and suddenly realised that the car had gone. "Thank God. He's not following me anymore."

"Good. He has probably given up now that he knows you are driving home."

They disconnected their call and went back to their respective evenings. Rob tried to calm himself. He didn't see the car again all the way home.

52

"What is he up to?"

After the success with tailing Rob to Janice Silverman's, he was a little bit more motivated than usual, despite his father's constant disapproval.

He had been following Rob as he normally did, but today he had not taken his customary route home from the hospital. Instead of heading west he had started towards the centre of Reading. He was excited. Was Rob finally going to lead him to whoever his father thought was helping him?

But, after tailing him for about a mile through the incessantly slow rush-hour traffic, he suddenly turned west and headed back towards his usual route home.

How odd.

He suddenly wondered whether Rob knew he was being followed. Had he been spotted? Had he spooked him?

He followed him until he reached the Caversham Bridge and started up the hill through the residential areas that would eventually lead to the A4074 and home. That was enough. Whatever had just happened was now a dead end. Rob was going home.

He decided against texting his father.

Somehow, despite this being only the second potential lead they had after the boredom of following Rob day in and day out, he knew his father would find some way to blame him for what had just happened.

Fuck him. I will get you Rob and when I do, I will revel in the glory of my father having to be grateful. For once.

*

William Hardacre sat impatiently in James' office at Number 10. Something had gone wrong with the Chinese trade deal and he was livid. Waiting was not improving his mood. After ten minutes of stewing on his own juices, James finally arrived.

"Dad, I won't say it is a pleasure. I am very busy. What are you doing here?"

"You know damn well what I am doing here. What the hell has happened to the Chinese trade deal?"

"Well it passed the Commons vote but the first round of negotiations have not gone as we hoped."

"That is the understatement of the bloody century. I was supposed to be on a plane to Beijing yesterday, ready to meet my representatives and get all these contracts signed. Your incompetence is costing me millions."

"I am sorry but you can't always control how these things go. The trade minister has hit some hurdles but he will get them sorted. You just have to be patient."

"God, you are pathetic. I don't do patient. I don't pay people what I pay them to be patient. Getting you to PM was supposed to be the final piece in sorting out all these loose ends but you are as ineffective as PM as you are as a man."

"Get out."

William Hardacre stood up, regaining some of his composure.

"You get this sorted or I will take you down as quickly as I got you here. And don't forget, I will not hesitate to expose your dirty little secret. I am sure Annabelle will be chuffed to know the truth about you."

With that he slammed the door behind him and left.

James Hardacre sat down and put his head in his hands.

Everything was going wrong. He was going to lose everything. He picked up the phone to the trade minister. Time to kick some serious butt.

*

The doctor was buzzing. Bianca and Sam's first round of treatment had worked. He would ring his contact and give him the good news.

He was on his way. On his way to getting out of this hell. To indulge in what he really wanted to do. This time next year, he hoped this would all be a distant memory.

53

Sunday came and it was time for Rob to put their plan into place. Shake off the tail, assuming he was even following him today.

Rob got out of his car in the hospital car park and scanned around as subtly as he could. He thought there was a good chance this man was watching him. As he started to walk towards the hospital entrance he thought he caught a glimpse of a black 4x4, about 100 yards beyond where he had parked and slightly back behind one of the pillars. Rob froze. What should he do? Was he about to be killed? He shook himself out of his stupor and rushed into the hospital.

His beautiful Anya was still lying there, quiet and serene but still no closer to waking up from this nightmare. How many weeks was it now? Rob was losing count. He did the usual and nattered on about everything and nothing, reading stories from the Sunday newspapers about the latest celebrity gossip. She just lay there as the machines beeped and pumped in the liquids that were keeping her alive.

Rob grabbed a quick lunch and did as Clark suggested, ordering a taxi from the main entrance, well away from the underground car park. He kept an eye out and was reasonably satisfied that no one was watching him. He kept looking back as the taxi pulled away and drove through the centre of Reading. No black 4x4. He relaxed a bit and enjoyed the short journey.

Rob got up to Clark's flat.

"Did it work? Were you followed?" exclaimed Clark. Slightly hyper and clearly concerned for his own safety.

"I think so. I didn't see anyone following me and no black 4x4's. I think we are in the clear."

"I don't like the word 'think' Rob. I would rather you were sure."

"For God's sake Clark. I am sure as I can be."

Clark calmed down a bit and they settled in the man cave with the normal coffee pot ready and waiting.

"You know Rob, this is a really intriguing development. I am sure that they are onto you and this man in the black 4x4 has obviously been told to follow you, but why hasn't he tried to kill you? After all it can't be a coincidence he is in the same type of car that has been linked with all the murders."

"Jesus, how can you be so blasé about this? I am pretty sure he was in the hospital car park watching me. I didn't know whether he was going to jump out and kill me at any moment. Do you have any idea how that feels?"

"OK. I am sorry."

Rob went quiet and Clark sensed that his obsession with keeping himself off the grid, whilst Rob was exposed to whatever threat this man posed, was pissing Rob off. He tried to calm the potential flashpoint.

"Look Rob, I am sorry that you are taking all the risks here but I really don't think it would help anyone if I was exposed."

"Clark, I just want Anya to wake up and end this nightmare. I will keep doing what you suggest but you'll have to forgive me if I am a bit tetchy about having an alleged multiple killer on my tail!"

Clark quickly changed tack.

"I do have some good news."

"What?"

"My mate has hacked the bank!"

"Oh my God. How did he do that?"

"Well, to be honest, he is a better hacker than me. This man is a genius. It took all his brain power but he has done it. He has mimicked the security controls of an internal bank employee meaning we can hack in and move around pretty much at will."

"Who is he? Can you trust him? Will he stitch us up and get us caught?"

"I don't know who he is. He is one of the members in our hackers' community but I have worked with him for years now. He has never let me down."

"Hold on. So, you are trusting a person that you have never met, who could literally be anyone in the world. How the hell do you know he is not a police officer?"

"We have a code. We trust each other because we share our resources. We help each other with hacks, we share intel. If he was a copper, I would know by now."

"Christ Clark, I have already moved so far out of my comfort zone and you are expecting me to trust a complete stranger with something like this?"

Here they were again. At another of Rob's moral crossroads. Clark had learned to let it rest. He got up and poured them both a coffee.

Rob moved into the living room and sat down, lost in his thoughts. Lost in his anguish. Clark just waited.

*

Something was wrong. It was way past lunchtime and Rob had not returned to his car. He usually only visited for half a day and went home. Sundays were different but still, it seemed odd. He decided to risk going up to the ward to see if he could see Rob in the room. He went up the several flights of stairs that led to the back end of the floor that the ward was on. He peeked out of the door and the coast seemed clear. He walked quickly up to the ward door and peered in. He could see Anya lying in the bed. No Rob. He risked glancing further into the ward to see if he was talking to the nurses or doctors at the nurses' station. Nothing. He dashed back down the stairs hoping they hadn't crossed paths. Rob's car was still there. What the hell was going on? Where was he? He decided to wait some more.

*

"Where should we start?"

Clark was jolted out of his daydream. As usual Rob had just needed some time to process the latest in a long line of personal challenges.

"Oh, umm. Well, let's hack in and see if we can find the account that the statements came from. Can you hand me the printout on the desk?"

Rob picked it up, glancing at Anya's face on the board as he did. He knew she would expect him to do all he could. Soulmates for ever.

Clark navigated his way to the main bank account and found the transaction history that matched the statements. So far so good. Snap's protocols were holding. No security alerts. No one trying to stop them moving around. Yet.

He clicked onto the account details. The account was registered to an FM Holdings PLC, registered in the Caymans.

"Hmm. FM Holdings. Could that be Fairport Medical?"

"I would think that is a pretty good bet," mused Rob.

Clark clicked on another screen to see whether there were any named directors of the company to which the account could be attributed.

"Well, well, well. The account executive is listed as George Walker. We have the connection we were looking for."

"What about the Hardacres and Dr Normandy?"

169

"No, interesting. They are not mentioned. Maybe George Walker is the money man and has been left to manage the accounts. Give me the numbers for the other numbered accounts on that statement printout. The ones where the money was transferred into. Let's see if we can tie the others to those accounts."

Rob read out the numbers one at a time and Clark went to the transaction history to tally them up with the main account and looked at the relevant information.

They started with the account that had the five payments of £200k, which they guessed was the doctor's pot. The five payments were there and the two more recent payments of £225k. The information was exactly the same as the main account, registered to FM Holdings PLC with George Walker as the executive.

"That is odd," said Clark, "I was sure that each of these accounts would have a different name attached to them. Let's look at the next one."

They looked at the account that had five payments of £50k. Again, they were there and two more recent payments of £100k. The account information was the same.

They checked the third account, looking for the five original payments of £125k and two more recent ones of £175k. The transactions were there but also a number of smaller amounts of money going out, a few thousand at a time over quite a long period. The account information was the same.

"This is not what I hoped for," said Clark. "So far all these are registered to FM Holdings PLC with George Walker as the account executive. Now whilst that is good in linking him with the conspiracy, I was hoping to see the names of our other conspirators listed against the accounts. What is interesting though are these smaller transactions going out. I think this confirms that this is George Walker's personal account and, if he is the fixer, he is using it to pay other people off, such as our cop Mr Chandra. I am guessing that he is managing all these accounts on behalf of our gang of criminals and must be giving them access through some other means."

"What about this last one?" said Rob.

"Yes, this one should be interesting as I am guessing this could be the account the Hardacres are using as it has the biggest amounts in it."

Clark navigated to the account information and once again it was the same. No surprise. A look at the transaction history made curious reading.

In the same period that the other accounts had five payments, this one only had four of £175k. There were two recent transactions of £225k. These did match the transactions listed on the main account. What piqued Clark's interest though was a payment going out for £375k, which matched one of the payments into the main account.

"What the hell is this?" said Clark.

"What have you found?" replied Rob.

"There is an anomaly on this account. I remember thinking this was odd when I first found the statements. If this *is* the Hardacres' pot of money, they seem to have received one less payment than all the others but have made a payment back into the main account."

Rob and Clark looked at each other, searching for inspiration to explain this anomaly. Suddenly Clark's face changed.

"Oh, my fuck!"

"What is it?"

"Jesus, if I am right, this puts a whole different complexion on this conspiracy."

"What? What do you mean?"

"I think the Hardacres might be one of Dr Normandy's customers."

54

Rob and Clark stopped and made some more coffee, trying to take in what they thought they had found. Could it be true? Could the Hardacres be customers of the doctor? It might explain why James' name was copied into the original email. The problem was, apart from Snap's brief online profiling and this one email, the Hardacres' involvement was pure conjecture. The evidence was flimsy at best. What was it about this conspiracy that made it feel right that the Hardacres were involved?

It was now late afternoon and they needed to make a decision about what to do next. They decided to order Chinese and crack on. Rob would take out a mortgage to pay the hospital car-parking fee, but it would be worth it if they could find some more details today.

After wolfing down the Chinese and trying to process all this new information, they settled back down to finding more evidence. They decided to look at the detailed transaction history of the amounts coming into the main Cayman Island account. If they could track these payments back to the UK bank accounts, they could really open up this conspiracy.

"Now this should be much easier," said Clark. "If we can find the UK sort code and account number against each transaction, I have a hacked list that will basically give me the account holders from any bank in the UK."

"I am really not going to ask how you got that," said Rob wearily. He tried to ignore how complicit he was now being in each act of criminal behaviour that investigating this conspiracy was forcing them to undertake.

Clark smiled inwardly. There was no turning back now.

Having conjectured that the Hardacres had made one of the five original payments, they looked at the other four.

They drilled behind the payment details of the first payment and for once found a nice, neat trail. The sort code and account number were present. It was from a Barclays account in London. Clark went to his hacked information and found it belonged to a Mr Arthur Baltimore. He immediately switched to his search engine to find out who this man was. Rob watched on with anticipation.

"Right, our Mr Baltimore is a property developer, thirty-two years of age, a portfolio of London properties. Seriously rich. Lives in Holland Park with his wife and three-year-old son and… very interesting, a major donor to James Hardacre's leadership bid."

They looked at the next one. This one was from Coutts in London. That rather told them before they looked what sort of person this was going to be. The account holder was a Geoffrey Pottinger. Again, they searched the web.

"Geoffrey Pottinger is thirty-six, a CEO of a major chain of luxury hotels across the UK. He lives in Kensington with his wife and three-year-old daughter. He seems to be rich, well connected, particularly with William Hardacre. There are lots of photos of them together at various swanky functions in Mayfair and Park Lane."

"So, more evidence of the Hardacres' involvement?"

"Well, their associations are interesting but all the evidence is still circumstantial. James Hardacre's name on one email is still not going to be enough. We need more."

They looked at the last two of the original payments. The first one was from another Coutts account and belonged to a

Rupert Blakeney-Smyth. He was thirty, a merchant banker, living in Surrey with his wife and three-year-old daughter. No obvious links with the Hardacres but working in the type of environment that would almost certainly expose him to the rich crowd.

They started looking at the last one and as Clark flicked to the account details, he froze.

"What is it?" said Rob.

Clark looked at him with disbelief.

"Would you believe our last payment came from Hassan Chandra."

55

He was now really pissed off. Rob's car was still in the car park and he had sat around almost all day waiting for him to return. He had no idea where he had gone and was worried that Rob was somehow onto him and had deliberately given him the slip. He would have to return at some point as the car park didn't allow overnight parking.

Fuck this. I am not wasting any more time. I am going home.

As he drove home he got a call from his father.

"Have you made any progress?"

He didn't really want to tell his father about the day's events. He would only give him more grief.

"No, still doing my same old boring routine. Nothing new."

"Well it is a good job that one of us is doing something useful. The people monitoring Rob's phone calls have highlighted another problem."

"What?"

"They say that over the last week he has received four phone calls from different mobile numbers, each of which can be traced back to a police officer involved in the investigations of the girls' accidents. Our police contact has checked with his contacts in each force and whilst none of these officers are on our payroll he has been able to glean that they were asked to phone Rob and provide details of the status of the investigations. Rather regrettably it seems each of these officers told Rob outright, or let it slip, that the cases had been handed over to our contact and his agency."

"Oh, that is a problem."

"Too right. He is spitting chips and wants this dealt with. However, if we kill Rob we lose all possibility of finding out for sure whether he is getting help. This is getting alarmingly out of control and I really don't have time to be dealing with this. I will give some thought to our next steps and call you. In the meantime, keep tracking him and see if you can find anything else. I want results!"

The call was abruptly ended. He put his foot down on the accelerator and tried to control his rage.

I'm done.

56

What is the definition of obsession?

'The state of being obsessed with someone or something. An idea or thought that continually preoccupies or intrudes on a person's mind.'

Yep. Clark was there all right. His dad's picture a constant reminder of what was driving him. His lively relationship with Rob, spurring him on as each day they found more and more.

We are going to do this, Dad. We are going to crack this conspiracy. I can feel it.

He couldn't wait for Rob to turn up again. He wanted to crack on with the bank now he had free access and Snap's protocols seemed to be holding.

Right, let's have a look at the two new transactions.

Clark went into the main Cayman Island account and found the UK sort code and account number for the first of the recent payments. The account was Lloyds Bank, Windsor and belonged to a Charles McKenna. A search of his online records identified him as fifty-five years old, living in Windsor with his wife. He seemed to have two grown-up children and had a number of chairperson and non-executive director roles, including one of the companies owned by William Hardacre and the Berkshire General Hospital.

Clark was not surprised to find the Hardacre connection but the hospital one worried him. Was this a happy coincidence for the conspirators that Anya happened to be in the hospital where Mr McKenna was a non-executive director? Could he be keeping an eye on Anya's progress and feeding updates to them?

He looked at the final payment. It was from a Barclays account in London and belonged to a Castro Popadopalous. His online records identified him as a twenty-four-year-old city trader. He was of Greek origin, living with his partner in a swanky apartment complex in Battersea. No children. There were no obvious connections to the Hardacres but he was an active member of the local political party. Could he be linked with the local MP... George Walker?

He added the client names to the ever-expanding murder board. It was good. They did have something. Clear evidence of big amounts of money changing hands and, he was sure, people being murdered to protect the secrets. God though, it was frustrating because Clark knew that a good lawyer could probably knock down everything they had found with some clever words.

Clark stewed on it some more. What had they found? A clear money trail, six clients plus maybe the Hardacres, but paying for what? The evidence trails clearly implicated Dr Normandy and George Walker but the Hardacre links, whilst prevalent, were still circumstantial.

He agonised. Would the bank transactions be enough to implicate and prosecute the 'clients'?

Clark knew the answers to these questions... *no*... they needed more. They needed to get in the clinic. Maybe that was the only way they could prove what was going on. Catch the bastards red handed.

He had a break and tried to clear his mind. He played a bit of FIFA 18, won as usual, against some online opponent called MessyRunaldo... oh dear, what a lame arse.

Come on brain. Get yourself sorted. What can I do next?

Clark looked again at the board. The clinic? What about the stuff that Janice had told Rob? His vigour was back.

OK Janice, let's see if what you told us can help. Now, where can I find the plans to this place?

Clark searched the public records and found the basic internal and external plans of the Loughborough Clinic. He downloaded the plans and studied the layout.

The plans showed the main clinic layout, the outside space and the secure perimeter. Janice had said there was a private clinic, well away from the main clinic, towards the back of the site. The plans showed a large area that seemed to have a number of rooms within an enclosed area. The detail was a little light and Clark couldn't conclusively confirm that this was the area Janice was talking about, but it seemed a pretty good bet. There seemed to be access routes from the main clinic to this area, which meant it wasn't a separate secure location.

Clark decided to have a bit of fun and hacked back into the Fairport Medical servers. He found the CCTV feeds and discreetly piggybacked onto their live CCTV management system. He used the plans to navigate between the different camera feeds to try to orientate himself with what he was seeing.

There were camera feeds at the main entrance, the ones that would have picked up Anya and Rob on their failed attempt to get in. There were feeds around the perimeter, in the main reception and along all the main corridors. There were a couple in what looked like treatment clinics but, cross referencing with the plans, it was clear that not all rooms were covered by CCTV. Critically there did not seem to be any cameras in the private clinic.

Clark looked again at all the corridor cameras and managed to navigate his way from the main clinic to the area where he thought the private clinic should be. Sure enough there seemed to be relatively free access along these routes, only broken by normal fobbed security doors that he could see staff going through relatively unrestricted. He stopped on the camera that was in the corridor that the plans said skirted the private clinic. The images were sharp but still inconclusive. He couldn't work out whether there was an entrance door along this corridor and, as no one was allowed in the clinic, there was no real traffic at this end of the building.

He was just about to give up this little ruse when a figure appeared from behind a small alcove along the corridor.

Shit. That's Dr Normandy.

The CCTV camera was not picking up the door that he had come out of, because of the alcove being set back from the line of the main wall, but Clark was sure this was the entrance.

Thank you, Janice. I think we may have something here.

57

Clark had the bit between his teeth. He didn't care how ropey some of their evidence was. Everything he was finding added more weight to the conspiracy. It was real. It was live. He had to keep going. A Proton message flashed up on his screen.

SNAPDEVIL: How's it going Krypto? Is the bank revealing its secrets?
KRYPTO: Amazing dude. Your hack is holding. No alerts. No problems. You is a genius.
SNAPDEVIL: Ahh, you say the nicest things.
KRYPTO: No, respect man. This conspiracy is live. The bank has given us more evidence.
SNAPDEVIL: How long till you go global.
KRYPTO: Not yet. More to do but plans in place. Will let you know if need more help.
SNAPDEVIL: No probs. Seez you later.

It was getting late but Clark was running on pure adrenalin. He had to finish off looking at the other things Janice had told them. The courier deliveries and the drugs from Poland.

He started off by hacking into the Fairport Medical finance system to see if he could identify the courier firm they used. The current supplier was called 'Justin Time', apparently named after the founder of the company, Justin Little. *Lame*, thought Clark.

According to the finance system they had been a supplier for seven years, which meant there was a pretty good chance they had been the company that delivered Dr Normandy's suspicious packages. The Fairport Medical records did not reveal any history other than the payments made to the company. There were a number of invoices over this period but it was difficult to judge which related to the deliveries he was looking for.

Clark changed tack and hacked into the Justin Time systems to see if there was more detail. He looked over several months around the periods that Janice had mentioned. He found one requisition that had details of a collection from a Mayfair address to the clinic at about the right time with a package description of 'Medical Supplies'. He researched the Mayfair address and found it was an exclusive members' club that, surprise surprise, had William Hardacre as an executive director. Another compelling connection.

Clark looked for more around that period and managed to find a series of deliveries with the same details and delivery route. Whilst these records didn't really give up the secrets, it was at least another piece of circumstantial evidence to cement a trail between the Hardacres and the clinic.

Clark was just about to give up on this piece of investigating when a thought came to him. He had been looking at the old deliveries because they were the ones that Janice was around for.

I wonder if there are any recent deliveries, related to the two new girls? he mused to himself.

It didn't take Clark long to find what he was looking for. A recent delivery had been made from the same Mayfair address to the clinic, with the same 'Medical Supplies' description. Clark jumped back into the Fairport Medical systems to see if there was any more information. Apart from a record of a delivery note, nothing. He hacked into the secure Cayman Island server and looked through Dr Normandy's private files. Nothing obvious.

"Damn," Clark muttered to himself. "This has to be more evidence but again, it is not enough."

He carried on. Mania was setting in.

All that was left were the drug deliveries from Poland. A quick search of the finance system confirmed what Janice had told Rob. No orders placed to a Polish firm, no invoices paid, no delivery note records and no suppliers that matched what Janice thought she had observed.

Right. This tells me that this was off the books.

He searched the private folders again. This time he found something promising. A folder called 'Medical Supplies' containing various documents and image files. A sub folder entitled AHDPolska caught his attention.

He opened up the first file in the folder and was presented with what looked like a contract for services. As he read down the page, bingo!

It was a contract between Dr Normandy, not Fairport Medical, and a company called AHD Polska for the supply of drugs. The contract covered the supply of barbiturates, benzodiazepines and a methadone derivative. A quick trawl through the internet identified these as drugs which could be used for medically induced comas, drug induced memory suppression and drug addiction recovery. More importantly, a trawl of the UK drug licensing records showed that the specific brands Dr Normandy was ordering under this agreement were not licensed to be used in the UK. He looked at the other documents in the folder and found a series of orders around the time periods when the original five girls were in the clinic. What really made Clark smile though was an order from last month. This supported the evidence from the courier company that the doctor was running the same scam.

Gotcha, you bastard. Real evidence. Finally!

Clark was buzzing. He had to calm down. This was getting frighteningly real. He decided to phone Rob. He had to offload all that he had found. Rob was suitably stunned.

"Christ Clark. What did that bastard do to Anya? Illegal drugs. Fuck me."

"I know. We need to get in the clinic and expose this thing. Everything we are finding is just making me more sure that we have uncovered something big. Have you had any problems with 4x4 man?"

"No. I didn't see him after we gave him the slip the other day and I haven't seen him around recently."

"Good. Let's hope he doesn't suddenly escalate. How is Anya?"

"No change."

"Have you tried music? Don't they say that can often be a trigger for coma patients to wake up?"

"No, I haven't. The doctors tell me she can probably hear us so I just gabble on about my day, what is in the paper and sometimes what we have been doing if no one is overhearing our conversation. I will try it though. It can't hurt. I'll just have to download some Take That to my phone. It was always her favourite and I am sure I can cope with a bit of cheesy boyband stuff on there."

They ended their call. The game was definitely on and tomorrow Anya would get Take That.

58

The dreams. The flashbacks? They were invading Anya's mind once again.

LEX... LEX... LEXI... LEXIC... LEXICON. She could see it. LEXICON. The whole word. LEXICON, but what was it? Where was she?

No!... The images were fading. The sounds were changing.

What was that noise?

Anya was still surrounded by the blackness but could hear... Take That.

Was this another weird dream from the clinic? No, there had never been music playing in those horrible dreams.

Was this part of that disconnected world where she could hear Rob's voice, and other unidentified voices talking to her, unable to respond, trapped in her body, not able to see? Yes, she could hear Rob and Take That. What was happening?

*

As Rob watched Anya, he was sure her eyelids moved. My God, was this working? He stared at her, holding his breath, willing her to fight through it. There it was again, a small but perceptible movement around the eyes. He shouted for the doctor. She rushed in with the ward sister not far behind.

"She is responding," Rob screamed at a pitch he had never heard come out of his mouth.

The doctor watched her for a few minutes as the music continued to play.

There did seem to be some eye movement. She examined her. Her vitals were normal.

"This could just be some enhanced brain activity, stimulated by the music. Keep playing it and we'll monitor her."

An agonising thirty more minutes went past as the greatest hits of Take That continued to belt out of Rob's phone. He was sure he had been breathing, as he hadn't keeled over, but everything around him seemed to be stopped, hushed, waiting for something to happen. He couldn't take his eyes off Anya. There was now a regular movement of the eye area. Whatever was happening, this was the most progress they had seen in the three months that Anya had been in the coma.

"Come on Anya, wake up."

*

She could still hear Take That. It was 'Relight My Fire'.

Howard was always her favourite and she loved this song. She could hear Rob again. What was he saying? Something about waking up?

Her eyelids fluttered. What was that?

Suddenly the darkness was interrupted by a thin shaft of light. Faint shadows, outlines. What was happening?

Rob? Could she see Rob? And, oh my God, what was that noise?

Rob let out a scream at a decibel level that once again he didn't know could ever come from his body. "She is waking up!"

The doctor and nurses rushed in. Anya *was* waking up.

The images were clearer now. Faces all staring at her. Rob and three people she didn't know. She struggled to speak, just a grunt came out. One of the new faces spoke.

"Anya, don't try to speak, just take it easy. You have been in a coma. You need to let your body adjust."

She looked at Rob. Tears were streaming down his face. He grabbed her hand. She smiled back.

"Hello handsome," she squeaked, barely audible.

Rob was beside himself. Anya had come back to him. The doctor and nurses busied themselves, checking Anya over as she watched on, slightly bewildered by all the fuss. They gave her a sip of water. She coughed hard. "OK, take it easy," said the same new face that had spoken to her the first time.

Rob was just staring at her, holding her hand like his life depended on it. Anya suddenly realised where she was and tried to ask Rob what had happened, but another inaudible squeak came out.

Rob instinctively knew what was going on in Anya's mind.

"Don't try to speak Anya. You are in hospital. You were in a car accident and have been in a coma for the last three months. These are the doctor and nurses that have been looking after you so well. Oh my God, I have missed you. Thank you for finding your way back to me."

Anya's face dropped. The accident, that man in the black car who drove her off the road and then hurtling down the hill towards that tree. Her baby! The machines started to beep. Her heart was racing, she was at risk of tachycardia. The doctor shouted some instructions to the nurse. An injection in her IV. Rob frozen in time. Anya looking terrified and trying to speak again.

"What is happening?" demanded Rob.

"She is getting distressed. Her heartbeat has increased rapidly but we have just given her something to calm it down. Give it a minute."

Anya's heartbeat returned to normal. She beckoned Rob to her. She wanted him to hear what she was trying to say. He put his ear to her mouth.

"Our baby," she whispered.

Rob looked at Anya with complete shock. "What did she say?" asked the doctor.

"I think she said 'our baby'. Are you trying to tell us that you are pregnant?"

Anya smiled and nodded.

The doctor put on that face, the one where bad news had to be delivered.

"I am sorry Anya, but you are not pregnant. We checked all this when you were admitted and I am sorry to tell you that you were not pregnant and there were no signs that you were and lost the baby. I am afraid you were probably just a bit late."

Anya beckoned to Rob again.

"I want a baby. I need a baby," she whispered in his ear.

The doctor asked Rob to relay the message again.

"She really wants a baby. We have been trying for a while and no success. We are both scared it is never going to happen."

Anya grimaced at the doctor, who could see it meant a lot to her.

The doctor was clearly troubled. Rob and Anya could see it on her face.

"What is it?" said Rob. "What is wrong?"

"Could I speak to Miss Novak alone for a minute?"

Rob looked at Anya. Confused and hurt. She nodded for him to go.

"I'll be right outside."

The doctor sat on the side of Anya's bed.

"This is something I wanted to check Miss Novak, I'm a bit confused. Although there's nothing in your medical records about a previous pregnancy, you do have what looks very much like a C-section scar and there is evidence of stretch marks on your abdominal skin. I think you have been pregnant before, but for some reason it is not on your medical records."

59

The scars. That scar. Anya sat dumbfounded by what the doctor had just told her. When she left the clinic, her body was covered in cuts, bruises and scars. That bastard doctor had blamed it on her violent withdrawal rages but she never believed him. The abuse she had suffered at the hands of Bradley and all the other men had not helped. She was always nursing some injury in between getting her latest fix, to numb the pain. Her body was ravaged by the three years of hell but there had always been something about that particular scar that she couldn't explain. It always felt and looked different to the others but her brain could never process what it was. Now it all made sense and maybe, somewhere in the awful nightmares and patchy memories, she always knew.

After telling Rob what the doctor had said Anya asked, "Where is my baby Rob? What did that clinic do to me? Do you think it died while I was in there?"

"I don't know, but there is so much I have to tell you. That man that wrote to you was right. His name is Clark Kent, it wasn't a joke, and he has uncovered a massive conspiracy which you were part of. Your accident was all part of it. Someone tried to kill you because we went back to the clinic. While you have been in a coma, I have been working with him to get all the evidence. We have found so much but have not worked out what

189

the doctor did to you. I don't know now whether it has anything to do with your baby."

Anya was devastated. She lay in bed, tears running down her face, unable to comprehend all that had happened to her. What had she done in her life to deserve such heartache?

"I need to phone Clark, Anya, and let him know that you are awake. I need to update him on this situation as well. We will get you better and then we can go through everything. I know this is distressing but please try to get some rest. I will come and see you tomorrow. I love you and I am so relieved you have come back to me. We will get to the bottom of this, I promise."

Anya gave Rob a weak smile and shut her eyes. She could not believe what had happened but did need to fully recover from the trauma. Despite being in the hospital bed for so long, she was suddenly really tired. The doctor and nurses were still giving her injections and checking her vitals every hour. She did at least feel safe in the hospital.

It pulled at Rob's heart strings to leave Anya but he knew he had to update Clark and she needed to get some rest. The sooner they could get her better, the sooner they could put the final phase of their plan into action. Rob was acutely aware that Anya waking up probably put both their lives in greater danger, but he could only worry about one thing at a time. He phoned Clark.

"Hi Clark, it's Rob. Anya has woken up."

"Oh my God, that is absolutely amazing news. Why do you sound so solemn, I thought you would be bouncing off the walls?"

"I am absolutely stoked Clark but something else devastating has happened."

"Oh no, what is it?"

"Anya thought she was pregnant when she had the car accident. When she asked the doctor about it, after she came out of the coma, the doctor told us that she wasn't. But, as the conversation progressed about us wanting a baby, she dropped a bombshell that Anya has already given birth. She has a Caesarean section scar."

"What the hell. What happened to the baby? Did it survive?"

"We just don't know Clark, but this can't be a coincidence. Surely, it has to be linked to the clinic."

There was a silence on the line as Clark tried to process what he had just heard.

"Clark. Clark. Are you still there?"

"Yes, sorry. I am just trying to make sense of what you just told me."

"No shit Sherlock. How the hell do you think Anya and I are feeling?"

"I know. Sorry. It must be such a shock."

"Well that is the understatement of the week!"

"Look Rob, you clearly need time to process all this and look after Anya, but I have to agree with you. This puts a different complexion on what we have found. Is it possible we have just stumbled on what this conspiracy is all about?"

60

He got another call from his father, who launched into his usual tirade as soon as he answered.

"My contacts at the hospital tell me that Anya has woken up, which means that we have a real fucking mess. We need to deal with Anya and her boyfriend and sort out the loose end with that ex-employee. My problem though is I am convinced they are getting help from someone and, if we kill them, we may still be exposed and never find out who it is. My technical experts have been searching for anything around Anya and Rob that might help but there is no digital footprint. Either I am completely wrong or the person that is helping them has some serious technical wizardry that is stopping them being identified."

"What do you want me to do?"

"Kill that Janice person. We need her out of the way now. You need to monitor Anya and Rob for a bit longer. The doctors say she will be out in a couple of weeks. If they are really onto us, I am sure they will be actively pursuing whatever they think they have found. We need a break and hopefully with two of them out and about, one of them will slip up."

"OK. I will deal with Janice tomorrow."

"Oh, and son, don't fuck this up as well."

Once again, he was left with a stinging rebuke, festering in his ear. His anger was rising.

Well, maybe Dad, I won't do your dirty work anymore. Or, maybe I will do it my way. Do it how I want to do it and fuck whether you get caught. Hmm, yes. I think it is time I took control.

*

He woke up the next day ready to get more blood on his hands. He was going to sort out Anya and Rob the way he wanted but, for now, he was happy to tidy up this loose end.

He drove up to where Janice Silverman lived. He parked up about 100 yards down from her house and waited. He saw her pottering about in her front garden and, as he sat watching, something dawned on him.

Shit, there is no car in the drive.

She didn't have a garage and he couldn't see any cars parked outside her house. He was going to have to change his M.O.

He pondered his options and decided he would have to go for a more direct solution. He got out of the car and walked towards her house. As he approached she was still tending her front garden.

"Excuse me," he said, "I wonder if you can help me. My car has broken down up the road and my mobile battery has died. Could I quickly use your phone to call my recovery service?"

Janice eyed him suspiciously. After Rob had arrived on her doorstep unannounced she had become paranoid and nervous. She stared at him. He gave her the most unthreatening smile he could. She was a bit nervous but he looked quite harmless, tall and rather handsome with the look of good breeding. She told herself there wasn't anything to worry about. She had to stop being paranoid. He was wearing gloves though on quite a warm day. Curious.

She made a decision after what seemed an eon of hesitation.

"OK, come around the back."

He went through first and as they walked through the back gate and along the side of the house, passing through an area that was shielded from the prying eyes of any neighbours, he pounced. He turned quickly and thrust the knife deep into her chest, piercing her heart. It was so quick, there was no sound as she slumped to the floor, dead. He dragged her body out of sight and quickly left, putting on his dark glasses to minimise the risk of people being able to describe his facial features. He was lucky. The street was quiet and he got back to his car and drove off without further incident.

Good. Now it is time to deal with my other little problem. Get ready bitch and your prick of a boyfriend. I am coming for you.

As he drove away the adrenalin started to leave his body and he began to shake. Not with fear but excitement. All the others had been done with the car. This felt so much more personal and it excited him. It was the same feeling he had when he was strangling that bimbo the other night. He had eventually let her go and she had stormed out, screaming at him, crying uncontrollably, terrified by what he had done to her. Now he had gone the whole way and it felt like nothing he had done before. Yes, Anya would have to be killed like this. Up close and personal. He smiled to himself and drove home.

61

Each visit to see Anya was now a new set of stresses. Rob was overwhelmed that his darling Anya had come back to him. Out of the coma and seemingly none the worse for her three months of incarceration, but the horror of the new revelations and Anya's impatience to get answers was causing a strain in their relationship. Every conversation started the same, with Anya offloading.

"Where is my baby Rob? What have you and this man found? I want to get out of here NOW!"

Rob had to draw on all his powers of tact and patience. Since she had found out about her baby, something had fundamentally changed in their relationship. It was like he wasn't important in her life anymore. The baby was everything. He ploughed on, trying not to let it affect him.

"Anya, I know this is horrific but we don't have all the answers. I need you to meet Clark as soon as we get you out of here. If we can show you what we have found and talk through it, I am sure you can help to fill in some blanks and help us bring this to a conclusion."

"What do you mean a 'conclusion'? Call the bloody police and find my baby."

"Look Anya, we can't do that. We don't know who we can trust in the police but we do have a plan. We just need more time."

Anya glared at him.

"Just go Rob. I don't want you here unless you are going to take me home or give me some answers."

She turned away from him and closed her eyes.

Rob was gobsmacked. The ungrateful bitch. All the hours he had sat by her bed and she treated him like this. He got up and left, before he said something he would regret. He wasn't going to give up on her but they needed some space. He drove home and called Clark.

"Hi Rob, how is it going?"

"Not well. Anya is impossible. She is bitter and angry. I can't say anything to her. She wants us to go to the police. I have tried to explain why we can't do that but she just wants answers we can't give her. I need to get her out of there and over to you, so we can show her what we have actually done."

"Well, I guess it is understandable. She hasn't had the time we have had to process the horror of this thing and, at the end of the day, she is the victim here, Rob."

"Yeah, I know but it makes it so hard. I watched over her every day for three months and just when I get her back, we have to deal with this. When will this end Clark? I just don't seem to be important to her anymore."

"Look Rob, we have to look at the positives. This baby situation just might be the missing piece we have been looking for. We have lots of evidence but if we can get in that clinic, I am sure we can find the answers and work out what happened to Anya's baby."

"Do you think they just killed it?"

"I don't know. It is possible but what if the baby was the reason she was targeted?"

"What? So, you think they are stealing babies?"

"I think it has to be a possibility. Maybe all the girls were pregnant when they went in. Their lifestyles seemed to be pretty loose as they got more addicted. There has to be a good chance they were sleeping around as well as taking drugs, meaning there must be a good chance they could have all been pregnant."

"But hold on. If any of the girls had a baby while they were in the clinic, wouldn't it also be addicted?"

"Yes, that it is true. Why would they want addicted bab—?"

Clark stopped in mid-sentence.

"What is it Clark?"

"Oh my God Rob. Turn on the local news. Quickly."

They both watched in horror as the reporter spoke.

"Police in Warwickshire are appealing for witnesses after a fifty-two-year-old woman living in Warwick was found murdered in her home this afternoon. She had been stabbed once in the heart and preliminary reports suggest she died instantly. Police want anyone who was in the area to contact them about any vehicles or people they saw between 10 a.m. and 2 p.m. today."

"Shit Clark, that is the street where I visited Janice."

"I thought as much. That is why I freaked when I saw the news story coming through. Jesus, this is getting serious. They are clearing up the loose ends."

"How did they know about Janice?"

"Well I am sorry to say it mate but you were obviously not careful enough. You must have been followed."

"I was not followed. I told you that."

"Are you sure? How else would they know about her?"

"Well thanks a lot mate for just making my day that little bit worse. So, you are saying I am responsible for getting Janice killed?"

"Look Rob, I know this is shit and regrettable about Janice but you have to focus. This means that you and Anya are in real danger."

"God Clark. I just can't do this anymore."

There was a brief pause as they both didn't know what to say next. Clark broke the awkward silence once again.

"Well, well, well. This day just gets weirder."

"What?"

"I have just had an email alert from the Loughborough Clinic. They are advertising for a cleaner. This is our way in!"

62

William Hardacre sat in his first-class seat, quaffing champagne and tucking into his filet mignon. He was finally on his way to Beijing to sign a series of trade deals that would add more to his billion-pound portfolio.

His pathetic son had finally delivered the Chinese trade deal that he had put so much effort into. All the bribery and greasing of palms had finally paid off, handsomely. He finished off his last mouthful and stretched out his legs as he watched the female flight attendant walk by.

What a cracking arse, he thought to himself. *I wonder how much money it would take to get her bouncing on my balls?*

He smiled to himself. Money really did make the world go round.

He could forget about his other little 'problem' for a few days. He had left clear instructions for the loose ends to be tidied up. He just hoped that he wouldn't be let down again. He didn't tolerate failure.

*

James Hardacre sat at the table for a rare moment of family time with Annabelle and Sophie. He had got his dad off his back for a week or two but he knew he would be back for more. More being manipulated to do his bidding. More things that would tear at the heart of the very integrity that should be the foundations of any good PM. He tried not to show his angst but Annabelle was beginning to notice.

"James. What is the matter?"

"Oh, nothing, just a lot on my mind."

"You have been like this for weeks and it is always worse when your bloody father is around."

"Well you know what a wonderful man he is," he replied sarcastically. "Anyway, he has gone to China today and won't be around for a few weeks."

"Good, why do we need him in our lives anyway?"

"Oh, Annabelle, don't be naïve. His business interests are so tied up with most of my political agenda. I can't avoid him."

"Well keep him away from me and Sophie. I don't like him. He is a sleaze bag and I am sure he is cheating on your mother again with some bimbo in his office."

"Just leave it Annabelle. I don't like him either but I just have to tolerate him. Especially now."

"What do you mean, 'especially now'?"

"Oh, nothing, just forget I said anything."

James stood up and walked out, leaving Annabelle hanging. She was not impressed.

He walked back to his office, agonising over what to do. He had got himself in a situation with his father that he was struggling to get out of. Annabelle would never forgive him if she knew the truth and James knew that his father would have no hesitation in using the ultimate sanction if he didn't comply. Exposing his dirty little secret and wrecking the most precious part of his life.

Shit!

63

A couple of weeks had passed and the doctors were happy to discharge Anya, with a warning to take it easy. She was booked back in a month later for an outpatient check-up.

Rob and Anya were still talking. Just. But, the last few weeks had put a massive strain on their relationship. Anya did not agree with Rob and Clark's approach and wanted answers.

"Where is my baby? Where is my baby?" The mantra of every conversation they had over the last two weeks.

Rob drove her home and as they walked back into the family home in Goring, Anya stopped to take it all in.

"My God, it seems so long since I was here."

"I know. Come and sit down and I'll make a cup of tea."

"Rob, stop fussing. Just leave me alone."

Rob did as he was asked. He knew he had to tread carefully. Anya would not settle until he could get her to see Clark. At least he had a plan. They would go tomorrow. Elisha was still being amazing looking after the gallery whenever Rob needed her. His feelings for her were confused. She was being his rock and with Anya being so distant, his mind and his underused cock were taking him places he didn't want to go but Anya was his soulmate... wasn't she? He agonised over the change in their relationship. Did soulmates really build a relationship based on lies and deceit? Had the events of the last few months exposed their relationship as a sham? Anya's obsession with her baby, her reluctance to open up to Rob about her addiction and the time in the clinic was definitely shaking the foundations. He tried to ignore the inner turmoil and busied himself.

After a couple of hours back in the house, Rob walked back into the living room hoping that Anya would be more civil. As he walked in, she looked at him. Her expression was different. No longer was it the pained, angry countenance that seemed to be permanently etched on her face since she had come out of the coma. There was something else. Fear.

"Are we in a lot of danger Rob?"

This was no time for lies.

"We are Anya. In very real danger. Whatever happened to you in that clinic was criminal and the people involved are trying to clear it up."

"Will they try to kill me again?"

"Yes. We think they will try to kill both of us. We think the only reason I am still alive is because they have been tailing me, hoping that I would lead them to Clark."

"So, have you been careful? Is Clark exposed?"

"No, Clark is not exposed. We have been careful but we have made a mistake."

"What?"

"We found a disgruntled ex-employee. I visited her to try to find out what she could tell us about the clinic. A few days after I visited her, she was murdered."

"Oh my God Rob. No. This is all my fault."

"What? No. If it is anyone's fault it is mine. I must have been followed by the man that tried to kill you. I am responsible for her death."

They both sat staring at each other. For the first time since Anya had come out of the coma, they seemed to be connecting again.

Anya was now looking scared and vulnerable. The fight of the last two weeks seemed to have gone out of her. Her next sentence was delivered in a tone Rob had not heard for a while. One of genuine love, concern and a small bit of vulnerability that had always melted Rob's heart.

"Are we going to see Clark tomorrow?"

"Yes Baldrick. I have a cunning plan."

Anya grimaced at the bad joke but invited Rob to sit down next to her. She wrapped herself in his arms and fell asleep. Rob was pleased but something about this didn't now feel right. What the hell was happening?

*

Clark sat at this computer, creating a new identity for Rob. The deadline for the cleaner job at the clinic was rapidly approaching and he had to create a killer application. One that could not be ignored. They had to get in that clinic. Clark was convinced it would tie together all the missing pieces of their extensive evidence trail. As he put the finishing touches to it, he got a text from Rob.

'Anya is home. We will meet tomorrow. Can you be in the main Pangbourne car park at around 2 p.m.?'

He texted back.

'Great. I'll be there. I'll borrow my neighbour's car. Look out for a Fiat Panda.'

Rob smiled at the text. A Fiat Panda. That was so Clark.

64

Anya came down the stairs after a restless sleep to find Rob making breakfast and packing a picnic hamper.

"What is that for?"

"It is all part of my cunning plan to get to Clark's without being tailed. Now eat your scrambled eggs on toast and I'll explain what we need to do."

It was late morning by the time they had finished breakfast, cleared away and got ready. It was a lovely sunny day, perfect for what Rob had planned.

They got dressed for the occasion and finished packing up the picnic hamper. As they left the house they didn't get in the car but headed for the river.

They tried to be as casual as possible as they walked through the village but kept trying to spot the black car or anyone acting suspiciously. For once this plan really needed them to be followed.

As they got closer to the lane that led to the river, Rob looked around without being too obvious. As he scanned left, he thought he could see a black 4x4, parked slightly back behind a tree about thirty yards down the road. He looked away quickly and hurried Anya forward.

"I think our tail is in place."

"I don't like this Rob. We are exposed."

"Just keep walking. We are nearly at the boat."

Suddenly, they heard the roar of a car engine starting up and moving at speed. It was coming their way.

"Rob. He is coming."

"I know. Walk faster. It is just around this corner."

They changed to a fast walk, reached the end of the lane and turned right towards where the boats were hired.

*

He sat in his car waiting, fully expecting to see Rob and Anya driving out of the village but he suddenly spotted them on foot, carrying a picnic hamper and going towards the river.

What the hell are they doing?

As they disappeared, he fired the car up and drove quickly to the end of the road. As the lane came into view he saw Rob and Anya turning the corner towards the boat-hire place.

Shit, they are getting on a boat. How do I follow them now? God they are pissing me off. Time to follow them, find them and kill them. Fuck you Dad.

He knew the road followed the river for long stretches. He would get ahead of them and track their progress. They would have to stop sometime and then he would end this thing. Once and for all.

*

They made it to the boat hire place and began to execute part one of the plan. Rob had told Anya that they were going to go on a boat ride and stop for a picnic, hoping that the tail would follow them in the car and try to keep an eye on them from the road. They hired a boat and got set, looking like a loving couple that were out to enjoy the warm spring sunshine, lazing about on the river and having a picnic.

They set off, looking behind them to see if anyone was following them on the river. Rob hoped not. This would blow his plan. He needed the tail to follow them in the car.

Rob and Anya navigated down the river towards Reading at a leisurely pace, keeping well in view of the road at the points where the river could be seen. After about half an hour they arrived in Pangbourne and moored up to have their picnic, making sure they could easily be seen from the road. Part two of the plan. They got out the picnic and had a lovely meal, lounging on the boat, sitting in the sun. They both had their shades on because they wanted to look across the river to the road without making it too obvious they were watching. They chatted and ate, trying to look cool and calm but desperately hoping to see the black 4x4 on the road, watching them.

"There it is," exclaimed Anya. "It has just pulled into one of the spaces along the river. I can't see the driver but he looks like he has stopped to keep an eye on us."

"Excellent, just what I wanted," said Rob. "Let's enjoy our lunch and make him wait."

*

He had followed the road to Reading from Goring and stopped a couple of times en route to see if he could see Rob and Anya on the river. He was much quicker and had got ahead of them, stopping now and then and waiting for them to come along. Each time, they came into view within a few minutes. After the last stop he sped to the next place where the river was in good view. Pangbourne. He drove along the road and couldn't quite work out where it was best to stop. As he began to reach the town centre he realised he had probably gone too far and would have a better vantage point further back down the road. He turned around and went back the way he came. He drove along to some parking spaces, right next to the river with a wide view of the whole thing. As he parked up he could see that they had already stopped on the opposite side. They looked like they were having a picnic. He got out a chocolate bar which had gone soft in the heat of the car and tried to eat it without getting totally messy, all the time watching what they were doing. Waiting to kill them.

*

The plan was working. They were leading him on a merry dance but the last stage of the plan was the riskiest. They decided to sit around for a while as they had to keep up the pretence that this was just a lazy Saturday, messing about on the river. At around 1.30 p.m. they fired up the boat and turned around, apparently heading home. They furtively watched the car and sure enough, they could see him starting up and pulling off. Excellent, this is just what they needed. The first half a mile back up the river was exposed to the road but after that there was about a mile where the river flowed behind a wildlife park, stopping anybody being able to see the river from the road. This was the moment. As soon as they entered this area, blind from the road, Rob turned the boat around and headed back towards Pangbourne. They texted Clark: 'Meet us in Pangbourne car park in 20 minutes'. This was it. They had to get back down the river, get out of the boat and into the Pangbourne car park before he realised what had happened. Rob pushed the boat's speed up to the maximum they could go without breaking the river speed rules.

*

He saw them start up the boat and turn around, heading back to Goring. He skirted the river for a short while before the road bent away as the water meandered around a large wooded area and some sort of animal attraction. He would get to the next vantage point that he stopped at on the way. He parked up and waited.

No sign. They were usually there within about five minutes of him parking up. Seven minutes. No sign. Ten minutes. No sign. Had they stopped again? Fifteen minutes. No sign. It suddenly dawned on him. He had been played. They had turned around and were heading towards Reading. He got in the car and went as fast as he could without catching the numerous bloody speed cameras that blotted the whole of this road.

*

Rob pushed the boat as fast as he dared and Pangbourne soon came into view. They headed for moorings by the town centre. Clark was ready, waiting for them in the car park. They moored up and got out, desperately hoping not to see the black 4x4. This was the point they were completely exposed and would blow the plan if they were seen. They hurried off the boat towards the car park. No sign of the car. They rushed to the car park, desperately looking for Clark. Suddenly, Rob spotted him as he stepped out of a small, black Fiat Panda. Anya saw him for the first time. A dishevelled, lanky student type with mad fly-away hair and the cutest smile. They bundled into the car without ceremony, shut the doors and took a breath. Had they got away with it?

Clark broke the silence. "Hi, I'm Clark," he said to Anya, "you don't know how much I have been looking forward to meeting you."

"Get down," Rob suddenly shouted. He had spotted the 4x4 driving past the car park. They all crouched down. "Not you," Rob said to Clark. "He doesn't know what you look like."

"Oh yeah." Clark adjusted his position to the normal-sitting-in-a-car pose without it being too obvious that he was coming back from a crouching position.

"Can you see him? Has he seen us?" Rob asked nervously.

"No, I don't think so. He is just doing a complete U-turn around the roundabout and heading back the way he came."

"Can you see what he looks like?" asked Anya.

"Fair-haired dude, dark glasses. That is about all I can see. He has gone."

There was something about the vague description that made Anya uneasy. She couldn't put her finger on what it was.

"Let's get out of here," said Rob. Clark fired up the car and they headed to his flat in Reading to take Anya through all they had discovered. It was going to be a long afternoon.

*

He had sped back along the road to Pangbourne. No sign. As he approached the town centre he was frantically scanning for any sign of the boat, Rob or Anya. Nothing. He reached the mini roundabout by the car park and scanned up and down the roads. Nothing. He didn't know what to do next. He had bloody well lost them and this was now absolute confirmation that they knew they were being followed. How long had they known? As far back as that day he spent waiting in the hospital car park. Probably. He was pretty certain he had been played that day but couldn't be sure. He was now. God, he was going to enjoy killing these two for making him look like a mug. He did a U-turn at the roundabout and went back the way he came.

65

They had got away with it. As they drove out of Pangbourne towards Reading, there was no further sign of the black 4x4. Their tail didn't know what car they were driving but they were happy that he was not still around searching for them. They got to Clark's flat within twenty-five minutes and Clark invited Anya into his lovely waterside home for the first time. Anya was frantic to get on but couldn't help but be impressed. Clark clearly knew how to keep a home.

They sat down in the living room after Clark made a big pot of coffee and started to talk about what they needed to go through with Anya.

"Anya, we need to take you through our whiteboard which has all the photos, connections and key information written on it. It is in my office. However, I think I should outline the details and depth of the conspiracy first."

"Look Clark, I am sorry if you think I am being rude but there is only one thing I care about. Where is my baby? I don't like that you and Rob have been playing your little conspiracy games and not going to the police with this. I am really struggling to understand what the hell you have been doing."

Clark sat and took the barrage. *Rob 2.0*, he thought to himself. Anya and Rob were clearly cut from the same bolshy, argumentative cloth. He pressed on with his most diplomatic tone.

"Anya, I am sorry this has happened to you and I promise that we will find out what happened to your baby. Your revelation has given us an angle that we hadn't considered but it doesn't change the fact that the four girls that were in the clinic at the same time as you were murdered and two of them were your friends."

"What? Who?"

"Rachel Hermitage and Lisa Benbridge."

"Oh my God. No."

"Yes, and worse than that, we think it has started again. We think there are two more girls in there now."

"What! Well call the police. Catch them at it!"

"We can't. We have evidence that there are some dodgy police officers involved. We need to play this carefully. If we call the police, there is a really good chance that this will get covered up. There are seriously heavy people involved in this and millions of pounds changing hands. They are murdering the victims and paying people off to protect their secrets."

Anya looked at Clark, looked at Rob. Her face etched with the pain of not knowing. Rob had kept quiet, letting Clark take the lead, but it was not going as they hoped. Anya was not happy to listen to the long explanations that Clark had prepared.

"Show me this board," she commanded.

Clark realised he was not going to manage this conversation the way he had planned. He relented. Anya was highly volatile and he had to adapt to her highly charged state.

"OK, come through."

They walked into Clark's man cave. Anya spotted the whiteboard at the end of the room and walked right up to it. It was full of pictures, writing and arrows linking the people. Her picture was there, next to Rachel and Lisa's but it was the face in the centre of the board that made her stop. Her legs gave way and she fell to the floor.

Rob and Clark rushed to catch her but only succeeded in stumbling over each other. Rob picked her up.

"Anya. Anya. Are you all right?" he said as he lightly tapped her face, trying to rouse her.

She stirred.

"What is it? What did you see on the board? You fainted."

Anya sat up. Tried to clear her head. After a few minutes she was cognisant enough to speak. From her position, sitting on the floor by the board, she looked back at the picture.

"That is Bradley. Evil Bradley. He is the reason I became a drug addict. An evil raping bastard."

"What do you mean?" pleaded Rob.

"I told you about the drugs, Rob, and being admitted to the clinic but this was preceded by months of abuse. Verbal and physical abuse. Sexual abuse, by that bastard. He was pure evil. The more drugs I wanted, the worse it got. If I was late paying him for the drugs, he took it out on me. Raping me. Sometimes with other men too."

Rob was gobsmacked. He didn't know what to do. Why had she never told him? More lies. More deceit. He was consumed with rage that someone could have done that to Anya. He wanted to hit something or someone, but all the while his mind was conflicted by being lied to again. The foundations of the relationship being attacked again. His tumultuous mind blurted out the first thing that came to him.

"Could he be the one that made you pregnant?"

"Oh my God Rob," she said through sudden convulsive sobs, "I hadn't even thought of that. It has to be a possibility – or any of the other creeps that raped me. I can't believe my baby was fathered by one of those evil men."

Clark had let this play out. He knew they needed to handle this carefully. The real horror of this hadn't really hit him until he was confronted with a genuine victim of this terrible situation. Anya had suddenly made it more than ideas on paper, online records and words on the board. He tried to take back control of the conversation.

"Look, we don't know anything for sure. All we know is that you had a baby. We don't know whether he was the father or not, but what we can be fairly sure about is that he is still around and almost certainly the driver of the 4x4."

"What? Why do you say that?" Anya exclaimed.

"I only saw the guy in the car briefly today and he had dark glasses on, but I am sure it was him. The man in that picture."

"So, what does that mean?" asked Rob, running on autopilot now as he still tried to reconcile what Anya had told him.

"I think it confirms that he is key to this conspiracy. Based on what Anya has told us, I reckon he is the finder. He has groomed the girls, got them hooked on drugs and delivered them to the clinic for the doctor to do his evil work. After that he has almost certainly been the one doing the killings. I am not sure how he is connected to the doctor, George Walker or maybe the Hardacres but I am sure he is the one trying to tidy everything up."

They all sat for a minute stunned by this revelation. Anya could not believe how her life had been so controlled by this man, from the minute her parents died and her first meeting with him in the uni bar.

After a few minutes, Anya stood up and looked at the board again. She had stopped crying and steeled herself to look at more of the horror. Her recent life laid out before her like some unreal nightmare. The lost years.

She looked at the picture of the doctor.

"That is Dr French."

Clark was shocked but not surprised. He knew getting Anya to see their murder board would help join the dots and boy, was she doing that.

"Well Anya, that is actually Dr Normandy. He is the CEO of the Loughborough Clinic and clearly implicated in all this. We have a clear money trail leading to him and now you have confirmed that he is in fact the doctor that treated you, albeit with some weird pseudonym, we have him squarely in the middle of this conspiracy. What we don't know is what he did to you. I think with your baby revelation, he is doing more than curing drug addicts. He is also a disgusting paedophile."

"What! Oh my God. Is that what happened to my baby? Did they sell them to paedos?"

"No, no. We don't think so. We found pictures of his depravity on the Fairport Medical server but they were in one of George Walker's folders. We think they are using his depravity to leverage him to do what they want."

Anya sat there. Her eyes darting between Clark and Rob, not knowing what to believe or what to do next. The horror was coming at her in waves. After a few minutes she spoke again.

"I don't care what that man is. He is evil. Horrible. I knew there was something wrong with him and, my dreams, they have never been about drug recovery. It has always seemed like I was in a hospital bed, hooked up to drips and machines and that creepy man hovering around, violating me."

"This is why we need to get in the clinic and catch him at whatever he is doing. We can't rely on the police to expose this thing."

There was a pause while Anya took this all in. Rob and Clark both held their breath. She was highly charged and they now began to understand why. The full horror of what had happened to her was beginning to reveal itself and Anya was here, having to relive it, whilst not remembering exactly what had happened to her or the baby.

"I am still not happy about waiting, but what is your plan for getting in? We can't just walk in, as Rob and I discovered."

"We are going to try to get a job there. I have created a new identity for Rob and have applied for the cleaner's job they have advertised. The deadline is Monday and with the killer application I have put together, Rob will definitely get an interview. Hopefully it will be quite soon."

"And how is that going to help?"

"If Rob can get in there, he can recce the place. We have been given some idea where the private clinic is, which is probably where you were treated. I have hacked their CCTV and got a good idea of the layout, but we need someone on the ground to confirm. Once that is done, we can work out a plan for getting in the private bit and hopefully exposing this thing."

"And finding my baby!"

"Well, maybe finding out what happened to your baby."

Anya was still finding it hard to tolerate Rob and Clark's apparent lack of urgency. They just didn't understand what she had been through. The pain of not knowing where her baby was. It was an emptiness she had never experienced. She went back to the board.

"Why have you written 'Anya's parents?' on the board?" probed Anya.

Rob looked at Clark. He didn't remember seeing that written on the board.

"Eh, yes Clark why have you written that on there? I don't remember us talking about Anya's parents."

Clark knew this moment was coming. He knew it was probably a mistake to have kept this from Rob but, if he was right about their accident, this was going to be difficult for both of them to hear.

"OK, I am sorry if what I am about to say upsets you but I have a theory about your parents' accident, Anya, and it is not a pleasant one."

"What? Tell me!"

"I looked at the reports of their car accident and I think it is very likely that your parents were murdered, probably by Bradley causing the same type of accident that resulted in the other girls' deaths."

"That... that can't be true," sobbed Anya, once again overwhelmed by this whole situation. "Why?"

"All the other girls they chose after you were only children with parents that were either dead or in poor health. I think they realised that they had to find girls who were alone with no one looking out for them. I truly believe they murdered your parents to put you in that position. After you, they realised it was just too much trouble to keep creating this situation and groomed girls who fitted the profile. I am sorry Anya. I know this is just a theory but it seems to fit."

Anya let out a howl of pain like nothing Clark and Rob had ever heard emanating from a human being.

She stood up, grabbed her bag and bolted for the front door, screaming out the same mantra over and over.

"This is too much. This is too much."

Within seconds she was gone.

Rob sat looking at Clark, stunned. Immobilised by the sudden horror of the revelation and not reacting when Anya took flight, he suddenly came to his senses and glared at Clark.

"What have you done? Why did you keep this from me? I need to find her. You had better hope this has not pushed her over the edge and she does something stupid."

With that tirade, Rob charged through the front door and went after Anya.

Clark sat in his den. *Shit*.

66

Anya flew down the stairs of Clark's complex and out the main door, onto the small promenade that ran along either side of the river which flowed through the centre of Reading. She turned left and just kept on walking. Her head was exploding. How far back did this terror go? Were here parents really murdered? She thought that meeting Rob and rebuilding her life would allow the past to stay in the past. How wrong had she been? The dreams, the nightmares had taken her back to the horror of her lost years and the more that Clark and Rob were filling in the gaps in her memories, the worse it got. Her parents, her baby, people trying to kill her, her friends dead. The familiar yearning for a fix invaded her thoughts. She knew you were never really cured of your addiction.

She kept on walking, further and further away from Clark's flat, following the river and then cutting into some dingy backstreets. She suddenly realised how alone and vulnerable she was. The road she was in looked and felt like poverty. Badly maintained houses, burnt out cars, rubbish everywhere and small groups of youths hanging around looking menacing. She suddenly froze as a hand touched her shoulder.

"Now what is a nice ho like you doing in a place like this?"

She turned to see a tall, heavily tattooed, mixed-race male staring at her with a big grin, embellished by two gold teeth.

He had the loose, baggy clothing so typical of an urban male. His hands and neck were festooned with gold, or something that looked like gold. He was holding a six-inch blade, which he played with casually to maximise the intimidation.

"Umm. Nothing. I am just walking."

"People don't walk round this hood. Either you are here to score or you are threatening my patch. Now which is it?"

"I am just passing through."

He grabbed her neck and got his face up close. The various groups of youths watched from a distance with increased amusement. They knew not to get involved in Zebu's business.

"Look bitch. Maybe you is not understanding me. People don't pass through my patch. You either do a deal or I will cut you open."

Anya was scared but perversely he was offering her the one thing that her current emotional state was driving her toward. She desperately needed a fix.

"I need a fix."

"Ah, so you are here to score. Lucky for you. What is your poison?"

"Cocaine."

"Walk with me."

He let her go and gestured for her to follow him into a small yard that contained a series of garages. He opened up the one nearest the road they had come from. He went in and a few seconds later came out with a small wrap, containing white powder.

"Now this my beautiful one is your grade A Colombian. £200."

Anya froze. She wanted a fix and saying she did had stopped her from being stabbed, but she didn't have £200. She made a play of rummaging in her bag. Her heart was racing. Her mind trying to process how to get out of this terrible situation. She got her purse out.

"I only have £100."

"Well that is just not going to cut it bitch. It's £200 or I cut you."

"Please, just give me what you can for a £100."

He glared at her and then his face changed to a smug arrogant grin.

"Well there is another way that bitches like you can pay their way. If a ho can blow, I halve the cost of the transaction."

With that he unzipped his trousers and they dropped to his ankles, with his CK pants quickly following.

Anya stared at an impressive cock, which was growing by the second. He looked at her, expectantly, leering at her body.

"You could show me those lovely tits first, before you start to blow."

Anya was numb. The memories of Bradley and all the evil men that had sexually assaulted her, making her do these sorts of sordid sexual favours, came flooding back. She had one chance. He was vulnerable, expecting her to flash her tits and get down on her knees. She didn't do that. She did the only thing she could. She aimed the hardest kick she could at his balls, which hung invitingly below his erect penis.

She connected. His eyes bulged and he screamed in pain. Anya bolted. The trousers round his ankles and the excruciating pain slowed his reactions, giving Anya the few seconds she needed.

She ran out of the yard, back towards where she came from. The groups of youths suddenly seemed interested in what was going on and started moving in her direction. She ran as fast as she could. She got to the river and turned back in the direction of Clark's flat. She looked behind her to see if he was following her, but as she faced forward again her momentum sent her crashing into someone. They both sprawled to the floor.

"Anya!"

"Rob! Oh my God Rob."

She hugged him harder than she had ever hugged him. Suddenly, about 100 yards back in the direction she came from, a voice shouted.

"You are going to die bitch."

He was there with a small group of youths, clearly revelling in what they thought was about to happen.

"Run!" shouted Anya to Rob.

He stared at her with disbelief. What the hell was going on? Before he could process the possible answers to that question she was off, running back in the direction of Clark's. The threatening man that had shouted at Anya was also on his heels. Rob set off after Anya.

The promenade by the river was long and straight with no exit points. They ran, all the time hearing the distant pounding of feet chasing them. They didn't have time to see if they were being caught.

Suddenly, a gap in the wall appeared, leading into to the shopping area.

"Quick. This way."

Rob had no hesitation in following Anya's instructions. He was amazed at how fit she was and how lame his attempts had been at keeping up with her.

They emerged into the main shopping street and bolted into the first big shop they could see, which sold all sorts of fashion and accessories. They stopped and tried to hide themselves, whilst trying to keep an eye on the road. About twenty seconds later the man and his little gang emerged. They stopped and scanned the area. Rob and Anya stepped back, more into the shop. They could see him talking to his gang and using his phone. After a few agonising minutes they turned around and walked away.

Rob looked at Anya.

"We better get back to Clark's and you bloody well tell me what the fuck that was all about."

67

Clark opened his front door. Rob and Anya stood there, looking tired and stressed.

"You had better come in. I have ordered some pizza. I knew you would be back."

"Oh, so you are a bloody mind reader now as well as a liar."

Clark tried to ignore Rob's obvious rage.

"I am sorry. I probably deserved that and I am sorry Anya for upsetting you so much. This is all so horrible but I sometimes forget that this is your life, your traumatic experiences. Until today this had all been words on paper. Meeting you has made it all terribly real but we are going to have to confront the truth if we are ever going to crack this and give you some closure."

Rob's rage had not subsided.

"Stop. Just stop Clark. I am so sick of your fancy monologues and false platitudes. Anya almost got herself killed because you have no idea how to deal with people. With their emotions."

The two stags were rutting again. Anya steamed into the confrontation.

"Rob. Don't. It is not Clark's fault. I know you have both been bursting to tell me all that you have found but I just can't process everything that has happened. You are filling gaps in my memory that I never wanted to remember. I was so desperate for information but, my parents, that was just too much. It can't be true."

The tension was palpable. Rob and Clark didn't know whether to fight or hug and make up. They were trying to take their cues from Anya but she was the most messed up of all of them. They were beginning to understand why.

"What just happened?" asked Clark, trying to move the conversation on.

"I just ran. I didn't know where I was going and ended up somewhere I shouldn't have been. I needed a fix and ran into a wanker who thought he was the local drug lord."

"What happened?" they chorused.

"He pulled a knife and threatened to cut me if I didn't buy drugs. I was terrified but strangely calm. I did want the drugs and I hoped I could get myself out of the situation without being hurt."

"So why was he chasing you? Threatening to kill you," said Rob.

"I couldn't pay. He wanted sexual favours and dropped his trousers expecting me to give him head. I took my chance and kicked him in the balls. Suddenly a fix didn't seem all that important. I ran for my life."

"Jesus Anya. What the fuck were you thinking?" said Rob disapprovingly.

"Oh, fuck off Rob. Like you have any idea what I have been through. What it is like to be a drug addict, to be sexually assaulted, to have massive gaps in your memory. Meeting you was supposed to be a new start, but now because of you and Supernerd here playing conspiracy games, I am having to relive all this horror."

This was not going well. Clark and Rob sat like a pair of naughty children, chastened by Anya's anger. The doorbell rang. The pizza delivery man had saved the day.

They sat eating the pizza, quiet and lost in their own individual thoughts, nobody really knowing what to say to ease the tension. Clark knew they had barely touched the surface with Anya in terms of telling her what they had found. Her highly emotional state meant that the information they had given her was haphazard and unfortunately had hit on the most traumatic aspects of the conspiracy. Anya broke the silence.

"How much did they pay for my baby?"

"Look Anya, we don't know if that is what happened."

"How much?"

"There is no point speculating... "

"HOW MUCH?"

"OK, OK. Around half a million pounds changed hands, but we don't know what they were paying for. The money seemed to be split between several people."

"Who?"

"Well, we have clear evidence that Dr Normandy was paid to do something to you. George Walker is clearly implicated in handling the money, probably the fixer. Now that you have identified Bradley, he is almost certainly the finder. We have a guy called Hassan Chandra who seems to be the main corrupt police link. The final conspirator is still unclear. We have one email that had James Hardacre's name on it."

"What! *The* James Hardacre? The prime minister?"

"Yes."

"Holy fuck. How can he be involved? That just defies belief."

"We don't know that he is. We only have his name on one email, albeit it was the one that had yours and the other girls' names on it. I got my mate to look into him and his family. The really dodgy character is his father, William Hardacre. Seems like he used his considerable influence to get James the PM job, but we can't tie him into the conspiracy, other than lots of circumstantial links."

"What do you mean?"

"My mate managed to find a way to hack the Cayman Island bank that these bastards have been using to launder the money. It led us to the identities of all the so-called customers who paid money for whatever service they are selling."

"Stealing babies!"

"Well, maybe, but whatever, all the customers had strong links with the Hardacre family."

"God, that is horrific. Do you think the Hardacres are pulling all the strings? Running whatever is going on?"

"The evidence is patchy but I would put money on it. There is one other thing though."

"What?"

"There was a strange anomaly with the bank transactions. One of the pots of money had one less payment than the others and seemed to have paid a large amount of money into the main account."

"I don't understand. What do you mean?"

"Well Anya, although all our evidence is still circumstantial, if our theory about the Hardacres is right, we believe they might be one of the customers of the doctor's services."

Anya put her head in her hands. "My God. This is too much."

*

They gave Anya some time to take in the latest information. They couldn't afford for her to bolt again. She was still a bit unpredictable but Clark felt that they were finally beginning to get through the evidence trail. Rob had also calmed down and seemed happy to let Clark and Anya talk. It was getting late though and they did have more to cover. Clark didn't want them to leave.

"Why don't you stay here tonight? You two can have my bed and I will sleep on the couch."

"Oh, sorry Clark, it is late. We should go."

"No, I want you to stay. We have much more to discuss but I know this is traumatic for you. We can stop for today and do more tomorrow. It's Sunday tomorrow, so none of us have to work. Please."

Anya and Rob looked at each other. They both knew Clark was right.

"We don't have a change of clothes or even a toothbrush."

"Don't worry. I have some new toothbrushes in the cupboard. There are clean towels in the airing cupboard and I am sure your clothes won't mind if you wear them for a second day."

His quirky enthusiasm was infectious. It had been a difficult day for all of them but Rob and Anya knew it made sense to stay. After all, they were probably in the safest place they could be. Away from the glare and threat of evil Bradley, if they were indeed right that he was the one-man killing machine.

*

He was raging. He had gone back to Anya and Rob's house, expecting them to return at some point after they had played him like some two-bit mug job. They hadn't come home and it was well past midnight. All bets were off now. They were dead the moment he saw them. Sod his father and all this game-playing. Judgement day had arrived. These loose ends needed to be tied up. He made his favourite booty call to the Swedish twins who were always up for a debauched night of drink, drugs and wild sex. It would soothe his anger and get him ready for his next killing spree.

68

Anya and Rob woke the next morning in Clark's flat to the smell of bacon and coffee. After freshening up they walked into his small kitchen/breakfast room to poached eggs on muffins, bacon and coffee. Clark was sitting there, eating his breakfast and smiling.

"Enjoy. Please."

Rob and Anya were impressed. This guy clearly knew how to make breakfast. As they enjoyed the freedom of being safe, not thinking about being followed and Anya not having any bad dreams, Clark threw them a curve ball.

"Why don't you stay here for a bit. It's safe. We know you weren't followed here, which means that your tail doesn't know where you are. If you go home, you are at more risk. It would give us more time to discuss what we have found and our plans for getting in the clinic."

Through mouthfuls of poached egg, Rob said, "But what about the gallery? I can't just leave it."

"Could the lady that has been helping you look after it full time for a few days?"

"I don't know. I suppose I could ring her and ask."

Anya interjected. "Look, sorry to state the bleeding obvious but you disgusting men might be happy to wear the same pair of pants for several days on end but I am not. We have no clothes."

"Go out and buy what you need. The shops are just around the corner."

Anya and Rob looked at each other. Was this a good plan? Could they really hide out here for a bit? Buy a temporary wardrobe and live at Clark's?

As they pondered what to do, Clark pushed on his with master plan.

"I can take a week off work. I am owed loads of time and they are always hassling me to take my leave. It will give us time to really move this forward."

After a few minutes Anya spoke up.

"Let's do it. Rob, give Elisha a call and give her some flannel about me needing some time to recover. I am sure she will do whatever you ask, as she is clearly smitten with you."

Rob put on his surprised, slightly hurt expression.

"Oh, spare me Rob. If you can't see that girl is madly in love with you, you must have a thicker skin than I thought. Don't worry, I am not jealous. I have a few more important things to worry about than some ditzy mooning artist type."

Rob finished his breakfast with no further comment. Embarrassed and a little bit chastened by Anya's insight. She was right about Elisha. He knew she liked him and he thought she was incredibly cute. During the dark days of Anya's coma, he had been tempted.

Rob made the call and, as Anya had predicted, she was delighted to help. They spent the morning buying clothes and supplies for a few days. Clark bought some more food and drink to keep them going alongside the inevitable takeaway menus.

After a lazy lunch, where the tensions of the previous day seemed to have dissipated a bit, they reconvened around the whiteboard. Anya gazed at the board, numb but trying to crack on.

"Why do you think it is happening again now?"

Clark perked up. Anya was calm and seemingly focused. He had to grab this opportunity.

"Oh, well, when Rob and I were looking at the bank transactions we noticed two new payments going into the main account, followed by payments out a few days later. It followed the same pattern although the figures had increased."

Anya started to bite her nails. She always did it when she was nervous. Clark pushed on.

"I looked at the admissions records and found two girls who fitted the profile. Their records were hidden, just like yours. Also, just like when you five were in the clinic, there had been confidential deliveries around the time of their admission."

"Deliveries?"

"Janice told us that two strange deliveries happened when you were in there. One was for illegal drugs from Poland that induced comas, supressed memories and treated drug addiction. The other was something in cold storage. She was sacked when she tried to open it."

Anya put her face in her hands. "Oh God. Janice. That is the lady that got killed because of me."

Rob jumped in. "No Anya. I told you that was not your fault. It was my fault for not being careful enough about being tailed by your friend."

"FRIEND! FRIEND! Fuck me Rob. Have you listened to anything I have said? He was not a friend. He was an evil raping bastard."

Rob held his hands up. "Sorry. Poor choice of words."

Clark jumped in to stop the tension between Rob and Anya escalating.

"Anya. Janice's death was a tragedy but the information she has given us is invaluable. I managed to track the illegal drug orders which gives us clear evidence of criminality against Dr Normandy. We don't know what the cold storage packages contained but she did give us a big clue about the private clinic. When we get in there, Janice's help will make a huge difference."

"God. I don't know. This is all too much. We should go to the police."

"No Anya. Look at this man." Clark pointed at Hassan Chandra. "We have spoken to four police officers that handled the girl's accidents. They confirmed that he took over the investigations and nothing happened to catch the killer, because he is part of the conspiracy and was covering it up. What is worse is that he is one of the customers of this sordid affair."

"What?"

"Yes, he paid the doctor and if you are right, stole a baby."

"God, this is too awful for words."

Anya sat for a while trying to compose herself. She seemed to be gaining some inner strength and ploughed on.

"So, Clark. What are your theories about my recurring dreams of the letters LEX, which I am sure is the start of the word LEXICON? I saw it one of my recent dreams."

"Sorry, I have no ideas about that. There is nothing in the evidence trail that explains those letters or the word LEXICON. Like many of the gaps in our investigation, we suspect that is something that will be explained when we get in there."

Anya sat down, still staring at the board, trying to absorb all that Clark and Rob had found. She turned to Clark again.

"Why are you doing this Clark? Why are you looking out for me?"

Clark picked up the picture of his father and showed it to Anya.

"Because of him. My father. He committed suicide when I was young because some corporate bastards asset stripped the company he had worked for all his life and left him with nothing. They stole his pension pot and fled the country. The police and the politicians did nothing. Since that day I had resolved to seek out these people and expose their dirty secrets. I started looking at this case when George Walker was in the news. It led me to you and this conspiracy."

"Wow. Well I am sorry about your father and sorry that I have got you involved in this."

"It really is no problem. If I can, in some small way, avenge my dad I will be happy. The friend that helped me hack the Cayman Island bank and investigate the Hardacres found some sort of business connection between William Hardacre and the bastards that took my father down. I would love it if I can disrupt their evil practices, even by association."

"Who is this friend you keep talking about? Where is he? Can we trust him?"

Rob had remained quiet during these exchanges, happy that Clark and Anya had seemed to be bonding, but he couldn't let this one go.

"Well Anya. The man doesn't really exist. He is a cyber friend. Clark doesn't know his name, where he lives or even if he is a police officer. We are taking a massive gamble using him."

Clark bit back. "We are not taking a gamble. I have worked with Snap for years. He is part of our hacking community and I trust him completely."

Anya looked at Clark. She looked at Rob.

"Jesus, you two don't get on, do you? How on earth have you managed to get this far if you bicker all the time?"

Clark smiled. "Let's just call it creative differences. Rob has always had an issue with the way I have been finding the information about this conspiracy. He doesn't like breaking the law."

"Yeah well, you haven't given me much choice and anyway you are not the one taking all the risks. It has always been Anya and I in danger."

Anya interjected.

"For God's sake you two. If what you say is true, we are dealing with some pretty heavy criminals who are not frightened to kill to protect their secrets. It seems to me that we need to use all the help we can get in whatever way we can get it. And, maybe you should both remember that I am the one with the lost baby, murdered parents, murdered friends and a fucked-up life."

They both sat there, reprimanded again like naughty children. They both said sorry with a slightly sulky-teenager vibe.

Anya got up. "I am going for a walk. I need some air."

"Anya. Don't..."

She cut Rob off before he could finish his sentence.

"Look, just leave me alone. I am not going out to score some drugs. I won't make that mistake again. I am just going to walk into the shops and clear my head."

She left Rob and Clark to stew in their own juices.

*

He stirred and looked at his phone. He couldn't believe it was past three o'clock in the afternoon. They must have hit the drink and drugs hard last night. The girls were still there, sprawled across the bed, seemingly dead to the world. He checked his messages. Nothing from his father. Thank God. He didn't need that aggravation today. He would get back to killing Anya and Rob when it suited him. Right now, these lovely ladies looked like they might be up for another fun night. He smiled to himself and closed his eyes. Sex, drugs, drink and murder. Perfect.

*

The doctor checked on Bianca and Sam. They were both progressing nicely. He smiled to himself. A few more months and this would all be done and he would be off to Asia for his next encounter. He had been promised some nice young Thai boys this time.

69

Anya, Rob and Clark had gone out to eat the previous evening to try to get away from the confines of the flat and the constant reminder of the horror that was plastered all over the murder board.

They had all stocked up on supplies and Clark had got the week off. After breakfast, they decided to crack on.

"Anya, sorry to talk about Bradley again but I am curious as to how he links with the others. Can you remember anything else about him? What was his surname?"

"Umm, Williams, I think. Bradley Williams. I don't really know much about him other than he always seemed to have money."

Rob interjected. "He was a drug dealer Anya. They always have money."

"Yes, I suppose they do, but I mean he seemed rich. Posh rich, if you know what I mean."

"Yes, I know what you mean," said Clark.

Clark opened up his laptop and started dancing his fingers over the keyboard at an amazing pace.

"What are you doing?" asked Anya.

"I want to see what we can find about dear Bradley, either through legal means or otherwise." Clark glanced up at Rob as he said it, almost goading him into a reaction. Rob ignored him. Anya just watched Clark.

"OK, so his university records have him living in a flat in Oxford."

"Yes, that was the one I stayed in during… umm, during the worst of my addiction."

"Hmm, otherwise Bradley is pretty much off the grid, which just makes him more suspicious. He still seems to be registered as a student at Oxford Uni, even though he is twenty-five. He has no tax records, no car registered to him, even though we are pretty sure he is the one driving around killing people, and he has no employment records."

Clark continued to tap away, accessing different websites at an amazing speed.

"I have his birth certificate here. His mother is Jane Williams and his father is… oh, unknown."

"Eh, what do you mean unknown?" said Anya.

"Well it means his mother either genuinely didn't know the father or chose to leave his name off the birth certificate."

"Is she still alive?"

Clark flicked between numerous screens at a pace that Anya couldn't keep up with. Screens and information were constantly flashing before her eyes. She didn't know how Clark did it.

"Yes, she is living in Newbury and works as a care assistant in a local nursing home."

"Any connections to the other conspirators?"

"No, nothing obvious. She lived and worked in London in the early part of her career as a legal assistant. Seems like she worked for a number of different firms up to when she had Bradley. Looks like she took a career break to raise him, moved away from London and settled in Newbury. She has been a care assistant ever since."

Rob piped up. "Sorry to seem so judgemental, but she doesn't seem like the sort of person who would have lots of money or be posh rich, to use Anya's description."

"No, that is curious," said Clark, "maybe the father didn't want to be identified but looked after Jane and Bradley by giving them money or maybe she just inherited a lot of money from somewhere."

"We know Bradley went to Oxford Uni but where did he go to school?" asked Anya.

"Well this is interesting," replied Clark, "he went to a private boys' school in Oxford."

"That confirms it," said Rob, "there is no way she could afford to send him to private school on a care assistant salary. The father must have been paying for it."

Clark sat and pondered. "Yes, unless she has got family money from somewhere. The question still remains though. Who is Bradley's father?"

They all sat looking at the board, trying to piece together the bits they knew about Bradley. Clark suddenly started tapping away and brought up Snap's report on the Hardacre family.

"What is it?" said Anya.

"Hold on, something about Snap's report is niggling in my head. It's something he said in it. Hold on. Here it is. 'William Hardacre – rumours he can't keep his dick in his pants'. Jesus! Do you think Bradley could be his illegitimate child?"

Anya and Rob looked gobsmacked. Anya spoke first.

"Oh my God. That would make sense. If his father is as dodgy as you say he is, it follows that he has influenced Bradley to do his dirty work."

"That must be some heavy influence if he has murdered all the people we think he has," added Rob.

"Maybe he is just a psychopath and William is exploiting his unstable character," opined Clark.

They all sat and considered their theory. It did make sense but again was all conjecture. After a few moments Anya said what they all were thinking.

"This has to be right. It just makes sense that Bradley is William's son and the Hardacre family are running this conspiracy."

70

James Hardacre sat reading the papers for his Cabinet meeting the next day. His father was never far from his mind. James had finally delivered the Chinese trade deal for him and that had at least got him out of his hair for a few days, as he was adding more billions to his fortune with Far East money.

The problem was he was due to return from China in two days' time and James knew he would be back for more. He really had done a deal with the devil and could see no way out. Annabelle was being difficult and suspicious of everything he did with his father. She could never find out the truth.

*

He was stirring from another drug, drink and sex-induced sleep. Something was brushing his face.

"Wake up darling. Wake up. We need feeding."

He opened his eyes and smiled as the twins were hovering over him. He looked down at his cock and said, "Give it a minute to wake up."

They slapped him playfully. "Not that you randy sod. Real food. Order some room service."

"OK, OK, what do you want?"

"Champagne, strawberries and ice cream."

"Your wish is my command my beautiful ones."

He ordered the room service and checked his phone. No messages from his father. Thank God. He had a feeling he was out of the country, which probably explained why he had been given a few days without his usual aggravation.

His mind wandered to the unfinished business with Rob and Anya. He wondered whether they had returned home after their little adventure. He gritted his teeth at the memory of being played. They were onto him now but that would just make their deaths all the more enjoyable.

The girls snuggled up to him and a certain part of his anatomy had definitely woken up.

That little business can wait, he thought to himself. He was enjoying himself too much to stop this any time soon.

There was a knock on the hotel room door. The room service arrived and another night of fun was about to begin.

*

William Hardacre was just finishing off a fantastic meal at the Mandarin Oriental Hotel in Hong Kong. He had finished his business in China and was having a couple of days' stopover in Hong Kong before he flew back to the UK.

He was pondering what he needed next from his spineless son James, who sat nicely in the corridors of power doing his bidding, when an email popped up about the little problem he had left his other son to deal with. It was a report on a certain couple's digital activity.

Hmm, not sure this is telling me anything. So, they have been shopping in Reading. I do hope he is keeping an eye on them.

71

Anya and Rob woke to another amazing Clark breakfast. As they drank their first coffee of the morning, the conversation turned to the clinic.

"When do you think we will hear back about the job interview?" asked Anya.

"I don't know," replied Clark. "The deadline was noon yesterday and I am positive with the fake ID for Rob and the killer application, he will get an interview. It just depends whether they are one of these firms that takes ages to process applications."

"What do we do if he gets in?"

"As I said before, we need him to recce the place first. Get the layout sorted and find a way in so you can break into the clinic."

Rob interjected.

"Hold on Clark. Since when was Anya involved in this little clinic invasion of yours?"

"This was always going to be a two-person job. One of you has to be the insider. They will find a way to let the other one in, who will in turn break into the clinic and get the evidence we need."

"No. Sorry Clark. We never discussed this. I am not going to put Anya in more danger."

"For fuck's sake Rob, I am not a pathetic female that needs protecting by your old-fashioned ideas of chivalry. If there is evidence to find, don't you think I should be the one to find it? To find out what happened to *my* baby."

Rob didn't respond. He just moved away from the conversation and stewed. Since Anya had found out about her baby, he had become low on her list of priorities. Everything he had tried to do to support and comfort her had been met with hostility or an attitude that constantly undermined him. Clark didn't help either. He was so consumed by the desire to solve a conspiracy and avenge his father, he just bent to Anya's will and drove her on. He checked his phone. There was a nice text from Elisha asking how he was.

Clark and Anya had hardly noticed Rob moving into the other room as they carried on with their conversation.

"Clark. What do you really think is going on in the clinic?"

"Honestly, I don't know. Your baby revelation gave us something we had never previously considered. What I can't work out is exactly where the baby thing fits in. Rob and I discussed the one big problem with the theory that you were all pregnant when you went in."

"What's that?"

"Your addictions. It is a well-known fact that women who are drug addicts have a very high chance of delivering an addicted baby."

"Why is that a problem?"

"Well, let's consider the possibility that these clients were paying big money to 'steal' your babies."

"OK. Go on."

"Surely they wouldn't pay huge sums for a baby that had medical problems. They would want des—"

Clark stopped himself.

"What is it Clark? What is it? What were you going to say?" pleaded Anya.

Clark shook himself out of his sudden look of absolute shock.

"God. Sorry. I think I have worked out what happened to you."

72

He tore himself away from the Swedish twins and drove back to Goring. He wanted to see if he could conclude his little problem. The two nights with the twins had soothed his anger but driving here was just winding him back up. He was going to enjoy this. He was going to make sure they both knew exactly what was going to happen to them before he did it. Nice and slow and very painful.

He parked up around the corner from their house and tried to look like just another villager, out for a morning walk. He walked into the cul-de-sac and made his way up to Anya and Rob's place. The cold steel of the knife in his pocket was exciting him. Since Janice, this was the way he wanted to do it. The way he needed to do it. The car was just so impersonal. He wanted to see their fear. Smell it.

As he got closer, his anger grew. The car was outside but there didn't seem to be any life going on in the house. He risked getting a bit closer, straining to see through the front windows. It was quite a dull morning. The sort of morning where people might have had lights on, but there was nothing. They weren't in.

He walked away trying to work out what to do. Had they just gone out or had they not yet returned from their game of cat and mouse that he had most emphatically lost? Were they hiding? He had been played. They knew about him. They must do. It just added to his rage.

As he carried on walking trying not to totally lose it in the middle of the street, his phone beeped. His father.

'Have you found out who is helping them yet? My digital spies say they have been shopping in Reading over the weekend. We need a result.'

Reading? So, that is where they went and almost certainly where they are hiding.

He decided to watch the place in Goring for a bit. If they didn't return by lunchtime, he would drive to Reading. A big place, but he did have some chance of finding them if he was at least in the right postcode.

73

Anya was frantic. "What do you mean, you think you know what happened to me?"

Clark was suddenly incoherent. Words tumbling out of his mouth like some mixed-up dictionary.

"Designer babies. The cold boxes. The drugs. The money. The secrecy. It all makes sense."

"What do you mean?"

Rob walked back into the man cave to see what was going on. The pitch of their voices had suddenly reached a decibel level that only dogs could hear.

"Anya. Clark. What is going on?"

"He says he knows what happened to me but he is talking gibberish."

"Do you Clark? Do you know what happened to Anya?"

Clark looked at both of them. Seemingly immobilised by the sudden epiphany, he just sat there, staring at them.

"Jesus. Sorry. Just give me a minute."

"I don't have a fucking minute. If you know where my baby is, tell me."

"OK. OK. Look, I guess you could argue this is just another one of a number of possible theories but the more I talk to you Anya, the more the bits are falling into place. I am convinced I know what happened."

"What? Just tell me!"

"It was the bit about the addicted babies. The clients won't have paid half to three quarters of a million for babies that were addicted. That just doesn't make sense. If this is about stealing babies, the clients would want designer babies."

"What do you mean designer babies?"

"I think it is really obvious. You weren't pregnant when you went in there. The doctor cured you of your addiction and when you were clean, he created designer babies for the clients using you as the surrogates."

"Eh. How does that work?"

"Think about it. The cold boxes. I reckon they contained sperm samples from the men. The clients chose you to be the mothers of their babies. I bet they wanted a certain type of woman and Bradley found them. Someone wanted you Anya because you fitted a particular profile. I mean, you are incredibly beautiful and all the other girls were not bad to look at either. The ethnic profiling fits as well."

Anya was speechless. Clark was blurting out a mad theory but something about it was making sense.

"I... I... just don't know Clark. I guess it could make sense. What do you mean about the ethnic profiling?"

"Well, again, think about it. Is it a coincidence that Hassan Chandra is one of the clients? Marjit is the same ethnic origin as Hassan. If the doctor is creating babies for cash, this would seem to be a logical conclusion. And, one of the new clients is Greek."

"That Bianca girl. She must be Greek with a surname like that."

"Exactly."

Anya sat there. Trying to process it all. Rob and Clark just sat there in silence. They both knew soon the penny was going to drop, if Clark's theory was right. A minute later it happened. Anya had just worked out what Clark's theory meant.

"Fucking hell. My baby is alive and one of those bastards has him or her," Anya shouted as she pointed at the pictures of the clients that Clark had pinned on the board.

"Clark. Find pictures of their kids. One of them must be mine."

Rob interjected. He knew where Anya was going with this. "Anya. Don't. It is not going to help."

"And what the fuck would you know about it Rob? Of course it is going to help. If Clark is right, one of them has my baby."

"But, you won't be able to tell. Surely. You are just making more pain for yourself."

"I will know Rob. Clark, find those pictures. You can find everything else from this little criminal enterprise of yours. Find the pictures and find my baby."

With that she walked out of the man cave and sat in the living room. Clark and Rob looked at each other. They knew she would not let this go. They could hear her crying.

Within twenty minutes, Clark had found pictures of the children of each client. They were all the right age. Three years old. Exactly the right timescale to fit with when the girls were in the clinic. Clark knew this strengthened his theory but none of that mattered. What was important was that Anya believed it and now nothing was going to stop her finding her baby.

Clark had pinned the children's pictures up on the board underneath the men that they had identified as the clients. Five men. Five children. Five girls in the clinic. His theory had to be right.

They called Anya in and she jumped up like shot. Stony faced but determined. She went along the board like an identity parade. She walked along the line, taking in the features. She stopped at the picture of James Hardacre's 'daughter'. She stared for a while and then put her hand against the picture. The tears began to flow.

"Oh my God, this is my baby. Look at her. She looks just like me."

74

After the bombshell, Clark and Rob had left Anya alone. They had to admit that the Hardacre kid did look like Anya. Clark hoped he hadn't set Anya down a path that would ultimately cause more pain, especially if he was wrong. What if the Hardacre kid wasn't Anya's after all and they had got this conspiracy all messed up in their relentless pursuit of what they thought was the truth?

After about half an hour they went back into the living room to find Anya looking at her phone. The next thing she said made Clark realise that there was no turning back.

"They called her Sophie. I like that name. I won't change it when I get her back."

Rob and Clark looked at each other, not knowing what to say next. Anya was living this nightmare minute by minute and they had to tread carefully. Be guided by her highly emotional state.

"We have to go to the police. I can't stand another day without my daughter."

Clark guessed this was coming. He tried to deflect it.

"We need more Anya. You can't just rock up to the prime minister and say 'give me your kid as it's not yours'. Remember, if our theory is right, he is the father."

The look on Anya's face told them both that she hadn't assimilated that information when Clark had been blurting out his epiphany.

She stood up and started to pace.

"Oh my God. Oh my God. Oh my God. The father of my child is the fucking prime minister. What… what… what do I do? Shit!"

Normally this would have been the moment when Rob would have leapt in to comfort her but suddenly it didn't seem right. He just sat there and watched her dealing with the trauma, alone and in her own way.

"Clark. What about birth records? Surely, they would have to record me as the mother. Wouldn't they?"

Clark opened up his browser and started to tap away. In the words of Han Solo – he had 'a bad feeling about this'.

"I'll see if I can find a copy of the birth certificate and registration."

Anya stood hovering over him, ready to pounce on any information, like a praying mantis ready to snare its next meal. A search of the birth records found the name easily, Sophie Jennifer Hardacre, born the 28th March 2015. Clark looked at the birth certificate. Father – James Horatio Hardacre, Mother – Annabelle Emma Hardacre.

"This is what I feared," Clark exclaimed.

"What?" shouted Anya impatiently.

"They have faked the birth certificates as well."

Anya sat down. Deflated. The depths of this conspiracy were beginning to reveal themselves. She was convinced this put the Hardacres right in the middle of this nasty, sordid, heart-breaking situation but she knew Clark was right. They needed more evidence.

She started throwing more questions at Clark. Desperately searching for something they could take to the police.

"How have they got away with this? He is a famous person. Did nobody wonder how they suddenly had a kid?"

Clark started to tap away again.

"The thing is he wasn't the PM when this was done but he was a Cabinet minister. It might be that despite his role at the time, him having a kid just wasn't newsworthy."

"But what about his wife? Did nobody think it strange that she wasn't pregnant and they suddenly get a kid?"

"Hmm, you are right. Let me have a look."

Clark continued to mine information from various places.

"There are no pictures of her around that time. I remember Snap's report said she shunned the limelight. Maybe that is how they did it. Just kept her out of public view."

"That just seems ridiculous. Impossible. Can these people really cover up everything?"

Clark suddenly stopped. "Hold on. What is this?"

Anya leant over his shoulder to get a closer look.

"I have found an announcement in the *Telegraph*. 'James and Annabelle Hardacre are delighted to announce the birth of their first child, Sophie Hardacre, born on the 28th March 2015. A gift from God'."

"A gift. A GIFT! You bastards. My baby was not a fucking gift."

With that the tears began to flow again and Anya slumped in the chair. With every new revelation Clark and Rob felt more and more helpless. Not knowing what to do for Anya or how to comfort her from the horror that was unravelling before their eyes.

As they sat, waiting for Anya to guide them towards their next step, an email pinged into the fake email address that Clark had set up with Rob's fake ID.

"Oh my God Rob. It bloody well worked. The Loughborough Clinic have invited you in for an interview on Thursday morning at 9 a.m."

75

He had driven around Reading for most of the afternoon the day before and was now sitting in his hotel, eating breakfast, wondering what the fuck he was doing. How was he going to find them in such a large place? He needed a better plan but he knew he would need his father's help to get what he needed. He just couldn't bring himself to go there. He decided to walk into the main shopping area, where their credit cards had been used. Hoping to get lucky.

*

Anya was still livid with Clark and Rob. They both kept pushing the clinic invasion as the only way forward. To catch the conspirators in the act. She only cared about Sophie. She wanted to go to the police and force them to get Sophie away from the Hardacres. Do a DNA test. Prove that she was her daughter.

She sat eating what breakfast she could stomach and had to listen to Rob and Clark plotting. At least they seemed to have stopped shouting at each other.

"Right Rob, your new identity is watertight and I have called you Rob Stapleton. I thought it would be a good idea to give you the same first name to avoid confusion. You have a new life backed up by all the relevant online records. If they review your employment records they will find they all check out. If they offer you a job, say you can start straight away. We need to get this next stage done quickly."

Clark had furtively glanced at Anya when he said the last bit, conscious that she was not happy with their plan. He was worried she was going to bolt and take things into her own hands. She didn't react and he ploughed on.

"As soon as you start working there, I need you to get down to the secret part of the clinic. We need to find a way in. Something like a fire door would be brilliant. Once we have mapped the place out we can devise a plan to get Anya in there."

At the sound of her name Anya looked up and delivered her next line with a scarcely veiled touch of sarcasm.

"And what, Grandmaster Clark, is your plan for me then? How do we get the evidence?"

He ignored the obvious dissent.

"As soon as Rob gets the plans of the place I can guide you in. I will set you up with a device that records sound and pictures, relaying and recording everything back in real time to a secure server. I can disable the security as we go. No problem at all. They won't even know you have been there. We can get you in, capture all the evidence and get you out. Then we can send all we have to the police. I have already identified the private email address of the Met commissioner. I am praying he is clean and not on William Hardacre's payroll."

"And what if I get caught?"

"You won't. Trust me."

"*Trust*! What a fucking ironic word to use. I can't trust anyone. No one seems to know how I am feeling. No one knows the pain. If you did, you wouldn't ask me to trust you."

"OK, I am sorry. I will be listening in the whole time. If something goes wrong I will text Rob and if necessary ring the police. I won't put your life in danger Anya."

She didn't seem placated but just looked away and drank her coffee. Rob tried to steer the conversation in a different direction.

"I don't have a suit for the interview. I am going to have to buy one."

"That is fine. Just go into the shops today and get yourself kitted out."

Rob looked at Anya expectantly. Hoping for something.

"Do you want to come and help me find a suit?"

The response was emphatic.

"No. I want to stay here and help Clark put this evidence file together. I am not going to let anything slip. If we are *finally* going to get something to them, I am not leaving anything to chance."

Clark looked at Rob and raised his eyebrows. They both knew they should leave it there.

*

He was wandering around the centre of Reading, in the main shopping area, scanning the crowds hoping for a break. He knew this was a bad plan. Needle in a haystack time but he was not going to let his father know how much he had cocked this up. He would find a way somehow.

As he sat on the outside chairs of a non-descript coffee shop, a tall blonde with an amazing arse walked by and smiled at him. The sort of 'fuck me' smile he had gotten used to. He just had it. That electrifying combination of good looks, good breeding and confidence that seemed to draw women in. He wanted to go for it. More sex and maybe another chance to feel the buzz of... he stopped himself as he suddenly caught a glimpse of something he'd seen before. Someone he had seen before.

He leapt up from his seat, straining to see through the masses of people moving in front of him, obscuring his view. He had seen a man wearing a distinctive red jacket coming out of a clothes shop. The type of red jacket he had seen Rob wearing, almost every bloody time he had been watching him. He started to move through the crowd shoving people out of the way, ignoring the exclamations and expletives as he went. Could this be it? Had he been lucky or was he just seeing things? He kept straining to see as he navigated the crowds. Yes, there he was again. Walking away from him towards the river. He couldn't see the face but it looked like Rob from the back. Was he just willing it to be him?

He pushed on trying to close the gap but the crowds were stifling his progress despite his aggressive, desperate nature. He ploughed on; a gap opened up and he tried to break into a run but he bumped into an old lady, sending her bag flying. People started to look over. "Oi mate, leave that old lady alone," one concerned citizen shouted. It drew a reaction from others. They went to see if she was hurt. He just bolted. He had to. Hoping that no one would be brave enough to chase him. It wasn't as if he had mugged her. As he reorientated himself, he realised 'Rob' had gone out of view. Where had he gone? He ran to the point where he had last seen him. A covered walkway leading to the long path that skirted the river. He ran through it. Looked left. Look right. "Fuuuuuuck!" he screamed. He had lost him.

*

Rob crashed through the front door of Clark's flat, sounding like some bull elephant in must, breathing hard. Clark and Anya leapt up to see what the commotion was.

"Rob? What the hell are you doing?" shouted Anya accusingly. He tried to catch his breath.

"Brad..." Huff, puff. "Bradley. He was in the shopping area. Chasing me."

"What!" exclaimed Clark. "Where? Did he follow you?"

"No, I think I shook him off."

"You think! You think!" shouted Clark. "You had better bloody well know. If you have blown my cover, we are done. Finished."

Anya looked at Rob. Horrified. The doorbell rang. They all jumped out of their skins. A look of terror suddenly etched on all their faces. Anya's expression changed from horror to a look of hatred that Rob had never seen before.

"What have you done?"

They all looked at each other. Paralysed by fear. The doorbell rang again.

Clark moved towards the door and risked looking through the spyhole. Wasn't this where the assassin shot him in the eye as they predicted his move? The bullet didn't come. The shape in the doorway was not Bradley. It was the postman. Clark opened the door and took the parcel. He shut the door and slumped, sliding down the back of the door as all his energy sapped out of him. Rob and Anya just looked on, trying to get their heart rates back to normal. Clark started to laugh. Terror replaced by hysterics.

76

The near miss with 'Bradley' had shaken them all up. After the terror of the doorbell and the fleeting moment where they thought their worlds had come crashing down, they had to regroup.

Anya and Clark had spent the rest of the day pumping Rob for information, trying to ascertain whether it really was Bradley. All he could tell them was that he was walking back to Clark's when he noticed a fair-haired man with dark glasses moving quickly in his direction, shoving people out of the way and causing a commotion. His gut instinct had been to run. From a distance, the man looked so much like the pictures they had of Bradley and the same person that had followed him in the 4x4. In the end, Clark and Anya accepted he had done the right thing and were just relieved he had not led the man to Clark's door.

It was 6 a.m. and they were having an early breakfast, to make sure Rob could get to his interview on time, driving the car they had hired the previous day amongst all the drama. They were still twitchy. The car was in the underground car park attached to the complex that Clark lived in but they worried that this man was still lurking around. He knew the direction Rob had gone and Clark's flat was not that far away from the shops.

Rob put on the suit that had almost been their undoing and got ready to go. Anya wished him good luck with the kind of kiss your granny gives you. He tried to ignore the coldness and went out the door. He headed down to the underground car park, on high alert, desperately hoping not to see the man again. He got to the car without incident and set off for the Loughborough Clinic.

*

Anya and Clark cleared up breakfast without really talking, an air of impatience pervading every bit of Anya's mood. Her patience trigger seemingly coiled up like a snake waiting to pounce on its next meal. Clark knew he had to tread carefully. He had no control over the situation if she decided to bolt.

They sat back down in the man cave to finish off the hard-copy evidence file that they had been putting together. They continued to hope that the Met commissioner was the right person to approach. They had no real idea how far the Hardacres' influence and corruption reached.

The file was as comprehensive as they could make it. Their theory typed out like some executive summary of a board paper. The photos and backgrounds of the seven girls, their medical records, the reports on the car accidents and the links to Hassan Chandra, the clear evidence trails against Dr Normandy and George Walker, the emails, the disgusting paedo pictures, all the bank records from the Cayman Island accounts and the evidence of the clients, the illegal drug orders, the audit trail of the deliveries, the evidence from Janice and the news reports of her murder.

"Anya, thank you for helping me with this. I think this is as good as it's going to get but you know we need the evidence from the clinic to make this stick."

Clark had pushed the point to try and stop Anya from doing something crazy.

"I am not going to wait forever Clark. You are asking too much of me. You have to realise that my child is living with someone else. Do you have any idea how painful that is? I can't stand to waste another day without her. They have stolen so many precious years of my life, her life. I can't stand it."

"I know Anya and I am really sorry, but I am sure the evidence we get from the clinic will give us what we need. We just need to do this fast."

"Yes, Rob bloody well better get that job. If he doesn't I am out of here and I will sort it myself."

*

He was wandering around the Reading shops, near where he had lost Rob, hoping for a break. His rage was simmering. He needed to kill. To feel the rush again. He had been so close. His phone beeped.

'What is going on? Why have you not given me an update?'

*

The familiar gut-tightening feeling hit James Hardacre as soon as he heard his father's voice. He entered his private study where William was sitting. Waiting for his next favour.

"What do you want, Dad? Was China not enough?"

"We have a problem."

"And you think I can help... why?"

"It is not politics. It is our other matter. A certain individual is proving to be a problem. I have asked your brother to sort it but he has gone radio silent."

"I don't have a brother."

"Oh, for fuck's sake James. Don't be obtuse. He's involved. You're involved. Whether you recognise him as your brother or not."

"And what the hell do you expect me to do about it? Can't you control your little psycho love child?"

"I don't need you to do anything, you pathetic excuse for a man. You just need to know that if he doesn't get this sorted, your little secret might just get out there."

With that William walked out, leaving James feeling as helpless as he had ever felt.

He tried to compose himself and walked towards the conference room for the Cabinet meeting.

Annabelle Hardacre watched her father-in-law leave. A few minutes later, James came out of his private office. She had never seen James look the way he was looking right now. He was scared. Fear etched all over his face. What the hell was going on?

*

Rob arrived at the perimeter of the clinic, fifteen minutes before the scheduled start time of the interview. He parked in the same space as when they had come here before and pressed the buzzer on the intercom. The voice sounded the same. So, she was still here. He announced why he was there and was buzzed through the gate. He drove up the short gravel drive and parked in the visitors' car park. As he got out of his car he tried to take in as much of the layout as he could, without looking suspicious. He walked through the grand entrance to the reception desk and met the voice that had sent them away all those months ago. Janet Wall. Rob had grown a beard to change how he looked, just in case she had some form of photographic memory from watching the CCTV. He didn't need to worry. She hardly looked at him, handed him his visitor's badge and asked him to wait.

Pretty much on time, Rob was invited into a meeting room where he was to be interviewed by the head of facilities and the domestic supervisor. Everything ran smoothly. He seamlessly slipped into his new identity and managed not to make any obvious mistakes in recalling the work history that Clark had created. They were obviously impressed with his cleaning experience and asked when he could start. Rob made up some ruse about how he was in between roles and could start tomorrow if they wanted him to. After forty-five minutes they finished the interview and asked him to wait. He thought this was a good sign. Sure enough, after waiting fifteen minutes they offered him the job on the spot. Result. Rob had played his new role to perfection. The luck was still on their side. They asked if he could do the 1 p.m. to 8 p.m. shift the next day. Rob bit their hand off. The speed with which this was going was just what they needed. He thanked them and agreed to turn up for work the next day. He texted Clark and Anya.

'We're in!'

77

The plan was afoot. Clark and Anya were delighted that Rob had nailed it. For the first time in a few days, Rob actually felt some warmth from both of them. Like he was actually contributing something to this mad plan.

"Right, how is this going to work?" probed Anya. Clark tried to take control.

"Well Rob. You have a seven-hour shift today which should give you enough time to sneak away and recce the secret part of the clinic. You need to find a way in. As I said before, something like a fire door down that end of the building."

"OK, I will try but surely they will be supervising me closely on my first day."

"Surely not for the whole seven hours. You will find a way."

Anya pushed it. "You *need* to find a way Rob. I can't wait another day. We have to get in there. Please."

Rob looked at Anya. She was a shell of the person he thought he knew. His feelings for her had been shaken over the last few weeks but her desperation and whatever love he still had for her drove him on to help her.

"I will do it. Don't worry."

Anya put on a pained smile and hugged him. A proper loving hug. Like it used to be.

Clark pressed on with his master plan.

"I think you should both go and stay in a hotel in Warwick. It will make it easier to get to and from the clinic. I will stay here and manage the technical parts. Anya, I have sent you a link to your phone to run the app that will record the sound and images, once you get in there."

She pushed it further. "When? When is this going to happen?"

"If Rob gets what we need today, we can do it tomorrow."

"Good, come on Rob. Let's book a hotel and get up there. You have work to do."

*

They drove to the hotel and arrived just before 11 a.m. They checked in, had a quick lunch and Rob got ready for his shift. Anya decided to walk into Warwick to do some shopping. She had to take her mind off the hell she was experiencing every minute that went by without her daughter.

They were relieved that 'Bradley' did not appear to have found them or followed them up to Warwick. Whatever had happened yesterday had been a terrifying near-miss. They hoped their luck would hold.

Rob got to work. He was inducted into his role for the first hour and shown how and what to clean for the rest of the shift. He was doing rooms and clinic spaces towards where he needed to recce, but there was still going to be a risk if he was being closely supervised. He decided to play it by ear.

Rob was halfway through his shift and was now cleaning rooms towards the end of the building that was reasonably close to the mysterious clinic. He was on his own, although his supervisor was periodically checking up on him. He decided to wait until she checked in and then go for it once she left.

She turned up and checked Rob was getting on OK. She discussed his quality of work, gave him a few pointers, but otherwise seemed happy with what he was doing. Rob watched her leave and noticed she went back towards the main clinic. He knew this was his moment.

He quickly finished off the room he was doing and moved his cart out into the corridor. There was no one really moving around so he set off down the corridor towards the secret clinic. As he fobbed through the next security door, he met a nurse coming in the other direction. She just smiled and walked on. He went through another door and realised he must be in the corridor that Clark was talking about. He moved quickly, trying to look a bit lost, as he knew he was being picked up on CCTV. He moved towards the end of the corridor as it bent round to the left. There was the alcove Clark had mentioned. He walked past it and sure enough there was a security door, unmarked but almost certainly the door to the clinic. At the very end of the corridor was a dead end, with a fire exit door.

Bingo!

He had seen what he needed to see and quickly headed back to his work. As he walked back towards his cart, his heart sank. His supervisor was walking towards him.

"Where have you been?" she said with an accusing tone.

"Oh sorry, I was just trying to get my bearings whilst finding the loo," replied Rob, putting on his cutest facial expression. It didn't seem to work.

"Stick to where I have put you. No one needs to go down that end of the building. That is Dr Normandy's private quarters and he expressly forbids anyone from compromising his privacy. I don't want to have to sack you before you have completed your first day."

"I am sorry. It won't happen again."

She walked away with a disapproving look but thankfully it looked like he had got away with a mild rebuke. If he had been sacked, the whole plan would have died. He decided to keep his head down and finish his shift. He couldn't afford any more risks and he had what they needed anyway.

The shift finished with no major incidents and they confirmed that his next shift was 5 p.m. to 12 midnight. Rob bolted out of the clinic, relieved to get away.

*

He got back to the hotel to give Anya the good news. She was surrounded by shopping bags, including one from a local toy shop. She pulled out a cute teddy bear.

"This is for Sophie. I want her to have this as soon as I get her back."

Rob was unnerved. She seemed completely fixated on the moment when she would get her daughter back. There seemed to be an unshakeable belief that it was going to happen. Rob noticed that there was no 'we' in the sentence. Once again, he wondered where he fitted into these plans.

Anya seemed to jerk herself out of her daydream.

"How did you get on?"

"I did it. I found the secret clinic and there is a fire door just along the corridor. This is our way in."

Anya beamed.

"My God Rob. That is amazing."

With that she stood up, quickly removed her top and skirt. Rob was dumbstruck. It had been so long. She was a thing of beauty and standing there in just her skimpy underwear, Rob could not control himself. The rest of their clothes came off quickly and they had fast, passionate sex.

As they lay there recovering from the sudden surge of lust and passion, Rob's phone beeped. Clark.

'How did you get on? Why haven't you rung me? I am pacing the floors down here.'

Rob showed the text to Anya. She looked at Rob and laughed.

"Whoops! Maybe we should have phoned him before we... umm."

"I'm sure he will survive. Let's ring him now."

They put some clothes on and dialled Clark, putting him on speaker so they could all hear each other.

"Hey Clark. Rob and Anya here."

"Thank God. Where have you been? I thought you would have called me by now."

"Sorry, we got a bit tied up." They tried to stifle a snigger.

"Well, fine. What happened? Did you find what we needed?"

"Yes. I found the secret clinic and there is a fire door at the end of the corridor. It is a dead end so must go to the outside."

"Result. I thought that was the most likely layout. Any problems?"

"I nearly got caught by my boss but she just warned me away from the area. Her reaction kind of confirmed what we already knew."

"Brilliant. What time do you start tomorrow?"

"Not until 5 p.m."

"That is perfect. We can initiate the plan just as it is getting dark, somewhere around 8 p.m."

Anya piped up. "How am I going to get into the site?"

"Well, Rob can drive you in. You will just need to hide in the back. Put some coats on the back seat to cover you when you get near and make sure you park in a discreet part of the car park. I reckon from the plans and what Rob found, you need to park by the left-hand side of the building. It shouldn't be too far for you to get from the car to the fire door."

"What am I going to do for three hours?"

"Sorry Anya, but you are going to have to stay in the car until it starts getting dark. We can't risk you getting caught."

"Fuck me Clark. My mind doesn't need more time to stew. This is agony."

"I know. I am sorry, but tomorrow will be a success and we can go to the police with the last bits of evidence. Trus…"

Clark stopped himself from saying that word again. He just had to hope his optimism was not misplaced.

Anya continued to probe, clearly obsessed with every detail. If she had to wait another day, she was not going to let anything go wrong.

"Walk me through how you see this happening Clark."

"OK. Rob, start work as normal. A little before 8 p.m., I will text you both. Rob will need to make his way to the fire door. Anya, you will need to slip out of the car and make your way towards the back corner of the building, where this fire door is. Turn the app on, so I can hear what you are doing. When Rob reaches the fire door, he needs to text me. I will disable the CCTV and door security for a few minutes to get you inside and hopefully through the clinic door. It will alert their security team but if I can get them back on quickly, they should see it as a temporary glitch. Once you are in the clinic, record what we need and get out of there fast. I will disable the security again to get you out."

Rob looked concerned. "Sounds risky."

"This was never going to be without risk Rob. We just have to hope their security team are a bit lazy and don't fly down to the secret clinic the minute stuff goes off."

"Don't you think Dr Normandy will have them on high alert, especially around his precious 'private' area?"

There was an uncomfortable silence. Clark knew this was a high-risk plan with lots of variables. He had tried to remain upbeat for Anya's sake but they were both spotting the holes in the plan. Anya broke the silence.

"Ah fuck it. It is as good a plan as we are going to get. Those bastards are going to pay for what they did to me. I am going to find those girls and record what we need to put them in jail."

They ended the call. Rob and Anya went to get some food and Clark sat back in his man cave, pensive and worried. He knew there was a strong chance that something could go wrong. He would have to think of a back-up plan, especially if they got caught.

78

After a restless night, which at least did not have any horrible dreams, Anya woke, wired up like the addict she used to be. A high of different sorts but no less painful and tragic.

They spent the day trying to keep their minds off the opportunity that could make or break this conspiracy and get Anya's daughter back. They ate. They read every paper they could lay their hands on. Went for a walk. Time passed slowly, torturing Anya's soul.

*

He was still spending each day hanging around Reading town centre, hoping for another sighting of Rob or preferably that bitch, Anya. His rage was maxed out. He now had a gun to add to his killing options and he needed to kill again. The rush of excitement. The taste of blood. The power over life and death. The power over her life and death.

But, nothing. Nothing had happened since his failure to catch Rob. He couldn't contact his father. He was not going to get another bollocking for his failures. He was on his own. As he tried to calm his rage and work out what to do next, he heard the familiar beep of his phone. His father. Hmm, maybe he wasn't on his own. Maybe he could still be useful. The text message told him where they were.

The doctor examined Bianca and Sam. They were progressing nicely. Only a few more months and this would all be over. Thailand. Young boys. Waiting for his special attention.

*

The time finally arrived for them to leave for the clinic. To start with, Anya travelled in the front seat. As they got to the end of the lane that led to the clinic, they stopped and she lay down in the back as Rob covered her in the coats. Thankfully it wasn't a particularly warm late spring day, so she wouldn't cook. She had chocolate and water. It would keep her going on the long wait for darkness.

Rob set off down the lane to the clinic, picking up the CCTV cameras about a mile out. He desperately hoped that Anya was hidden enough and that there wasn't some sharp-eyed security person about to stop them and blow the plan before it started.

He drove to the gate, opened the car window to fob his way in. The gates opened and he drove through.

"We're in!"

Rob drove round to the left-hand side of the building and parked in the back part of the staff car park, as far away from the CCTV cameras as they could be. There were a few other cars in this part of the car park but they had to hope that anyone coming to their cars would not be interested in the contents of Rob's back seat. Rob parked up and started to get out, whispering to Anya.

"Be careful. I will see you soon."

A muffled "good luck" came from Anya as she settled down for a few hours' wait. A wait that would test every bit of her distressed, agonised mind.

Rob got into work, spoke to his supervisor about what she wanted him to do, got his cart out and started cleaning in the communal areas near reception. He would have to organise his cleaning rota to be down nearer the secret clinic around the time it got dark, as this was when Clark would text them both and start the plan. Rob felt this could be the longest three hours of his life as he worried about the risks. He tried to concentrate on the work and hoped time would pass quickly.

*

Clark settled into 'mission control', aka the Clark man cave, ready to help Rob and Anya storm the clinic and get the last bit of evidence they needed. He had the gateway into the Fairport Medical servers, ready to hack the CCTV and the security doors. He had all the protocols in place. It would be like turning a light on and off. He just needed Snap's help one more time to get the recording Anya would hopefully make secure and ready to send to the Met commissioner.

He logged into Proton.

KRYPTO:	Snap. Need you dude.
SNAPDEVIL:	Word up Krypto. What can I do for you?
KRYPTO:	The conspiracy. It's on. We crack it tonight.
SNAPDEVIL:	Much excitement dude. What do you need?
KRYPTO:	The girl has the Three Wise Monkeys app. She is going to record it all.
SNAPDEVIL:	And you need it securely streamed and stored.
KRYPTO:	You are way ahead of me.
SNAPDEVIL:	Send me her mobile IP and will get it sorted.
KRYPTO:	I need to send a link to the police so it needs to be real time and untraceable.
SNAPDEVIL:	Ah, the gold service. It shall be yours Cinderella.
KRYPTO:	Legend.

Clark had packaged up the hard-copy evidence file that he and Anya had put together and gave it to a courier with express instructions for it to be delivered to the Met commissioner between 8 p.m. and 8.30 p.m. The link that Snap was creating would be emailed to the commissioner as soon as Anya got out. He hoped it would be enough and that the commissioner was clean. They desperately needed him to believe what he was reading. It was high stakes but it had to work.

Clark sat back, obsessively eating Jaffa Cakes. He always did this when he was nervous. Now all he had to do was wait. For darkness and the moment of truth. He raised a Jaffa Cake to his dad's picture like he was making a toast.

This is it Dad. Redemption.

79

It was nearing 8 p.m. and it was beginning to get dark. Rob had manoeuvred himself so he was cleaning one of the clinic spaces which was quite close to where he needed to be. He hadn't heard the beep of a text message yet. The wait was killing him.

Anya was getting stiff. The car was comfortable but over three hours lying still in the same place was beginning to grate. It was almost dark outside, so she took the risk of moving, quickly eating some chocolate and swigging some water. At the moment their luck was holding. She had not heard anyone outside the whole time she had been lying there. She got her phone out, willing Clark to send the message that it was a go. She had the app up on screen ready to start recording.

Clark took a deep breath and typed out the text message. This was the moment they had been working towards.

'Go, go, go.'

Rob's phone beeped. There it was. Time to go. His supervisor hadn't been around for a while but he just had to go for it. He left his cart in the clinic room he had been cleaning, poked his head out the door and headed down towards the clinic and the fire door, where hopefully Anya would be waiting.

Anya's phone beeped. There it was. Time to go. She got out of the car on the opposite side from the CCTV. It was pretty dark and she began to move towards the end of the building where the fire door was. She turned on the app, put her phone in her top jacket pocket and started a whispered running dialogue, desperately hoping that Clark was listening and recording.

Clark could hear Anya's whispered commentary. She was out of the car and moving. He hacked into the building management system and disabled all the CCTV and fire alarms. Now the game had started. Would the security team catch them at it and ruin their plan at the first stage? Clark kept his fingers crossed. He ate another Jaffa Cake.

*

Jim Bartley, the Head Security Guard at the Loughborough Clinic was sitting nattering to the new boy, Gavin Wheatley, who was a bit of a prat and thought he knew it all. Jim would sort him out though. *The youth of today. Think they have all the answers to everything.* As they sat chatting about the weekend's football, all of the CCTV suddenly went blank.

"What the hell?" said Jim. Gavin looked on, vaguely uninterested. Jim tapped away at the CCTV management system. Nothing. The bloody thing had crashed.

"What do we do?" said Gavin, rather unhelpfully.

"I'll have to get IT to come and have a look. They might have to reboot the server to get it back online."

Jim phoned the IT guy, who said he would be there in a couple of minutes. They decided they would need to do a perimeter foot patrol and internal check if the IT guy couldn't get it fixed quick. They didn't want the wrath of Dr Normandy.

*

He had reached the hotel in Warwick where his father had texted to say Rob's credit card had been used. He decided to front it out and went into reception.

"Hi, I was wondering if Rob Simmons and Anya Novak are in the hotel. I am a friend of theirs and I was hoping to catch them. They said they were staying here."

The receptionist looked at him a bit suspiciously but still gave him what he needed. "Yes, they are still staying at the hotel, but they went out a few hours ago and have not returned yet. Can I leave them a message?"

"No, that is fine, I will ring them and arrange another time," he said in his most charming and unthreatening way, despite the rage rising once again.

*

Rob moved as fast as he could without looking too suspicious. Clark had texted him saying that the CCTV and fire alarms had been disabled. He got to the fire door and pushed the bar to open it. No alarm. He looked out. Anya wasn't there. He waited what seemed like an age, but was probably only thirty seconds, when she suddenly came into view. They embraced quickly, shut the door and headed for the clinic entrance. Rob told Anya to be careful and rushed back to his station. Anya continued her dialogue.

"I am at the clinic door, can you let me in?"

A few seconds later the door made an audible click. Anya pushed it tentatively. It gave. She pushed it some more and sneaked in as quietly as she could, entering into a corridor. She could see several rooms and other doors up ahead. "I'm in," she said and got the phone out of her pocket to start recording the sound and images that would nail this conspiracy.

*

Clark quickly switched back on the CCTV and fire alarms. Now, all he had to do was listen and watch the live feeds that Anya was hopefully going to record which would give them what they needed. Then he had to get her out, safe and alive. He wondered whether the Met commissioner had received his parcel yet. The tension was unbearable.

*

Rob got back to his station. His supervisor wasn't there. He had got away with it. For now.

*

Just as the IT guy got into Jim Bartley's office, the CCTV suddenly flashed into life. "Well, I'll be," said Jim, "you IT guys only need to walk in the room and things are fixed." Very strange. They had lost about four minutes of CCTV images but did a check on each camera and couldn't see anything untoward. They would double check things in their next routine patrol, which was scheduled in about twenty minutes. They made a coffee and sat back down, chatting and occasionally watching the monitors.

*

Anya's heart was beating much faster than usual. She didn't know if Dr Normandy was in the clinic, so she crept along the corridor as quietly as she could. As she moved further along the corridor, recording the images but trying not to speak too much, in fear of being heard, she suddenly came across a room that made her stop in her tracks. She gasped audibly. Clark was watching.

Lying in the room, apparently comatose on a bed, with a variety of tubes going into cannulas in her arms, was a young lady. She had the signs of a visible pregnancy bump under the covers. She was fair-haired and looked English.

"My God, are you seeing this? This is what we need." Anya walked into the room and recorded everything she could see. She knew she had been exactly where this poor girl was now. It was one of her visions. The tubes, the machines, the coma.

She peered out of the room along the corridor. All was still quiet. She reached the next room along and there was the other girl. She was in the same position, lying on a bed, apparently comatose with all sorts of wires and tubes hooking her up to the machines which were obviously keeping her alive but very much incapacitated. She also had a pronounced pregnancy bump. The girl had a slightly darker complexion, a beautiful Mediterranean glow.

"My God. This is awful but this has to be Bianca and the other one has to be Sam. We have found them. It's real. This is what happened to me. Oh my God. Oh my God."

She fought back the tears.

Clark watched on with amazement. Anya was getting everything they had hoped for. This was the last bit of evidence that would nail these bastards. He texted Anya.

'Get out. We have what we need.'

Her response made his heart sink.

'No. I need more. I need more answers.'

Anya looked down the corridor again. Towards the end was a door that looked like it went into a large room, based on what she could see from the small window in the door. Suddenly a head flashed across the door window. She ducked back quickly. It must be Dr Normandy. *Shit!* She turned the other way down the corridor and tried a large double door that was more or less opposite where Bianca and Sam were being held.

The door opened easily and as she entered, she was blinded by the bright lights all around the room. In the middle of the room was an operating table, with machines and monitors all set up for surgeries to be performed. Clinical instruments were all laid out ready. As she scanned the room, she saw it.

LEXICON THEATRE

Her legs almost gave way. The surge of emotion overwhelming every functioning part of her body. This was it. LEX. The visions, the nightmares. She had been here before.

Dr Normandy was sitting at his desk when one of the internal alarms went off. Someone had entered the operating theatre. He opened up his computer and looked at the camera that fed images from the theatre. He couldn't believe what he saw. Anya Novak was in his theatre. How the hell did she get in? He did what they agreed if this ever happened. He texted the one man that would sort this out.

'Code Red'

*

He was sitting in his car in the hotel car park pondering his options when his phone beeped. It was a text from Dr Normandy.

'Code Red'

Now he knew where they were. He sped off towards the clinic. Time to end this thing.

80

Mark Chesterfield, the Met commissioner, was still in his office and it was just past 8 p.m. It seemed the job of the commissioner never ended. He had been in the post just over a year, having accelerated through the ranks as an officer within the High Potential Development Scheme. His successes in various police forces, including significantly improving performance and detection rates as chief constable in his last force, had brought him to the attention of the home secretary and mayor of London when the post became vacant. He was doing a good job in London but his life was about to be turned upside down.

His poor put-upon assistant was also still there and she walked in the room with a package that had been delivered to reception at Scotland Yard with a message to get it to him urgently. As a matter of national security.

Mark frowned and took the package. He was about to go home to try to see his kids before they went to bed. It didn't look like that was going to happen again tonight.

He opened the large parcel and was confronted with a myriad of documents and a covering report. He read the report and started to look at the other documents and pictures. His gut began to tighten. He couldn't believe what he was reading.

This can't be real. What the hell is going on? How can the PM have stolen a child? This is nuts.

The more he read, the worse it got. Girls being exploited to produce babies for childless couples. Large amounts of money changing hands. Police corruption. Murder.

He sat back in his chair, trying to take in what he was reading. There were no contact details from the sender. It was anonymous. Was this just a crank?

He read it over and over. He decided he would have to keep this to himself until he could assess what the hell to do. The bottom line was he could not go and arrest the prime minister without watertight evidence. He told his assistant to go home, locked his office door and read it all again. Hoping for some divine guidance. If he got this wrong his career would be over.

*

Anya pulled herself together. There was another text from Clark willing her to get out. She put the phone in her jacket pocket and turned towards the door. In that instant the game changed.

Dr Normandy stood in the doorway.

"Well, well, Miss Novak. Just what the hell are you doing here?"

Years of rage welled up in Anya. Here was the bastard that had done all these awful things, standing right in front of her. In a movement so fast that Dr Normandy didn't have a chance to react, she picked up a scalpel and lunged at him, knocking him flying to the floor. He was small and scrawny, going down easily and landing with a heavy thud. Anya was onto him in a second, with the scalpel aimed at his throat.

"You absolute bastard. You sold my baby!"

Dr Normandy didn't try to struggle. She had her full body weight on his chest and was surprisingly strong.

"Anya, put down the scalpel. I will tell you anything you want to know. Please don't hurt me."

The rage was burning in Anya. She wanted to kill him, but she needed answers. The rational side of the brain suddenly kicked in and she dragged him up, dumping him in a nearby chair with the scalpel ready to strike. He sat there. Pathetic and seemingly defeated.

*

Clark could hear the commotion but there were no pictures as the phone was in her pocket. He could hear another voice.

Shit, she has been caught.

He was just about to text Rob to go to her aid when he realised Anya sounded like she was in control of the situation. It sounded like she was speaking to Dr Normandy and he was pleading with her not to hurt him. Go Anya!

He decided to listen and wait. If she could get him to confess to his dirty deeds this would be gold dust. It was worth the risk. At least that's what he told himself.

*

The scalpel still hovered close to his throat. Anya had never been more focused.

"You need to tell me right now where my baby is. You sold it to James Hardacre. Didn't you!"

"Yes, he was the recipient of your baby. You were always the special one, Anya. James' brother was paid to find the women at university and match them to the requirements of the clients. James wanted a beautiful baby because his wife couldn't give him a child, so he decided to choose what he wanted. He was transfixed by how beautiful you were when his brother showed him the pictures of you."

"And what about the other girls?"

"They soon realised they could do this for multiple clients and make a lot of money. They knew from the work I did at the clinic that I had perfected an accelerated drug addiction recovery programme and that I had the tools to keep patients sedated for long periods. I didn't want to do it but they had stuff on me."

"Yes, you are a disgusting paedophile."

"I can't help it. It's a sickness. They kept threatening to expose me."

Anya shoved the scalpel closer to his throat.

"Don't think for one minute you are going to get any sympathy from me. You are an evil, depraved man and anyway, we know that you were still getting paid, despite their threats."

"I... I... had to get someth—"

"Oh, fuck off. Don't even try to justify your part in this. Everything that comes out of your mouth is a lie."

Dr Normandy sat in the chair, tensed against the threat. He needed to bide his time. Strike back when she was off guard. He tried to continue the conversation hoping that an opportunity would present itself.

"Look, I know you won't believe it but I am sorry."

"Spare me your false platitudes. I want to know what you actually did to me."

"Well, OK. As I said, I devised an accelerated drug recovery programme. This got you clean much quicker than I had said. I needed you to think you were still recovering but really you were ready to start the process of making a baby."

Anya jabbed the scalpel at the doctor, trying to control her rage. He flinched at the sudden action. Tears were welling up in Anya but she knew she had to push on.

"And you impregnated me against my will. With the fucking prime minister's sperm."

"Yes."

Anya wanted to drive the scalpel into his throat and twist it. Make him feel even an ounce of the pain he had caused her but she knew everything he was saying was being recorded. She had to get him to confess all of what he had done.

"Why did you kill the rest of the girls and try to kill me?"

"That wasn't me. I used drugs that kept you in a coma for long periods but were also supposed to suppress memories. The problem was the memory suppression drugs weren't a hundred per cent effective. You all started recovering memories and they decided to have you dealt with. I told them I wanted nothing to do with that."

"Oh please. You are implicated in everything that went on. Don't try to pretend you have any sort of guilty conscience."

He just stared at her, trying to judge his next move. Anya was still poised with the scalpel.

"The drugs. They were illegal and you pumped them into us without a fucking care in the world."

"Well, let's just say that the UK licensing authority would not have seen my recovery programme as something they would have readily endorsed. They are so backward in this country. Despite everything, my work has real clinical merit."

Anya was dumbfounded by what he was saying.

"My God. You are a complete lunatic."

As she said it, she made a mistake. The weight of everything he was saying was pulling her down, emotionally and physically. She moved slightly back from her dominant position holding the scalpel. Dr Normandy saw his chance and lunged at her. The sudden movement caught Anya off guard and sent her sprawling to the floor.

The next ten seconds seem to happen in slow motion. As she tried to recover her position, scrambling and slipping on the shiny floor of the operating theatre, a sudden explosion of activity came from the doorway.

The noise was deafening. The door to the theatre had been kicked open and two gunshots, in quick succession, noisily reverberated around the hollow walls. Anya recoiled, fell over again and dropped the scalpel. For a split second her brain tried to process whether she had been shot. No. She looked up. Dr Normandy was sprawled on the floor. Dead. At the door, holding the gun was Anya's worst nightmare.

Bradley. Evil Bradley.

81

Clark heard the gunshots. No pictures, just a deafening sound. Something had gone badly wrong. Anya was in danger. He texted Rob.

'Anya is in danger. Gunshots heard. I think Bradley is in there! Go and save her.'

*

Rob's phone beeped. He jumped a mile. This had to be a message to say she was ready to go. He opened the text. It wasn't what he wanted to read. He started ranting at the phone message.

"Fuck! Fucking hell Clark. I told you this was too risky."

He dropped everything and made for the door of the room he was cleaning. He almost took out his supervisor in the rush.

"Where the hell are you going in such a hurry?" she shrieked accusingly.

Rob's heart sank. What the hell should he do? He could knock her out but then the game would really change. Anya was in danger. He went for politeness in the hope she would just go.

"Oh, I am sorry. I was just trying to remember which room I had to do next and was going to check the rooms I had done."

She didn't seem convinced and starting running through what he had to do for the rest of the shift. Rob was crushed. He stood and listened, hoping that Anya was not already dead.

*

Anya stared at Bradley with hatred in her eyes, as he walked over to her, gun aimed at her sprawled form.

"Well it is nice to finally get you in my sights Anya. You and your boyfriend have been making a real mug of me. I am going to enjoy killing you slowly for all the shit you have put me through."

Anya knew she was going to die, but she wasn't going to give him the satisfaction of showing her fear.

"The shit I have put you through? You are an evil, murdering, raping bastard Bradley. Abusing me, raping me, getting me hooked on drugs and selling me to that thing to violate my body with your brother's disgusting seed. Oh, and killing my parents to make me vulnerable to your questionable charms."

"Yes, I enjoyed killing your parents. So easy as their car careered off the road. You see Anya, I had been keeping an eye on you for a while before we properly hooked up. James was transfixed by the pictures I sent him and demanded I get you for his pathetic baby-making scheme. I could tell you were strong willed and would not easily be swayed. I heard you talking a lot about your parents and decided their tragic deaths were going to be the only way I could reel you in. And I was right. Wasn't I?"

This was killing Anya, but she remained defiant. Bradley rambled on.

"As for my questionable charms, I don't recall you complaining when you were snorting line after line of the cocaine I gave you, followed by you bonking my brains out at every opportunity."

"How can you live with yourself? You are a monster."

"Well, like I give a fuck what you think. I now have a shit load of money and the pleasure of watching you die, slowly and painfully."

Anya knew her best chance of surviving was to keep him talking. *God, what a cliché. You see this in the films, the narcissistic killer that just has to explain why he or she is so brilliant before they do the deed, only to be a victim of their own vanity as the hero saves the day.* But this wasn't a film. This was happening now and she desperately hoped that her phone was still recording everything that was going on and that Clark and Rob were somehow going to come to her aid.

"So why did you need to kill all the other girls and Janice?"

"Well, like you Anya, they started remembering things from their time in the clinic and tried to contact this useless piece of shit. We couldn't have that. They had to be silenced. As for Janice, that was your fault. If your boyfriend hadn't tried to find out what was going on, I wouldn't have had to deal with her."

"What about those poor girls lying there unaware of the horrors going on around them? You have killed the doctor. How are they going to survive without his support?"

"Do you know, I really don't care. He was a waste of space and my brother is just the same. Spineless idiots. They can clear up this mess. Once I kill you, I am gone. So, stop trying to keep me talking. Time for you to die."

Bradley fired.

82

Clark's heart was in his mouth. Bradley had somehow got into the clinic and was about to kill Anya. The stuff that was being recorded was amazing. Absolute confirmation that Bradley had been the one finding the girls and doing all the killings. But, it would all be for nothing if Anya was dead. Where was Rob? He heard another gunshot.

*

After about five minutes Rob's supervisor finally shut up and walked out of the room they were in. It was the longest five minutes of his life. Could Anya have survived somehow? He moved down the corridor as fast as he could, sending a text to Clark to let him in the clinic door.

*

The gunshot ripped through Anya's leg. Blood was oozing out of the bullet hole. Anya screamed in agony. Bradley just looked on, grinning.

"I said I would take my time with you Anya. Let's hope that one doesn't kill you. I need you to feel my pain. I think maybe I'll shoot you in each limb before I put one between your eyes. I hope you are enjoying these final moments with me Anya. It's almost poetic."

Anya knew she was badly hurt. She placed her hand over the wound. It helped a bit but blood was still seeping through her fingertips. Where was Rob?

*

Clark was waiting for Rob to reach the door but quickly decided that plan B had to be initiated. Rob and Anya were both in danger and Bradley was the only one with a gun. Shooting. He quickly logged onto Proton.

KRYPTO:	Snap. EMERGENCY.
SNAPDEVIL:	What?
KRYPTO:	Plan to bust conspiracy up shit creek. Lives in danger.
SNAPDEVIL:	What can I do?
KRYPTO:	Send the link of the live recording to the police email address I gave you.
SNAPDEVIL:	Done
KRYPTO:	Is it secure?
SNAPDEVIL:	Untraceable.

Clark wasn't sure he could do much else. He had to hope the commissioner believed what he read and what he was about to see. If he didn't, Rob and Anya were probably dead. He listened into the drama. Scared out of his wits.

*

Rob got to the door. He sent a text to Clark. The door clicked open almost immediately. He inched his way through and could hear muffled voices. They were coming from behind a door a bit further down the corridor. If they were talking, Anya had to still be alive. He moved quickly towards the door.

*

Mark Chesterfield, the Met commissioner, had now been reading the file and the contents for almost twenty minutes. The depth of the evidence trail was phenomenal. There was a complete money trail, mining information from a bank in the Cayman Islands and from local UK banks. He had no idea how the person who had put this together had got so much detailed information. He guessed it may have been obtained illegally, hence the anonymity.

He couldn't ignore it though. It was alleged that the Loughborough Clinic, under this Dr Normandy, was creating designer babies for childless couples, using unsuspecting girls who were all now dead. And not just dead but murdered. Except for one. Someone called Anya Novak.

The alleged conspirators were listed. The doctor; James Hardacre; the MP George Walker; someone called Bradley Williams, allegedly the half-brother of James Hardacre, and a police officer in the National Major Crime Agency called Hassan Chandra. His heart sank at the last name on the list. William Hardacre. A man who ran with the rich and famous, and a personal friend of his father.

What added to the absolute fucked-up nature of what he was reading was the allegation that at least five police forces, including his own, seemed to have corrupt officers in their roads policing units who were working with this Mr Chandra to cover up the police investigations.

The evidence file was good and despite his reluctance to believe the prime minister was crooked, he had to act on this. Not least because the file said that this Anya Novak was still alive and in danger, as were two girls who were allegedly in the clinic now, having the same awful things done to them. He was about to ring the most trusted members of his command team, to share the burden of the most sensational thing he had ever encountered, when an email popped into his inbox.

He opened the email, which contained a link and a message.

'This is happening NOW at the Loughborough Clinic near Warwick.'

He clicked on the link. The live feed had no pictures, just sound. He could hear a man and a woman. The woman was screaming at the man. He was goading her, threatening her, revelling in the moment he said he was going to kill her.

This was the moment. Did he believe all that he had read and was now hearing? Or did he ignore it? Was he being scammed? If he went into action would this end his career? The Hardacres. What could they do to him if he got this wrong?

He decided he couldn't wait. Even if he just reacted to what he had just been sent, he would only be doing what he had been trained for. What he had pledged to the Crown when he joined the police. To protect life.

He contacted the control room at Warwickshire Police. The duty inspector answered.

"Hello, Duty Inspector, can I help you?"

"Inspector. This is Mark Chesterfield, the commissioner of the Metropolitan Police."

"Oh, hello Sir. What can I do for you?"

"You have a threat to life incident happening now. You need to despatch as many units to the Loughborough Clinic, just outside Warwick, as you can. Get the ARVs there. There is a male live shooter, threatening to kill an unidentified female."

"Understood."

The inspector asked the commissioner to wait and went into action. He came back a minute later.

"All available units have been despatched Sir. The first responders are six minutes out. The ARV should be there in eight."

"Thank you, Inspector. I will send you a conference number in the next couple of minutes. I will set up a command call, which I need you on. I want to monitor this in live time. Can you Silver command this for the next couple of minutes?"

"Yes Sir. No problem."

The commissioner contacted his local control room and immediately initiated major incident command instructions. Within minutes he was on a conference call with his local Met commanders, who were still at Scotland Yard, and the Warwickshire control room inspector. He did not at this point explain the full situation. The first priority was to save lives and secure the crime scene. He hoped he wasn't too late.

83

Rob moved towards the door. He could hear a male voice goading Anya. It had to be Bradley. How the fuck had he found them?

Anya was alive and seemingly giving it back to Bradley, with both barrels. Thank God. How should he play this? He had no time to think.

Rob crashed through the door, hoping that Bradley was behind it, so the weight of the door and the surprise element would knock him down. The plan sort of worked but not well enough.

The door flew open and caught Bradley with a gentle sideswipe. It was enough to put him down but as he rolled, he recovered quickly, assessed the situation and fired in Rob's direction. The bullet tore through the top of Rob's shoulder, a straight through and through as the bullet finally lodged in the wall with an explosion of plaster. It was enough to distract Rob. Bradley was on him in seconds, pinning him to the floor with the gun in his face.

Bradley's rage had peaked. He screamed at Rob, spitting out every word with real venom.

"Thank you so much for saving me the trouble of finding you. This is the last time you make a mug of me. I can't tell you how long I have waited for this moment. To kill you and your slut."

In Bradley's rage he had not spotted Anya trying to move. Her leg was in a bad way but she slid herself towards where the scalpel had landed. She grabbed it, slid round and just about reached the back of Bradley's leg. Just as Bradley was about to pull the trigger to kill Rob, she plunged the scalpel into his leg.

Bradley screamed. The distraction was enough for Rob to push him off as blood started seeping from Bradley's wound. For a moment, they all froze. They were all bleeding. Anya couldn't stand, Bradley was temporarily incapacitated and Rob's shoulder was rapidly turning red as his wound reacted to the trauma. The gun lay in the middle of the room, in between all of them, like some weird spin-the-bottle game waiting for someone to take the next turn. Rob and Bradley lunged for it at the same time.

Bradley grabbed it first but Rob wrestled him for it, having the slight upper hand as his wound was the least traumatic. Rob leapt onto Bradley, they grappled and rolled. Anya watched on in horror, willing Rob to win the fight and finish Bradley off. All the while, Dr Normandy was still sprawled on the floor. Dead. A forgotten statistic in the horror show that was playing out.

Just as Bradley seemed to be getting control of the situation, having rolled Rob onto his back, the gun went off. Anya screamed. She froze as everything seemed to happen in slow motion. The sudden awful silence ended with Bradley moaning and Rob heaving him off. Rob had the gun. A large bullet hole was in the side of Bradley's stomach. He moaned again and passed out.

Anya crawled over to Rob, shaking with fear, but relieved that they were both alive. For a moment, Rob pointed the gun at Bradley, waiting for him to move. He didn't. He was alive but unconscious. Rob put the gun down and they both slumped against the wall. Hoping someone was coming.

84

Clark was still listening in. He had no idea if the commissioner had read the email or even believed anything they had sent him. The drama was still being recorded. No pictures, just the awful sounds of Bradley revelling in the moment he was going to kill Anya.

In that moment, the noises changed. Someone had entered the room with a loud crash. The police? No, it was Rob. Clark was holding his breath. There was shouting, noise of a struggle, screams and another gunshot. Then silence. No one was speaking. What had happened?

*

Mark Chesterfield was now in Gold command and running the job over the conference call he had hastily arranged.

"Inspector. What is the latest?"

"The first responders are two minutes out. The ARV is a few minutes behind."

He had the live feed from the email link, running on the screen in the conference room that had become a hastily arranged command centre. There was still only sound. No pictures.

"Command team. This audio is coming from a live feed in the Loughborough Clinic. There have been numerous threats to life and the inspector in Warwickshire is running Silver to deal with the immediate emergency. As you heard, local units are a few minutes away."

As he spoke, they heard a gunshot. They all jumped and looked at each other, horrified at what they were hearing.

"Inspector. There has been another gunshot. What is the status?"

"One minute out."

The Met Command team listened. There was a faint moaning sound followed by silence. They all looked at each other. Were they too late?

*

Rob and Anya lay slumped against the wall, bleeding from their wounds.

"We are going to die aren't we Rob? After everything we have done, it has all gone wrong. I am sorry. I am never going to see Sophie."

"Anya, don't talk like that. Someone is coming."

Anya realised the phone was still in her pocket. Was it still recording? She took it out. It seemed to still be working. She shouted at the phone.

"We are shot. Can you hear us? Get us help."

The app was only recording one way. They hoped Clark was still hearing them.

Their answer came thirty seconds later. Commotion at the outer door. A few seconds later, police officers piling into the room to a scene of utter carnage. One dead, one unconscious and two casualties injured and bleeding. The lead officer spoke.

"Sir. Madam. Are you OK?"

"We have been shot," said Rob. "We need medical attention immediately."

The officer and the rest of his team had assessed the scene quickly based on the updates coming from the control room.

They called for ambulances for Rob and Anya, handcuffed the unconscious Bradley and checked that the doctor was actually dead.

Rob looked at Anya as the officers secured the scene and managed the communication with all the other units.

"It's over," he said.

*

Clark wasn't sure he had been breathing since the silence descended on the drama at the clinic. He must have been as he hadn't keeled over. The silence was killing him. Minutes passed that seemed like hours. No sound until... Anya spoke. She was talking to Rob. A few seconds later images suddenly appeared. Anya must have taken the phone out of her pocket. The pictures blurred as she grappled with the phone. Suddenly her faced appeared and she was screaming down the phone for help.

"I can hear you," Clark shouted back, feeling helpless. He knew they couldn't hear him but it just felt better. Like when you shout the quiz answers at the TV contestant who is 'being a bit thick'.

He hoped the Met commissioner had believed what he had heard on the live recording and was about to save them. Could he risk calling the police himself? They would want to know who he was.

Shit!

Just as he was about to ring, he heard lots of noise. The police had arrived.

Thank God.

85

In the command centre at Scotland Yard, Mark sat with his command team. Three assistant commissioners and his detective chief superintendent in charge of Major Crime. One of the assistant commissioners spoke.

"Mark. What is going on? Why are we managing a Warwickshire job?"

"Ladies and gentlemen. What I am about to tell you is unprecedented in all my time in policing. In anybody's time in policing. The local Warwickshire police response you have just heard was triggered by an evidence file that was couriered to me anonymously. It landed on my desk just after 8 p.m. I could not believe what I was reading and, to be honest, almost dismissed it as a hoax, until this was emailed to me."

He pointed back at the screen where the live feed had been playing. He put it back to the start of the recording and paused it.

"I haven't seen the first bit of this recording but, as soon as it arrived, it was obvious from the audio that a threat to life situation was occurring at this Loughborough Clinic. The email stated that what I was hearing was happening in real time. I made the decision to protect life before doing anything else. I am assuming the events before we all started hearing the recording will give evidence to support what is in this file."

The same assistant commissioner, Richard Washington, pushed back again.

"That is all very noble Mark. You have saved some lives, but I still don't understand why we are involved."

Mark glared at him, unimpressed by his insubordination.

"Well Richard. I will explain. This file alleges that the Loughborough Clinic was the centre of an illegal baby-making scheme. Rich clients were paying huge sums of money for the doctor at the clinic to create designer babies using unsuspecting and unwilling girls as enforced surrogates. It appears all these girls were admitted to the clinic as drug addicts, cured of their addiction and then violated. It alleges that the doctor used illegal drugs to keep them sedated for long periods and supress any memories of what happened to them. Four of the original five girls are dead. Allegedly murdered by the man that was shooting in the clinic. The fifth girl, Anya Novak, was the woman he was trying to kill. Somehow, she had got in the clinic, trying to find two new girls who were allegedly having the same thing done to them."

Richard had clearly not picked up on the vibes from his boss as he pushed back some more.

"Yes, sounds terrible Mark. Still doesn't explain why we are involved."

Mark's anger rose and he slammed his fist on the file.

"Because the fucking prime minister of this country is alleged to be one of the clients of the clinic."

The room descended into complete silence. Shock across everyone's face. Richard broke the silence.

"Fuck me. I am sorry Boss. That is fucking unbelievable."

"I know. The evidence is very comprehensive, albeit almost certainly containing information that was obtained illegally. We need to watch this recording. It should cement everything that is alleged."

Mark clicked the play button and they all watched as the horror slowly revealed itself. They watched as Anya entered the clinic through an outside door. Spoke to her partner and asked to be let in the door. They all clocked it. Someone was helping them remotely.

She was recording the images as she entered a clinical white-walled corridor. The full horror appeared soon after. One girl, pregnant and hooked up to all sorts of machines, not awake. Followed by another girl, in another room but with the same set-up. The gasps of Anya as she came upon the scene were loud and reflected the shock in the command centre.

They watched as she left the girls and went into another room. An operating theatre. They watched captivated as she looked around the room and seemed to stumble, followed by a haunting comment.

"I have been here before."

The images stopped as she placed the phone in her pocket. The sound of the doctor's voice came over loud and clear. There was sounds of a struggle. Anya sounded like she was in control. The doctor was spilling his guts. Confessing to all the crimes, including being a paedophile.

The gunshots started. Commotion. Bradley Williams and Anya arguing. The point that Mark had first starting listening to the live recording. Another gunshot. More arguing. More threats to kill from Bradley. A crash at the door. Anya's partner entering the scene. A struggle. Gunshot. Silence. The police response.

After taking in all that they had just seen, they listened to Mark as he continued to outline the full extent of the alleged conspiracy. The team began to understand why this was going to be the defining moment in their careers.

"Jesus Christ Mark. Do you believe that this is all true?" asked Rachel Brownlow, one of the other assistant commissioners sitting round the table.

"I fear it is. We can't deny what we have just seen and heard. The doctor and Bradley Williams have pretty much confessed to their crimes. We have to arrest all the clients, George Walker and

Hassan Chandra on conspiracy charges. They will all have to be interviewed under caution and we need to get investigation teams looking at each aspect of this evidence file while we do that. I will Gold, Richard you will Silver and we need to get our Bronzes in place ASAP."

"What about the children?" asked Rachel.

"Can you contact the head of social services? I think we have no choice but to immediately extract the children from their families and put them into temporary care."

"Are you sure that is wise? What about the mothers?"

"Well, as harsh as this sounds, according to the file, none of them are the real mothers. Whether they are aware of their husbands' parts in this is unclear but the kids are not theirs to keep."

"OK, I will speak to her when you have finished the briefing."

Simon Norton, the final assistant commissioner present, tried to deal with the 'elephant in the room'.

"What about William Hardacre?"

Mark shuffled nervously.

"I really don't know. The file alleges his involvement but of all the alleged conspirators he is the one that seems to have the least concrete evidence against him."

Jennifer Ragnor, the DCS in charge of Major Crime, piped up.

"Are we really surprised? We have been trying to nail this bastard for years. His name comes up in so many of my teams' major enquiries but we have never got close enough to nail him. He is a professional crook. His influence is phenomenal. He got James the PM job and has undoubtedly been pulling his strings. This has his dirty fingers all over it but I agree Mark, there is no point pursuing him if the evidence is flaky."

Mark rubbed his face.

"Thanks Jenny. We can't move on William yet. It is going to be bad enough that we are arresting his two sons. Let's get the first round of arrests done, start the investigations and see where it takes us."

"So, Boss," said Richard with a certain amount of mischief in his tone, "who is going to arrest the PM and how do we do it? I don't think I have a SOP for that!"

Mark ignored the attempt at levity.

"I will do it personally. I will need to contact the home secretary, the mayor and inform the Palace. This is not going to be easy and the press coverage is going to be off the scale. Richard, can you get the director of comms briefed urgently and get her team and the Mayor's comms team moving on this as a priority."

"Will do Boss."

"Right, Rachel can you come with me to Downing Street. Richard, can you get your Silver command running, sort out comms and get your Bronze investigation commanders in place. Simon, can you personally supervise the arrests of the other conspirators and get them all booked in here. I don't want any other stations dealing with this. Jenny, can you go up to Warwickshire and take control of the interviews with Anya, Rob and Bradley."

They all agreed and left the room. This was going to be a long night.

86

Mark Chesterfield and his assistant commissioner, Rachel Brownlow, drove into Downing Street. They were met at the door by the close protection officer, who let them in. James Hardacre was in his private office finishing his work for the day. As they entered the office, James knew the game was up. As Mark began to read him his rights his wife came into the room.

"What is going on? Do you not know who you are dealing with?" she exclaimed with an indignation that was soon to be completely torn down.

Mark was as polite as he could be. "Madam, I am sorry to have to do this, but your husband needs to come with us. I am also sorry to tell you that you will shortly receive a visit from social services and they will almost certainly take your daughter away."

Annabelle Hardacre couldn't believe what she was hearing.

"James, what are they talking about? What has this got to do with Sophie?"

Despite all his power and self-confidence, James was beaten.

"Annabelle, I am so sorry. I have been a fool. Sophie is my child, our child, but I broke the law to get her. I am so sorry. So many people have been hurt. I need to go with these officers and sort this out."

"You're sorry. YOU'RE SORRY. What in God's name does that mean? This isn't just some minor mishap James where sorry is enough. This is our daughter. What have you done?"

Mark tried to lead James away. Annabelle grabbed James and glared at Mark.

"No, you bloody don't. He is not leaving here until I get an explanation."

"I have to go Annabelle. I am under arrest."

"I don't give a flying fuck. You damn well tell me what you have done. This is to do with your father, isn't it? What has he made you do now?"

Mark decided that discretion was the best approach.

"Look Mr and Mrs Hardacre. I do need to take Mr Hardacre with me, but I can give you five minutes in your private study, so you can sort things out."

Annabelle Hardacre seemed mildly appreciative of the gesture despite her burning rage. They walked into James' study and closed the door. The volume of the conversation made it clear that this had come as a complete shock to Annabelle Hardacre.

As Mark and Rachel waited outside, feeling awkward and mildly voyeuristic at having to see and hear the complete meltdown of the PM, they discussed the immediate implications of what Annabelle had said.

"Well, Rachel. Interesting that Mrs Hardacre immediately accused his father of being involved?"

"Yes, there is clearly no love lost there and suggests he has been far more involved in James' professional and personal life than she wanted him to be."

"I wonder whether she will make a statement against him?"

"Hmm, Jenny would be stoked if we could get something on him."

Within a few minutes the shouting subsided and James came out, ashen faced. "Let's go," he said in a barely audible tone. The sound of a defeated man. Annabelle stayed in the study, the sounds of her complete devastation evident in the tears and moaning that emanated from her.

"Rachel, will you stay with Mrs Hardacre and supervise the situation when social services arrive?"

"Of course, Mark."

With that, Mark led the PM out to the waiting car. They spared him the indignity of being handcuffed. James got in the car, head bowed as they sped away.

Whilst all the arrests had been executed as discreetly as possible, the home secretary and mayor of London had no choice but to hold an urgent press conference, the like of which would never be seen again. The worldwide media frenzy was unprecedented. It seemed as though the press had all the sordid details within minutes of the arrests being made. The press teams at the Met and the Mayor's office were perplexed at how the news had broken so quickly, which had put them on the back foot from the off. They didn't have time to work out whether they had a leak. This was DEFCON 1 in anyone's PR nightmare.

*

In a flat in Reading, a man sat eating Jaffa Cakes, very pleased with himself. They hadn't discussed leaking the details to the press but he had decided it was a good insurance policy against the risk of further police corruption. He watched as the news channels and main TV channels around the world ran constant updates about the unfolding events.

*

Rob and Anya had their wounds attended to. Both of them were stabilised and given separate private rooms with armed guards. They had been made aware that the press was hounding the hospital to let them make a statement but they had been advised to rest by the doctors. They had been told by the local police that a senior officer from the Met was on the way to take over the investigation. It was all academic. All they wanted to do was sleep. After that, all Anya wanted to do was to get her daughter.

87

Mark Chesterfield sat in his Gold briefing. It was 9 a.m. and he had got barely three hours' sleep. The press scrutiny was immense. The press teams had been working all through the night, trying to contain the clamour for information and explanations.

The arrests had been executed efficiently and the investigations were well underway. Jenny had Bradley Williams secured in the local hospital after surgery had saved his life. Anya and Rob had armed protection while they recovered.

The briefing quickly went through the main points and Mark tasked out the most immediate and urgent actions, including the formal interviews with the prime suspects, which were scheduled to start that morning. As he brought the briefing to a close, his PA walked in the room, looking tense.

"What is it Kathy?"

"Sir, William Hardacre is in reception. He is insisting on speaking with you now."

Mark steeled himself. William Hardacre was on his way up to his office. He had to think on his feet. Potentially, one of the prime suspects of this conspiracy was about to walk freely into his office, but he knew William Hardacre never did anything without some ulterior motive.

William bounded into his office with all the arrogance of a man who thought he was untouchable.

"Mark. Great to see you. How is your father?"

"What do you want Mr Hardacre?"

"OK. It's going to be like that is it?"

"Mr Hardacre. I am a very busy man, for obvious reasons. Is there something I can help you with?"

His demeanour changed.

"Well, quite frankly Mark, I would have thought it was fucking obvious. I want an explanation as to why you have arrested my two sons and kidnapped my granddaughter."

Mark had to stifle a laugh at the sheer audacity of the man.

"Are you seriously suggesting that you don't know why these things have happened?"

"I don't like your tone. What the hell are you implying?"

"Oh, come on Mr Hardacre. Your dirty fingers are all over this."

William stopped and fixed his most intimidating stare at Mark.

"You listen, you piece of shit. You are lucky my lawyer is not with me, otherwise I would have you for slander."

"My God. Are you really that arrogant? Do you really not think we can find something that connects you to this conspiracy?"

William regained some control. Sat back and looked at Mark with the smugness he was renowned for.

"Arrest me then. If you are so sure I am involved, why haven't you arrested me? You seem so sure that my sons are guilty of these alleged crimes and they are now in your cells. Why am I not in there too?"

Mark was losing the argument. William knew the answer to his question. Everything that had been supplied to the police about William's involvement was circumstantial and he knew it. Mark tried to gain ground.

"Your son Bradley has confessed to multiple murders on tape and James has admitted to his part in this, in front of his wife."

"Hmm, Bradley was always unhinged. I blame his whore of a mother. As for James, he was always a spineless idiot. If you think you can charge them with something, then get on with it. My lawyers will deal with whatever shit you think can stick."

"And what if we win? I think even your expensive lawyers will have a hard time refuting the confessions from both of them."

"Well, we will see, but quite frankly they are no great loss."

Mark was stunned at the complete lack of compassion shown by William Hardacre for his offspring. He was going to get them expensive lawyers but seemed to have no problem with throwing them under the bus if it ultimately saved his skin. Mark changed tack.

"Can you explain why several of the other clients of the doctor's illegal baby-making scheme are friends of yours? Geoffrey Pottinger for example."

"Sure, I know Geoffrey, but then I know a lot of people. Is that suddenly a crime?"

"No, it is not a crime but every client, including the ones apparently buying the babies from the two new girls that we saved from the clinic, has clear associations with you."

"Like I said, Mark. I know a lot of people. If you had a shred of evidence against me, we wouldn't be sitting here having this cosy chat. I would be in a cell, lawyered up, being interviewed under caution. So, why don't you stop wasting my time and deal with the only thing that I really care about."

"And what might that be?"

"My granddaughter. You need to return her to Annabelle immediately."

"That isn't going to happen. She isn't the girl's mother. The real mother is in a hospital in Warwick recovering from gunshot wounds inflicted by your son. Social services have every right to remove all the children from this sordid affair."

William stood up and fixed Mark with a steely stare.

"You really don't who you are dealing with boy. I will get her back if it is the last thing I do."

With that William stormed out and Mark was left wondering just what the hell was going to happen now.

88

DCS Jenny Ragnor had been stuck in Warwick for two days. She had supervised the lockdown on Bradley Williams' hospital room while he recovered from life-saving surgery and made sure that Anya and Rob were protected from all threats. The problem was that the doctors refused to let her interview any of them. She had kept up-to-date with events in London and Mark was regularly briefing her about key information. He had told her about his unexpected visit from William Hardacre. The sheer mention of the man's name made her gut tighten. She had four years left and she wondered whether she would ever nail the bastard before she retired.

As she started her third day hanging around the hospital, consuming another cup of brown liquid that purported to be coffee, the doctor looking after her three 'clients' finally offered her some solace.

"Detective Ragnor. I am happy for you to speak to Miss Novak and Mr Simmonds today, as long as you don't spend too long with each of them. Mr Williams is still too ill for any sort of interrogation."

"Thank you Doctor, that is really helpful. I will just complete some preliminary enquiries."

She walked in to see Anya, who was sitting up drinking a cup of tea and staring out of the window.

"Miss Novak, my name is DCS Jenny Ragnor. I have been put in charge of looking after you and taking your statement. You have caused quite a stir."

"Where is my baby?"

"Your daughter has been removed from the Hardacre household and is with temporary foster parents."

"So, you do believe she is mine?"

"The evidence that we have been supplied seems to support that assertion. Social services will need to review the case carefully and will probably need some DNA tests completed, but I am reasonably confident it will be proved that she is your daughter. There is one thing though."

"What?"

"My boss had a visit from William Hardacre. He was threatening all sorts of things to get her back to Mrs Hardacre. I think he is going to take this through the courts."

"What! Why haven't you arrested him?"

Jenny shifted uncomfortably in her chair.

"Miss Novak. I, more than anyone, would like to nail that bastard. The problem is the evidence against him is flimsy. There just isn't enough in the evidence file and nothing on the tape that was sent to us of your little clinic visit which directly implicates him."

Anya's rage began to grow.

"That is ridiculous. He is all over this. Both his sons are involved. Bradley confessed to all his crimes as he was threatening to kill me. You must have that on tape."

"We do, but there is not a single reference to William's involvement in your conversations with the doctor or Bradley."

Anya couldn't believe what she was hearing. Her mind immediately wandered to Clark. She knew he would be devastated if William Hardacre got away with it. Jenny pushed on, taking the opportunity to gain back the momentum, as Anya paused to take in what she had just been told.

"There is one thing that we all found rather curious, Miss Novak."

Anya snapped out of her daydream, trying to suppress her anger.

"Oh, what is that?"

"Who was helping you?"

"I don't know what you mean."

"Someone other than your partner was helping you. They overrode the security doors and cut the CCTV feeds. They also sent the live feed of your clinic invasion to my boss. Anonymously. I presume this is the same person that sent him the hard-copy evidence file?"

Anya knew this was the moment. She had to protect Clark. They hadn't discussed how they would handle this. She had to think on her feet. She had to lie.

"Erm. My guardian angel. We never met this person. He wrote to me, telling me they had found this conspiracy and that my life was in danger. We didn't believe him at first but, when Bradley tried to kill me in that car accident, we started to believe. We corresponded by post and via email. You will never track him down though. He is a master hacker. He got the evidence in ways you probably don't like but quite frankly, I don't give a fuck. He saved my life and convinced your boss that this conspiracy is real. He is my fucking hero."

"So, you know it was a man? Do you have the letters and the emails?"

"No, he told us to destroy every piece of correspondence after we had read it. He said he was keeping all the evidence securely and would release it to the police at the right time. During our investigations he found that two new girls had been admitted and we knew we had to catch the bastards red handed. To prove everything else we had found. He set up all the technical links to record everything you saw and heard. He did hack the clinic security, but as I said, thank God he did. I am alive because of him."

"This is all very convenient Miss Novak, but I am sorry, I don't believe you. I think you are covering for someone that is clearly a criminal. I really don't want to arrest you for perverting the course of justice, just as you might be getting your daughter back."

Anya was frantic. This woman was going to ruin it all. Just when she was so close to getting Sophie back. She decided to go for bravado.

"Well, that is all I am going to say on the matter. If you think you can prove what I am saying is untrue, then go for your life."

Jenny looked at her, sizing her up. This woman was clearly a tough cookie. She had risked her life to find out the truth about the conspiracy and get her daughter back. She kind of admired her but equally hated to lose. She started to walk out and left Anya with some final words that chilled her to the bone.

"I don't like criminals Miss Novak, regardless of the circumstances. I will be interested in what your partner has to say about this."

Anya sat in her bed, gripped by fear. She would kill Rob if he betrayed her and Clark.

89

Before she went in to interview Rob Simmons, Jenny Ragnor phoned Mark Chesterfield.

"Sir, it's Jenny. I have just interviewed Anya Novak. She is refusing to give us the name of the person that helped her. She claims she never met him. Said he was a master hacker that found the conspiracy and tipped them off about her life being in danger. She claims he helped them find all the evidence and got them in the clinic. Conveniently, she says she has destroyed all the correspondence between them, at his instruction."

"So, you don't believe her?"

"Not for a minute. She is lying through her teeth."

There was a short pause and Jenny wasn't sure what it meant. The next thing her boss said took her legs away.

"I need you to back off from this line of enquiry Jenny."

"What! Why?"

"Look, I know this guy obtained a lot of this stuff illegally and that is not going to help us when this gets to trial. The Hardacre lawyers in particular are going to challenge the legal admissibility of a whole load of what we have. If we are seen trying to pursue the guy that got us this evidence, it will play into their hands. It would also be a PR disaster. My advice from our director of comms is that we should play on this guardian angel line, whilst not condoning what he has done. The same applies to Miss Novak and Mr Simmonds. We have to treat them as the victims, not criminals."

"But Mark…"

"Jenny, I am sorry. This is just how it has got to be. We have a similar problem with the women that received these babies. They are all claiming that they did not know their husbands had obtained the babies illegally. They had all been sold a story about willing surrogates. The PR team want us to paint them as victims as well. We need to keep clear lines between those we have arrested and the victims of this awful situation."

"OK Sir. Whatever you say."

*

Anya kept pushing the call button by her bed. She had to get help so she could see Rob before he said too much to that police officer. Eventually a nurse came, got her in a wheelchair and took her to Rob's room. As Anya was wheeled in, she held her breath, hoping that Rob was not in the middle of a full confession. She exhaled. The police officer wasn't there.

"Rob. Have you spoken to the police officer?"

"What police officer?"

"Oh, thank God. That detective woman. She was asking lots of questions about who had helped us. I had to lie to protect Clark."

"I haven't seen anyone. Who is she?"

"She is some senior officer from the Met police, sent up here to protect us and take our statements, but she seemed more interested in finding out about Clark. She knew I was lying and said she was going to speak to you. I have been frantic. She said she was going to arrest me if she could prove I was lying. I didn't know what to do. We didn't discuss how to handle this."

"What did you say to her?"

309

"I said we never met him, that he wrote to us about my life being in danger, said we didn't believe him until Bradley tried to kill me."

"OK, well not all of that is a lie. What else?"

"I said we corresponded by post and email. That he uncovered all the evidence and helped us get in the clinic when we found out about the two new girls. I also said he told us to destroy all correspondence because he had the master information and agreed to send it to the police at the right time."

"Well, sounds like you did a great job, but then you always did find lying easy, didn't you Anya?"

Anya was gobsmacked. The bitterness she had felt from Rob since she had come out of the coma was laid bare in that one sentence. Just as she was about to lose it with him a familiar voice came from the doorway.

"Miss Novak. I do hope you are not plotting with your partner."

Anya froze. She was facing away from Jenny Ragnor, looking straight at Rob. She fixed him with a 'don't you dare betray me' stare. She turned around, complete with her best 'Veronica Mars' smile.

"Detective Ragnor. Would I do that? I was just seeing how Rob was."

She walked into the room and sighed.

"It's OK. You have nothing to worry about. You don't need to tell me anything about your dirty little secrets with your hacking dude. The commissioner has asked me to back off this line of enquiry and just get your statements. You are in the clear."

Anya looked at Rob, a massive sense of relief all over her face. He just sat there. Stony faced.

*

A week after they had been admitted to hospital, Rob and Anya were discharged. The media pack had not let up, camping outside the hospital day and night, for exactly this moment. The moment they could interrogate and photograph the couple that had taken down the Prime Minister.

They emerged to more cameras and flash bulbs than a royal couple. They stopped to answer questions on the advice of the Met comms team, after being heavily coached at what to say. The questions were shouted at Anya, ten at a time.

"What you would say to the PM if he was standing here now?"

"Is it really your baby Miss Novak?"

"How did you crack the conspiracy?"

"Who helped you?"

"Are you going to get your baby back?"

Anya dealt with them brilliantly. Holding the line about not being able to answer their questions whilst the police enquiry was ongoing but very much looking forward to being united with her daughter.

After about ten minutes of fielding their questions, a reporter suddenly directed a question to Rob.

"Mr Simmons. How does it feel to be a hero?"

The sudden change of focus surprised Anya. She looked at Rob. He didn't seem like he had heard the question. He had a broad smile on his face and was staring at a face in the crowd.

Anya looked at Rob. Followed his line of sight and saw who he was looking at. In that moment she knew.

90

TWELVE MONTHS LATER

Anya sat watching the news, gripped by the latest headlines about James Hardacre.

"After a fierce battle between the respective legal teams, the trial of James Hardacre concluded today. The judge handed down a custodial sentence of fifteen years for conspiracy charges after a conclusive guilty verdict by the jury. His father stood outside court with the Hardacre lawyers, stating they would lodge an appeal. His estranged wife Annabelle did not attend court. This sentence seems to be the last the police are to pursue against the conspirators in what many have come to know as the 'cash for babies scandal'. Many observers are surprised that William Hardacre was not up on charges himself. Rumours are rife that the police and CPS could not construct a sound case against him due to a lack of clear evidence implicating him in this sordid affair.

This verdict comes after the eight life sentences handed down to his stepbrother Bradley Williams, a fifteen-year sentence for George Walker, the ten-year sentence for Hassan Chandra and sentences ranging from two years to eight years for the corrupt police officers and clients of this scandal.

The real victims of this scandal, the five children born from the deeds of these evil men, have all been the subject of protracted legal arguments. Unlike Miss Anya Novak, the lady that helped blow this conspiracy wide open, the real mothers of the other four babies are dead. The custodial sentences handed down to the male clients has taken away any legal right they had to their offspring, despite it being proven that they were the actual fathers. The legal battles still rage on as to whether the women who received these babies should be allowed to keep them, as it is alleged they knew nothing of their husbands' crimes. Miss Novak's custody trial was concluded last month, despite a fierce fight from the Hardacres' lawyers. Her daughter was returned to her soon after.

Sam Clarke and Bianca Mavroudis, the two women who were in the middle of being exploited when this conspiracy was cracked wide open, have both given birth to healthy baby girls.

There will be more on this story on BBC News 24 and on our website. In other news…"

Anya's concentration was broken by a sudden outburst.

"Mummy. Why is there a picture of my old daddy on the telly?"

Sophie stood there. Arms crossed. Developing her little madam pose with some aplomb.

"Come here Sophie. Sit with Mummy."

Sophie jumped on the sofa and snuggled in, her face fixed on Anya, probing for an answer.

"Look sweetie, you remember when you came to live with me, I told you that your old daddy had done some bad things and may have to go away for a while?"

"Yes."

"Well, a man called a judge has decided your old daddy won't be around for quite a long time as he has to be punished for what he did."

"O… K… so is he going over the sea to another place or staying in another house?"

"Yes, something like that and you won't be able to see him so it will just be me looking after you."

"Is my old mummy going away too?"

"No Sophie. Your old mummy didn't do anything wrong and I know she would like to see you some time. Would you like that?"

"Yes, that would be nice."

*

Clark had been watching the same news coverage. In fact, he had hardly been able to tear himself away from the constant coverage of the events since they had blown the conspiracy apart.

Every time he listened to the news he hoped for one thing. To hear that the police had finally arrested William Hardacre. But it never came. Clark agonised over it. He pored over the evidence file they had sent the police, watched and listened to the footage that Anya had got from the clinic over and over again, but there was nothing new. There just hadn't been enough and neither Dr Normandy or Bradley had implicated him in anything they said during their big confession speeches. He had got away with it by selling out his own family, despite all the window dressing of the expensive lawyers and talk of appeals. Clark looked at the picture on his desk.

"Don't worry Dad. I won't give up. I will get him. Somewhere. Somehow."

*

Rob cuddled up to Elisha, as they sat on the sofa watching TV. Rob knew he was now in the right place, with the right person. He thought he had found his soulmate when he met Anya, but their relationship had been built on lies and dishonesty. He knew it wasn't all her fault. She had been through the most terrible trauma and he reconciled this with the part he had played in helping save her life and getting Sophie back. But, at the end, they both knew they had no future together. Anya only had one priority and it was not her relationship with Rob.

*

A week after James Hardacre's trial verdict, William Hardacre sat on his yacht in St Helier harbour, enjoying one of the many tax havens he had squirrelled his fortune away in. He chinked champagne glasses with Dr Gerard Perdou from the Jersey Gladstone Private Clinic.

"I have some girls primed for you Doctor. I hope you are ready."

Acknowledgements

There are many people I need to thank for their support and encouragement during my first writing experience. Firstly, massive thanks to my family for their unerring support and enthusiasm for my writing. Your positive comments and numerous read throughs helped enormously. Specific thanks go to the people I call my alpha book reviewers – Ray Wade, Jacky Wade, Hannah Wade, Karen Warner and Anthony Cooper.

Thanks also to Jericho Writers for their support and guidance, with specific thanks to Russel McLean who completed a full manuscript review on a distinctly average first draft and set me on the right track to produce a much better read.

Big thanks to Kevin Morgan, Alyson Duckmanton and Tony Flower who completed significant reviews of later versions of the book, to shape it into what it has become.

Thank you to all those agents who didn't pay me the basic courtesy of even acknowledging my submissions. You helped me see that self-publishing was the way forward and thank you to the team at Troubador Publishing for an excellent service in getting my book designed, produced and marketed.

Finally, thanks must go to all those people who have listened to me bang on about my writing over the last year or so, for their good grace, encouragement and promises to buy a copy!